THE MEMORIAL

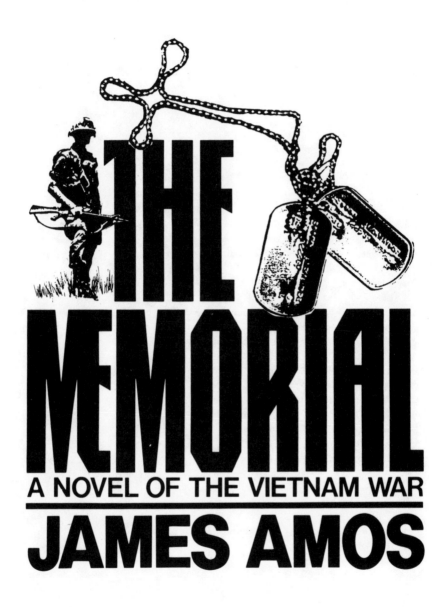

THE MEMORIAL

A NOVEL OF THE VIETNAM WAR

JAMES AMOS

CROWN PUBLISHERS, INC.

NEW YORK

F

Copyright © 1989 by James Amos

Published by Crown Publishers, Inc., 225 Park Avenue South, New York, New York 10003.

CROWN is a trademark of Crown Publishers, Inc.

Manufactured in the United States of America

Library of Congress Cataloging-in-Publication Data

Amos, James.
  The memorial / James Amos.
    p.   cm.
    1. Vietnamese Conflict, 1961–1975—Fiction.   I. Title.
PS3551.M63M46   1988
813'.54—dc19   88-38765
                                                                              CIP

ISBN 0-517-56971-X

10   9   8   7   6   5   4   3   2   1

First Edition

For Captain Barry Land, who paid the ultimate price and never stopped believing, and for my dad, James H. Amos, Sr., who instilled in me that ethereal love of country that allowed me to embrace, for a time, the proud title of marine.

CONTENTS

PART ONE

JEHOVAH'S
THROAT

My solution? Tell the Vietnamese they've got to draw in their horns . . . or we're going to bomb them back to the Stone Age.

GENERAL CURTIS E. LEMAY

It became necessary to destroy the town in order to save it.

MAJOR, DIRECTING FIRE INTO BEN TRE, 1968

I thought you knew. You sent me there.

LIEUTENANT COLONEL WALLEN SUMMERS,
WHEN ASKED WHY HE WENT TO VIETNAM

1

ABOUT AN INCH OF SNOW DUSTED THE Tidal Basin in Washington, D.C. The trees, somber and without evidence of life, stretched out along Independence Avenue, like a line of silent sentries guarding the slabs of dark granite that had somehow become a monument to a war without heroes.

To the east, the Washington Monument rose against the sky, surrounded by American flags snapping to attention in the biting wind. To the west, the stony eyes of Abraham Lincoln stared away from the Memorial Bridge and the Custis-Lee Mansion, where echoes of battles past whispered from tombstone to tombstone in a place called Arlington.

To Jake Adams, Vietnam was history. He was thirty-eight years old; it had been seventeen years since he last heard a round fired in anger. Early middle age threatened to make what was always a stocky build heavy. Yet he still worked out several times a week and managed to convince himself that the stressful life-style of a Washington consultant was offset by trips to the Arlington YMCA. That's where the handball players congregated.

He could not explain, even to himself, this deviation from routine.

Straining against the wind, eyes blinking away puffs of snow, he struggled to find the footpath that kept eluding him by disappearing as quickly as his reason for being there.

For months, Jake had been perplexed by the media's new love affair with the military. The most poignant example was the Marine Corps pullout from Beirut. Many of the marines coming home were being interviewed. The remarkable thing, to Jake, had been the flag-waving and the tears. The general acceptance of this short military operation by the public, and the resounding welcome accorded these soldiers, left him confused and resentful. Soon, the memorial would be dedicated and turned over to the government for maintenance. It seemed that it was again becoming fashionable to be patriotic. In fact, the homecomings described by the media were totally unlike what he had experienced so many years ago and produced feelings that were alien to him.

Jake convinced himself that he had escaped. The jungle boots, mosquitoes, M-16s, K-bar knives, and often unseen enemy had been replaced by this quest for acceptance and respectability. He had turned away, driven in a new direction that produced homes and cars and expensive suits. He worked at everything. Loving wasn't an emotion, it was a commitment. His wife, his daughters, even his colleagues, all had been the focus of this energy.

His overcoat was leather, pulled tight around his collar to ward off the cold wind blowing down the natural funnel of the Ellipse. In his pocket Jake clutched a crumpled telephone-message slip. Several names were scribbled on the reverse side. Each one belonged to the past he had refused to think about. Some would be engraved on the walls of the memorial. Others, for years, had been engraved on his soul. Now, Jake was about to look back.

It was 4:46 in the afternoon. The great commute had begun and bumper-to-bumper traffic already threatened to clog all routes from the city to the suburbs. With the new snow falling, experienced commuters knew it would be a long rush hour. Jake approached the Memorial mentally comparing this new relationship between the media and the military with the years of negative reports that, in his opinion, had focused on everything bad. He had heard an endless stream of stories: the "psychovet," the draftee being dragged screaming into uniform, the returning drug addict with hypos hanging out of his arm, the draft dodger, or, in general, the picture of the antisocial, aberrant Vietnam veteran on whom society had turned its back.

There was a spiritual void, deep inside him, that he had been ignoring all these years. It was an ache for the dignity accorded his father and his grandfather before him, as they returned from war to the respect and adulation of a people grateful and hungry to honor their own. But instead, for Jake and his fellow survivors, there was the hurt that came from being spit on by a group of hippies while walking through the airport concourse in their dress blues. It was always there, the hurt. It was the indifference of a country anxious to put the war behind it. It was the irony of being condemned for serving your country. It was a Harris Poll that indicated sixty percent of the people polled viewed the Vietnam veteran as a sucker. That's all there seemed to be: the hurt.

Jake pulled the message slip from the pocket of his overcoat and looked at the names. Each name was a reminder to him that there was a story the media never told, and he wondered why. He stood at the center of the Memorial where each wall stretched out 246 feet, 8 inches, east and west. The walls were 10 feet, 1½ inches in height. There were 70 separate inscribed panels, the largest having 137 lines of names, and the shortest, 1 line with 5 names to the line. The names of the first casualties, taken in July of 1959, were in the first line of panel number 1 on the east wall. They were listed continuously until the names of the last casualties formed the last line of panel number 1 in the west wall, dated May 1975.

The many had become one: 57,939 men and women who had given their lives or still remained missing, stretched out, collectively pointing exactly at the northeast corners of the Washington and Lincoln memorials. It seemed to Jake as if they were trying to reach out to the past and join hands with leaders who understood what total commitment was all about. Maybe in that effort, reason or sanity or some sense of justification would be given to this total sacrifice offered to a half-hearted cause.

The names of servicemen and servicewomen who became casualties in a given time period could be located by the time periods indicated on the panel. Jake turned and walked along the west wall, his eyes tearing in the wind. It was becoming very cold but he hardly noticed. Heightened

7

feelings and a sense of anticipation warmed him. December of 1968 was on panel 137, beginning with line 15. This was the starting point. Jake began searching the lines until he came to the first name on his list. No amount of preparation could have readied him for the emotion that pushed the breath from his lungs and tightened his chest. In spite of the cold, he removed his glove and reached out ritually, touching the name someone had gritblasted into the granite—Bowman, Harry Lee, Cpl. USMC.

2

H E HAD MET KAREN WHEN HE HAD moved with his parents from Ferguson to Pine Lawn, Missouri, in 1958. In seventh grade, it obviously wasn't marriage that they had on their minds, but they formed a relationship that would last. At fifteen and fourteen years old, respectively, a friendship was joined that would weather time and end in marriage in 1966. College had been two years without Karen and two years with Karen. Graduation came on the campus of the University of Missouri. With it, came a piece of paper declaring that Jake Adams had achieved an A.B. in political science and, more important to him, a second lieutenant's commission in the United States Marine Corps.

It was 1969. College campuses were echoing with cries of protest against the United States' involvement in Vietnam. In the past year, Martin Luther King had fallen to an assassin's bullet and now, as Jake and Karen headed east toward their destiny, the political career and life of Bobby Kennedy came to an end in a pool of blood on a hotel floor in California. America was casting off into a sea of uncertainty and so were Jake and Karen.

Two sister training companies, November and Oscar, would graduate simultaneously in 1968, from the Marine Corps Basic School in Quantico, Virginia. Karen would be taught how to be an officer's wife. Wives would play endless bridge games late into the night as their husbands learned the art of war. Yet, in the middle of demanding hours and little leisure time, passionate couplings would result in pregnancies. Some of these children, the fruit of that lovemaking, would never see their fathers. For others, it would be many months and, in some cases, years before families would reunite.

For Jake, the second graduation in less than a year would bring with it the military occupational specialty 0302, infantry officer. His destination was South Vietnam. All the field work, all the stress from trying to live up to both personal and peer pressure, all the training that could possibly be absorbed in nine months, designed to accomplish more than that of the first twenty-two years, would be necessary.

On the inside cover of their graduation cruise book, Second Lieutenant James B. Thompson, USMCR, had written these prophetic words: "Our eyes struggled against an unseen weight. They opened, blurred, unfocused, to accept the target's image, small and faint. Our feet pushed against an endless road. They ran and walked, fatigued, blistered, only to find more macadam, a heavier load. Our muscles strained over an unyielding obstacle. They pushed and pulled against a distant voice. They turned to receive the words, experienced, tested, which must be remembered, very important. But now it's all for keeps, the prep fires have ceased, and the challenge awaits to the south and the east."

3

H E COULDN'T BELIEVE THAT ONLY YES-
terday he had kissed Karen good-bye.
After having explained to her how to
pay the bills by following a chart that he had made to cover the thirteen
months he would be gone, Jake had leaned across the crib to kiss his
two-week-old daughter good-bye. He took off his wedding ring and
watch and gave them to Karen. Then, Jake's parents had driven him and
Karen to the airport, where he experienced emotions perhaps not unlike
those of ancient warriors in Caesar's legions as they left Rome; or of
Napoleon's troops when gathered by his marshalls; or of the Blue and the
Gray as they left the warmth of home; each with a purpose and inner
cause that moved them from all that was rational to all that was not.

His thoughts were of heroism and the ultimate test he faced. His
feelings were barometric, peaking in the anticipation of what was ahead
and ebbing in the uncertainty of separation. This was massive contradic-
tion.

Just getting on the plane brought a kind of peace to Jake. It was the
way it had been so many times before; great pressure and then great
calm. Jake often wondered if he were different from others or maybe

11

just plain selfish. Sometimes it seemed as if he could simply decide not to feel. He had a responsibility to his family, of course. He knew that his father was very proud of him but that it was also killing him, because he always seemed to anticipate the worst. Jake had a commitment to his country and the corps. Why couldn't all these commitments serve one another? Why did it seem they had to conflict? Jake angled his way down the cramped aisle of the plane while the acrid smell of jet exhaust followed him to his seat. It was not long before the stewardess was sealing the door.

He tightened hs seat belt, thinking about his classmates who had preceded him into Vietnam. Because Karen had been pregnant with their daughter, Harmony, he did not have to spend Christmas in Vietnam. He was grateful for having had the opportunity to see his daughter born but, strangely enough, he also felt a sense of guilt for staying behind. That's when he saw Wilbur.

Wilbur Dawson was a cool dude. All through the intensity of basic school, Wilbur knew he would make a great motor-transport officer, especially since it was a lot safer than being in the infantry. The problem was, although he was capable of good scores, Wilbur didn't produce them, and good scores were necessary to be able to pick your own military occupational specialty. Nonetheless, Wilbur was certain he would be given his chosen career. Yep, motor transport was the key. Wilbur came very close to going AWOL when it was announced that he was chosen to fill an 0302 infantry-officer military occupational specialty.

Jake moved up two rows and arranged a seating change so that he and Wilbur were soon involved in a deep rap session. Wilbur Dawson was five feet, eleven inches tall, with a jutting forehead and bushy eyebrows that looked like two large black caterpillars brushing against the rim of his sunglasses. Jake asked Wilbur where he was heading and Wilbur replied, "to Okinawa, man, just like you."

"Aw, I know that, Wilbur, but I mean, in the Nam. Are you headed up north or down south?"

"Well, I'll tell you, Jake, I got orders to the Third Marine Div..."

"Hey," Jake cried, "that's great, Wilbur, that's where I'm going."

Wilbur laughed. "Hold on, Chesty Puller. I'm not going to get my ass shot off. I hear that Okinawa is a great duty station. You wait, I'll work my bolt when we get on the islands and find myself some colonel with an ego that needs massaging and some little Okinawan sweetheart to massage me. You ever heard of a steam and cream, Jake?"

What in the world was a steam and cream, thought Jake. He hadn't even dated anyone other than Karen since he was fifteen, and it seemed as if his entire life had been dedicated to athletics, meeting someone else's performance standards, or becoming a marine. The fact was, he wasn't nearly as worldly as he would like to have thought himself. Sure, he had read *Playboy* as a kid and learned to masturbate with some of the neighborhood kids, but that was it. At the same time, he didn't want to seem stupid, so he replied, "I don't care about that crap, Wilbur, I just want to get in-country. I feel like I cheated some of the guys by going over late."

The stewardess was asking them if they wanted a meal and if so would they drop their trays. Wilbur just wanted a beer. He couldn't let Jake's comments go by without responding, however, so while the stewardess handed him his beer, he said, "You gotta be shitting me, Jake. You actually want to go over there. I delayed going over as long as I could but I could only stay on recruiting duty just so long. Listen," he continued, "I just want the lieutenant of marines on my record to enhance my political debut when all of this shit is over. But you, my God, you're serious. Look, Jake, what are you so gung ho about? You didn't buy all of that basic-school crap, did you? Let me give you a real lesson in strategy. When we get to Okinawa, we'll do an end run during processing and manage to land an administrative billet in the good old Ryukyu Islands. We wait out our tour with maybe a hop or two to Da Nang to try out some of that Vietnamese poontang and then we are real combat veterans."

Jake was astounded. This had nothing to do with love of country or commitment or loyalty or work ethic or anything, as far as he was concerned. He simply could not relate to it. What a man believed was his destiny, thought Jake. Jake could not understand this line of thinking.

"Look, Wilbur," Jake said, "I don't think you are going to understand this, but I need to find out if I can hack it. It's like practicing all year long and then ending up sitting on the bench. I want to know, when the time comes, how well I've been trained. Can I shoot a man? Will I run?

There's talk about whether this war is right or wrong, but frankly I haven't stopped to think about it. That's just not the issue. I am a professional and I want to prove it."

Wilbur, a self-proclaimed agnostic, looked as if a Roman Catholic priest had just performed high mass.

"What the fuck are you talking about?" he asked. "I think I need another beer and you, son, need a double of something."

Jake turned toward the window and closed his eyes. He would miss his meal because by the time the stewardess arrived he would be already asleep and dreaming of Karen. Wilbur would eat the meal meant for Jake and Jake would drift in and out of good memories, first dates, and hands being held during hay rides while frost crinkled the earth and hot cider warmed your throat. He dreamed of teenage hearts expanding beyond any ability of retrieving them. He dreamed of a heart offered and accepted.

The landing gear thumped as it locked into position. Jake and Wilbur got off the airplane together, more out of a need for mutual support than of any real closeness. The never-ending process of standing in lines that all military men have learned to detest had begun once again. To Jake, just being in Okinawa was a great adventure. He remembered how his dad had told him about being blown off a ship in a kamikaze attack right here in these waters during World War II. He had been fascinated with his father's description of the Japanese with the hachimaki wound around their heads, diving to their deaths in hope of taking others with them. Shimpu Tokubetsu Kogekitai—the Divine Wind Special Attack Force. The Shimpu, he learned later, referred to the Divine Winds of 1274 and 1281 that drowned the invading Mongol hordes, rescuing Nippon from destruction.

Now, here he was twenty-four years later standing in the same part of the world in which his father before him stood, ready to go to war in another effort, called by the mother country. God, he thought, this is wonderful.

4

THE SMALL SQUAT HOUSES WITH FLAT or slanted tile roofs, indecipherable Japanese calligraphy everywhere announcing something new and strange, exotic smells and sounds bombarding him, were all a part of his Oriental greeting. Jake, who had no idea how long he would be there, figured that he would have two or three days. But for the moment he was in the Orient and a long way from home.

As Wilbur had predicted, they checked into Camp Hansen on the fringe of Kin Village. Kin was the Oriental version of the nonstop merry-go-round of bars, pool halls, restaurants, as well as steam baths or *hotsi* houses that attaches itself to American military installations around the world. One thing was for sure, a marine could lose a lot of lonely in Kin Village.

Jake wanted to call home before leaving for Vietnam because he didn't know how long it would be before he had another crack at a phone. The best way to call home was through a system of short-wave and telephone hookups called MARS lines. The first day it was impossible to get through, due to the amount of traffic. Jake checked into the Bachelor

Officers' Quarters and decided he would wait to the last possible minute in the hope of getting his call through. Another day and a half went by before he got word they would try his call. Although standard phone equipment was used, radio procedure was observed. When his dad answered, Jake didn't know what to say. In fact, what was there to say? I love you, dad, or I love you, mom? He had said those things before. How about, I want to come home, which was true and yet it wasn't true and they wouldn't understand that anyway. Or, have a nice day, or I'll see you next year, maybe. It didn't make much difference. His dad was choking up when his mother took the phone. His mother, always full of faith and positive expectations. Then Karen came to the phone. Jake sensed that she felt abandoned in some way and, in truth, she had been. She had a new baby and he certainly wasn't there. The separation seemed as absolute as death, except that she couldn't mourn. She was left alone for the first time in her life, with a new baby and a new job. All he had to do was keep from getting killed. She had to wait with her life on hold for a year.

"Hi, poo," he said, using his pet name for her, "over." Static filled the receiver for a few seconds and Jake heard Karen respond, "Please take care of yourself, Jake, write and come home to me, over."

Once more, shouting through the increasing static, Jake said, "I will. I love you, over."

The connection was getting weaker but Jake heard Karen say, "I love you, Jake, I love so very much . . . over." His chest constricted and in spite of himself and in front of the corporal coordinating the MARS calls his eyes teared. "I love you too, Poo," he managed to whisper into the phone.

That was it. Karen, the girl he took out on her first date when she was a teenager. Karen, who was truly something special, was thirteen thousand miles away in another world.

Jake had one night left before going to Da Nang. Some men would have drawn on their faith and sought the face of God. Some would have gone to the club and attempted to drown whatever concerns seemed pressing. Jake went to Kin Village.

What seemed exotic from afar stunk godawful firsthand. Open *binjo* ditches drained raw sewage along the streets. Kin's being built on a hillside allowed the sewage to flow down to the bay. The streets were just wide enough for the modern-day kamikaze, the cab driver, to clear another vehicle coming the other way. Small stores, with sliding rice-paper doors fronting the entire building, lined the streets. Dried squid, fish, sashimi, sushi, soy, and octopus were all being hawked from the open doors. Huge vats of deep fry for tempura shrimp and vegetables crackled and popped in the doorways, sending odors that assaulted the senses of even the most indifferent passers-by. These were the sights and sounds that many of the old-timers called the bamboo complex. It was the lure and call of the East that slowly but surely entrapped young men, calling to them over and over again. Some would never leave.

Each block had several bars, each with a different theme and band playing perfect reproductions of the Archies' "Sugar, Sugar," or Bob Dylan's "Lay Lady Lay." Aspiring Glen Campbells, with jet-black hair and slanting eyes, wailed about what would occur by the time they got to Phoenix. Sounds of the Beatles, the Doors, Jimi Hendrix, Janis Joplin, all spilled out into the streets, reminding wandering soldiers and marines of home.

To Jake, it smacked of being back in Missouri at one of the small traveling carnivals that used to appear and disappear during the summer months. Around every bend was a new experience. Each door had a sideshow barker out front, announcing the delights hidden within. The American dollar rushed through the open doors, responding to, "Foo sho, foo sho, stateside foo sho, pretty *nassan*, come on in."

Time was running out. Jake walked one block south from the main gate at Camp Hansen and went into the first bar on the first corner he came to. It was the Hawaii Club, featuring a Filipino band and numerous bar girls, or *nassans*, who crowded around each serviceman who entered the door. It was dark and difficult to see. Several booths lined the left side of the bar. Jake selected the first available nook. This was hardly Hawaii, he reflected. Stale cigarette smoke and crushed tobacco along with years of spilled beer permeated the wooden floors. The small dance floor was so packed with bodies that collision was more common than dancing. The band was loud to the point of raucousness. In the midst of all the confusion, a raven-haired girl slid into the undersized booth beside Jake, who suddenly felt like a high-school freshman at his first dance.

"Hi, I'm Jake," he yelled, trying to be heard above the cacophony of sound.

"Hi, I'm Kaiko," she replied, offering her small hand. Jake shook her hand as she requested that he buy her a drink. That was the beginning of many two-dollar exchanges made for glasses of colored water that appeared before Kaiko. She was short, rather stout, and large boned, probably more Okinawan than Japanese. She surveyed Jake professionally and was soon lamenting the fact that she was forced into her occupation by a mysterious *mamma-san* who held her sister captive on some island in the Pacific. By that time, Jake had twenty bucks left. Kaiko said she was proud that he was going to Vietnam to *senso suru*, or make war. Jake was beginning to feel like a living chapter from *Sayonara*. Kaiko looked through the billowing smoke from her ever-present Salem menthol, trying not to show her impatience.

"You want to go short time, Jake?" she asked.

"No way," Jake replied, "I want to go for the whole tour. I'm not going to half-step. I want to see it through to the end."

Kaiko, squinting in question at him then began to laugh as she realized what he was saying. "No, no, Jake, you cute, neh. I mean to *ni/koi wo suru*, to make love. You and me, neh. How much money you got, Jake?"

Kaiko was wearing a red, very short cocktail dress. Her legs were short but well proportioned and she emphasized her remarks by reaching over and placing her hand on Jake's crotch. Oh, my God, he thought, it took me a year just to hold Karen's hand. There were less than ten hours left before leaving for Da Nang. Not time for the sifting through of morals or middle-class propriety or even how behavior related to both taught and self-images as to what an officer and gentleman should be. Kaiko took Jake's hand and rested it on her upper thigh just under the hem of her dress. In doing so, she nodded at her benny boy, letting him know she had another score.

They left the Hawaii Club and made their way down through Kin Village, passing rows of small two-story buildings where other *nassans*, perched on balconies overlooking the street, called out to marines and sailors, promising untold delights for the right price. Kaiko held his hand firmly as the mysterious sights and smells of this city in miniature bombarded his senses. They walked down the hill and then picked up a single lane below Kin that wound along the ocean. The lights of the small village dimmed, along with the mixture of music. They both walked along without speaking. A full moon shimmered on the calm sea, lighting up the night and stippling the beach, making it appear to be moving as they approached. A frieze of clay circles separated the *fu suma,* or shoji screen, of the house from the beachfront. An old woman Kaiko referred to as *oba,* or mother, sat in front of a small prayer niche Kaiko described as the *Tokonoma,* or shrine. Her mother was rendering a prayer to Buddha, muttering words that, to Jake, sounded something like, *"Dame, Dame, Dame nameoengenki."* Bending at the waist periodically, ringing a small bell, she ignored them completely.

Jake was uneasy about getting robbed or worse. Or maybe, as his inexperience began to surface, she had some kind of venereal disease. He really didn't know what to do or what precautions to take. A litany of awesome consequences began to float across his mind.

The little house had two rooms. The lower room was a two-*tatami* room, as Kaiko described it. Apparently the size of the rooms was measured by the number of reed *tatami* mats they could hold. Other than the *Tokonoma,* the only other evidence of furniture was a small hot plate for cooking rice that sat on a black lacquered table. The upper room, separated by another *fu suma,* or sliding screen, was a three-*tatami* room but also had thick futons, or padded mattresses, for sleeping and keeping warm.

Kaiko, deftly removing her dress, turned to Jake and said, *"go jiyu ni,"* which Jake took to mean make yourself at home. Kaiko's breasts were full, the first Jake had ever seen other than Karen's. The soft candlelight showed their fullness and accentuated the burnished color that made her dark nipples even more prominent. She was aware of the effect she was having on him.

"You take pants off, Jake. What are you waiting for?"

This was too much. In order for this to be right, he thought, and it had to be right, they had to talk. He decided that he must have some feeling for this girl. Apparently there was no conflict between worrying about her possible VD and still wanting a meaningful relationship. I'm not like all the other guys she goes with, he thought. Maybe she doesn't even do this with everybody she meets. Even if this is just one night, surely it can be more than just sex.

Kaiko broke his contemplation by asking him if he wanted to take a pee. Jake thought that was a good idea. She slipped on a short silk kimono and led him out the front door to a small cement square on the side of the house. In the center of this six-by-six square was a very small hole in the cement, which Jake was sure an expert marksman would have trouble hitting. He asked, "Is this where you go, I mean, um . . . do you do everything here?"

Kaiko had already squatted over the hole and was apparently a great shot. Jake lost his desire to relieve himself and was quickly losing the desire for more intimate things. This, he thought, will be more difficult than learning to eat with chopsticks. Kaiko, finishing, took Jake by the hand and led him back to the three-*tatami* room.

Once more she removed her kimono. Jake found he could not keep his eyes off the dark triangle that was the focus of the natural symmetry of her body. He noticed a Band-Aid on her right leg and that really worried him. I wonder if it would be bad manners to ask what the Band-Aid was for, he thought. Kaiko was going to waste no more time. She undid Jake's belt buckle herself and helped him remove his trousers. Kneeling before him she removed his Jockey shorts and circled his hardening penis with her lips. The sex was brief and efficient. Jake joined the ranks of brave young warriors defeated by lust. He paid Kaiko, wishing her well, and wanting to get away as fast as he could. In his anxiety, he almost fell off the stoop and into the clay frieze, trying to depart. Jake Adams, the brave young warrior about to face death for the first time, or at least to be aware he was facing it for the first time, walked back to the bachelor officers' quarters; broken in spirit, broke monetarily, broken from his personal commitments, having lost his first battle, a moral one. He felt ashamed as he returned the salute of the sentry at the main gate of Camp Hansen.

5

THE BOQ WAS A ROW OF ONE-ROOM concrete apartments, each one with cinder-block walls, two louvered windows, a steel wall locker, and a shower. Jake stripped off his clothes and threw them in a wastepaper basket. Standing in a scalding shower for as long as he could stand it, he prayed that if he had contracted anything it might burn away. He was shocked at the cracks in his commitments: to his wife, to himself, and to God.

Oh, Karen, I love you, he said to himself, forgive me.

But whether it was Karen or God he was speaking to, or maybe himself, Jake was not entirely certain. And whether either one could hear or forgive, of that he was also not certain. What was certain was that his conscience had spoken and something within him was responding.

He put on a pair of solid-green jungle utilities, brought from the basic school. There were only a few hours left in Okinawa, so even though he was very tired he walked up to the command center and cadged a ride to Kadena Air Base. Jake, although exhausted, found the early-morning air reviving him and a new sense of excitement and anticipation dissipating his guilt. He was beginning to feel the same sense of expectation he used to have when waiting in the early hours of the morning for his uncle Bud to show up, so he and his dad could join him in a hunting or fishing trip.

Jake thought he might run into Wilbur. Instead, he was greeted by lines of marines wrapped around the cyclone fencing, talking quietly in the semilight. There were small groups of officers and enlisted men standing around. Some, like Jake, were obviously new, while others were returning to Vietnam from R and R. Most were whispering as if someone might overhear what they were saying. They joked about everything, finding that their weak attempts at humor seemed to cut through the tension created by what tomorrow might bring. As Jake looked down the rows of men he could see the pulsing light of cigarette butts as they were intermittently drawn on by the men in line.

There was nothing remarkable about the short flight from Okinawa to Da Nang. Being on the ground in Vietnam, however, was remarkable. The first thing Jake saw as he got off the aircraft was Marble Mountain, dominating the terrain like a gray-white beehive rising abruptly out of the ground, except that the bees in attendance were hordes of helicopters. Surely they were the drones protecting some hidden queen within this great hive of activity. The heat had a physical presence, squeezing sweat from every pore. Dust, heat, and noise all made breathing a chore and brought with it disorientation and fear.

There seemed to be little organization to the activity of the sprawling base at Da Nang. A gunnery sergeant checked rosters of incoming personnel and, while the enlisted men were directed away, Jake was told to find a bunk in the transient staff and officers' hootch and be ready to catch a C-130 to Quang Tri the next morning.

Jake was still reeling and confused. Here I am, he thought, ready to do what a lifetime has prepared me to do. I'm confident, yet scared. I am supposed to be a man and leader of men, yet I sometimes feel like a little boy and would like someone to tell me what the hell to do. I'm a trained marine. I am still a civilian. Shit, here I am in Vietnam at last, all these gooks are supposed to be running around all over the place, and I don't even have a weapon. I'm still wearing stateside utilities that stick out like a sore thumb against the camouflaged utilities everyone else is wearing. I even look screwed up.

The staff hootch had a concrete slab for a floor with slat frame walls separated by patchwork screens. Cockroaches, bigger than any Jake had ever seen or heard of, ignored him and the war as they went about their business. They seemed to sneer at the activity all around them and its purpose, maybe recognizing that they were there before it all began and would be there when it all ended.

A standard army cot stood alone under a bare hundred-watt bulb hanging from a wire in the overhead. Through the partially screened windows Jake could see flares popping off in the distant sky and hear artillery shells bursting in some unknown quadrant. He was thirteen thousand miles away from home and anyone who might marginally care. From somewhere down the dirt road that ran by his hootch, Jake could hear emanating from some nameless hovel the guttural sounds of Janis Joplin straining at "Me and Bobby McGee." He sat on his coat tentatively and looked at the cloud of dust that lingered in the wake of his arrival. He lay back, looking up at the bare light bulb, and fought sleep throughout the night.

His fitful sleep ended abruptly as the sun exploded over Marble Mountain. Jake ate an enormous breakfast of eggs, bacon, coffee, and pancakes prepared at a mess hall close to the airstrip. The gunnery sergeant who had so peremptorily dismissed him the day before seemed not to have moved from his spot of the previous day. Jake approached him and was given his departure time. By 0900 hours he was on board a big gut-bellied C-130 heading for Dong Ha. Dong Ha, due south of Quang Tri, was on a coastal plain, but it was still dust and heat. A six-by truck left it behind as if with its departure the place would cease to exist. Jake was heading north to Quang Tri, still trying to cope with the heat and the ubiquitous dust that was mixing with his sweat and forming a semisolid coating, matting his hair, filling his nostrils, and layering grit over his teeth. He was brown all over with it.

Route 9 stretched westward from Dong Ha to Cam Lo, turned left at the Rockpile, moved southwest to Vandegrift Combat Base, and opened the doors to Khe Sahn and the Ashau Valley. Jake had no idea where he was going. He felt lost, as if events were propelling him to their own conclusion. Sure, he had made the decisions that brought him to this place, but now a sense of uneasiness filled his spirit. Once more he thought, what am I doing here in the middle of Vietnam, three thousand meters from the DMZ, and not even carrying a weapon?

He had to assume someone knew what they were doing. The big truck continued to rumble on, passing *mamma-sans* carrying huge bundles of wood and Montagnard tribesmen waving and smiling black through the betel nut they constantly chewed. Filthy children peered out from under coolie hats, living proof that this country might have a future. The question was, what kind? Jake rode in silence, barely noticing the three young marines bouncing around on the slat seats opposite him. A glance was enough to see they wore the camouflaged utilities and bleached-out jungle boots that identified them as having been here for some time. They stared at Jake and he was certain he could see the derision in their eyes as they looked at his stateside utilities, a dead giveaway to his lack of experience. Oh, how he wished he could become an old salt instantly.

They left, they were en route and they arrived. Jake hopped down off the six-by and made his way over to the S-2 batallion headquarters and found himself standing in line behind three other new lieutenants and trying to overhear where they were being assigned. All three of them were going to the Fourth Marines and Jake assumed that would also be his destiny. But when he stepped up to the major's desk, the smiling administrative officer said, "Lieutenant Adams, you'll be going to the First Battalion, Ninth Marine Regiment, the 'walking dead.' Do you want me to issue your purple heart now or later?"

6

QUANG TRI WAS A SERIES OF COM-
pounds enclosed by triple concertina
wire and intermittent guard towers.
Dirt roads led from one unit to another, the Ninth Marines to the
Fourth to the perimeter. From the air, it appeared as if a series of cells
began to form and split and multiply from a central core. Boardwalks
were built over the mud and dust between the hootches. Every second
building was separated by wide slit trenches that were rimmed by three
or four feet of sandbags. Each hootch was made of sandbags and canvas
or wire screening. The roofs were of corrugated steel or tin.

Captain Elias McCormack, of Battalion S-2, finally sent Jake over to
supply, where he picked up his 782 gear. Great, he thought, at least I'm
finally going to look like I fit in. A service automatic, Colt .45, four
clips, poncho, poncho liner, helmet, helmet liner, jungle boots, K-bar
knife, mess kit, and a standard-issue pack that Jake would soon learn was
considered by most marines to be far inferior to the army rucksack. In
addition, there was an entrenching tool, battle dressings, two hand grenades, flak jacket, and compass.

Captain McCormack was a mustang. He had gone up in rank as far as he was going to go and was retiring when he rotated from Vietnam. At forty, he looked more like an old gunny than a captain. Balding, overweight, he was gruff in manner and had dark piercing eyes that came together under a widow's peak. Jake soon learned that they called him "Old Hatchet Face." Elias McCormack was old, old corps.

Jake humped back from supply looking and feeling like a new recruit at boot camp. He threw all of his gear onto a cot in the staging hootch. James Clahan, a black lieutenant from somewhere in South Carolina that Jake didn't quite catch, stretched out on an adjoining cot. He eyed Jake as he dumped all of his gear. Even lying down, Jake could tell that Clahan was taller than he was and had the high hips of many blacks, and long, well-muscled arms. Jim Clahan was friendly but still distant. His hair was short, almost scrapped to the scalp on the sides. Propping himself up on one elbow and continuing to look Jake over, his face expressionless, he asked, "Have you been assigned yet?"

"Yeah," Jake responded, while busying himself sorting out his gear. "I'm going to the Ninth Marines." Jake saw a funny expression pass over the black man's face. Clahan got up abruptly and said, "Look, I'm going over to the slop chute for a couple of beers, you want to come along?" Jake wanted to very much because he wanted to fit in and feel like he belonged, but he rebuffed the offer, saying, "No, I think I'll clean my weapon and square my gear away. Maybe I'll join you later. I don't know when I'll be going to the bush and I want to be ready."

"Suit yourself," Jim Clahan said. "I'll catch you later."

As Clahan left, Jake wondered about other blacks he had seen passing the dap, the complicated handshake of the brothers, the yellow towels many of them seemed to sport around their necks, and especially the short-timer sticks with the black-power fists on the top. How could such a lack of discipline be tolerated, he thought. I wonder where Clahan stands on that stuff.

After changing into his camouflaged utilities and his new jungle boots, Jake began checking and cleaning his gear. He field stripped and reassembled his .45. The action was smooth and he hit the magazine release, never realizing a single round had gone home into the chamber. Jake pulled the trigger. The smell of cordite and smoke filled the hootch. Jake was stunned and amazed that he still held the pistol after the recoil. Shouts were ringing out in the compound.

The screened door flew open and Elias McCormack was silhouetted in the passageway. McCormack had spent part of his youth and all of his adult life in the Marine Corps. This was not the first green lieutenant he had ever seen, nor the first accidental discharge he had experienced in his long career. Several things went through his mind. First, to see if anyone was hurt in the adjoining hootch. The round had smashed through the bulkhead and apparently gone right into the next building. His deepest concern was his lack of officers in the bush. Lieutenant Crissman had just bought the farm. Alpha Company was without a platoon commander, and if this schmuck had just ruined his career, Alpha might have to go for weeks without a replacement.

"What the fuck is going on here, Adams?"

Jake was in a state of shock. Everything he had worked and dreamed for was on the verge of being crapped away thanks to a stupid mistake. A crowd began to gather around the door to the hootch and McCormack ordered them to stay out. Okay, he thought, first things first.

"Adams, go next door and see if you wasted anybody. If someone is wounded, call a corpsman. If someone is dead, don't come back. I don't give a shit where you go, but don't come back. If you lucked out and missed, get your ass back over here."

Without replying, Jake turned and went out the opposite end of the hootch. McCormack turned in the passageway and dispersed the troops. "It's okay," he said, "some brown bar wanted to find out if what he learned in his books about a .45 was true and, you know what, if you put a round in the chamber and pull the trigger, it will fire."

This was met with general laughter, and most just shook their heads and walked away.

Jake took both steps at one time and pushed through the door of the next hootch. As his eyes adjusted to the darkness, he wouldn't allow himself to anticipate the worst. The hootch was empty. The bullet had entered along the edge of the overhead and exited back through the roof. There was not time to feel relieved. He was grateful that no one was hurt, but he dreaded facing Old Hatchet Face.

Captain McCormack was waiting; in fact, he hadn't moved an inch.

"I assume since you are back here that you lucked out." McCormack said. "Okay, John Wayne," he continued, "you want to fucking shoot, you are going to fucking shoot. First light tomorrow, you join Alpha Company, First Battalion, Ninth Regiment. Now get your ass out of here and report to medical to complete your files so I can get you out of my sight."

Even though Jake knew he should keep his mouth shut he just couldn't help himself.

"I'm sorry, Skipper, it was an accident. Thanks for . . ."

McCormack was turning red around his widow's peak.

"Shut up, damn it," he said. "Don't thank me, asshole. I'm just sending you out to be cannon-fodder for the gooks. Why the hell should I court-martial you when I can let the gooners use you for target practice at much less expense? Now hit it, marine."

Jake wandered into the Fourth Marines area on his way to C-med. In less than a week he seemed to have failed in every area of his life that had once been important. As he approached the medical facility, helicopters were coming in and out of the landing zone at a steady pace. Stretchers were everywhere. A double-bay sliding door fronted the landing zone and inside four surgical tables lined one wall. Surgeons were working furiously to complete one emergency operation only to receive another medevac from the landing zone. Jake's mind went back to the books by Bruce Catton on the Civil War in which there were vivid descriptions of how arms and legs were stacked outside the medical tents. Not much has changed, he realized. It was just a different war and a more efficient way of killing, but the results were the same.

Walking out the double-bay doors, he was overwhelmed by the impact of the last few days. Less than a week ago, he was ordering tacos at Taco Bell on the Rock Road in St. Louis, Missouri. There was no rational relationship between then and now. Trying to make some sense out of what he was observing and feeling, he had turned toward the administrative section when he saw Captain Romero lying on a stretcher near the double door. Romero was a tank officer who had been one of the instructors at the basic school. Jake walked over and bent down to say something but Romero was incoherent. There appeared to be three fingers missing under the battle dressing on his left hand and Romero's head kept twitching every few seconds. An IV unit dripped life into his good arm while he waited for a table to open up just inside the double doors. Captain Romero had been one of the instructors Jake had particularly admired at the basic school. Back there, he had seemed invincible to Jake. He was not.

The heat was even more oppressive than on the previous day. The smell of aircraft exhaust permeated the area, while the dank fetid smell of the surrounding jungle lent a surreal atmosphere to the groaning of the wounded. Overhead, the whump, whump, whump of the helicopter rotors promised new casualties.

Jake took his leave of Captain Romero. What have I done? he thought. Is it possible to last through a year of this? Will I ever make it home again?

7

AT FIRST LIGHT, JAKE FOUND HIMSELF the grateful beneficiary of a piggyback ride from an army six-by-six truck. Once more he was headed farther west on Route 9. Alpha Company, along with the rest of the Ninth Marines, had returned from a major operation and then spent a couple of weeks in rest and relaxation, or R and R, at Cua Viet. There had been many casualties and it was a time for regrouping and wound-licking. The company commander, First Lieutenant Wayco Wolf, had also just returned from R and R in Hawaii. Thirty-seven years old, he had come up through the enlisted ranks and then received a field commission on his first tour in Vietnam. He had recently been selected as a captain but was not "frocked."

Alpha Company, First Battalion, Ninth Marine Regiment was situated on Hill 30 just outside Cam Lo, along the Song Cam Lo. The hill itself was high enough to offer a view of "Leatherneck Square," a rectangular piece of real estate that was so named by the marines who trudged through it. You could also see the three ridge lines beyond and into the DMZ from Hill 30. The company had been there about a week and expected to remain another two or possibly three weeks. As Jake got off the truck, he was surprised to see Jim Clahan. He had actually not seen him since the accidental weapon discharge in Quang Tri. Clahan greeted Jake in a perfunctory manner and explained that he was the company executive officer and had come out the night before. They shook hands and Clahan, grinning, said, "I guess you should have come with me to the slop chute, huh." Jake, looking sheepish at having been reminded of his screw-up back in Quang Tri just shook his head yes and quickly changed the subject. "I wonder if you could introduce me to the Skipper," Jake asked. Clahan allowed how he could and turned, saying, "Come on, I'll take you to his hootch."

Wayco Wolf was relatively short, about five feet, nine inches. His hair was cropped shorter on the sides but long enough on top to reveal natural curls. Broad in the shoulders, he tapered to the indented waist of a gymnast. Turning to shake hands with this new lieutenant he revealed a winning smile that must have been an asset in dealing with people throughout his life. The smile, however, was not the illuminating feature of Wayco Wolf. It was his eyes. What really caught your attention were the eyes. The icy blue gaze counterpointed the smile. The eyes were all business.

After shaking hands, Wolf told Jake that he was to take over the First Platoon for Barclay Crissman, who had been killed in the Ashau Valley. Jake didn't fail to notice the open emotion on Wolf's face as he talked about Crissman. Apparently, these would be big shoes to fill. It was during that same operation, Clahan later told Jake, that Wayco Wolf had been written up for the Medal of Honor. In-country he was close to being a legend.

It was a new family Jake was joining. The grunts, drawn together into a close-knit group, had all experienced a shared intensity of life and death that no outsider could understand. The concern, the comradeship, the courage, and the fear, all joined one to another.

Lieutenant Wolf took Jake over to the First Platoon sergeant, Staff Sergeant Samuel T. Jacobsen. He was now halfway through his third tour in Vietnam and was clearly trying to size Jake up as they met. Jake was feeling the insecurity that comes not only from new circumstances and people but new responsibility. He desperately wanted to make good. Jacobsen had the lanky look of a Wyoming cowboy. His ears, oversized, were unusually round rather than oblong and stood out from the sides of his skinned head like small satellite dishes, and when someone spoke his head seemed to follow the directions given by the ears. Jacobsen was aware of how much pressure could be taken off him if this boot lieutenant was any good. He also knew how much additional pressure would be there if this guy wasn't worth a crap. The skin on his face was weathered and leathery, and when he looked at Jake and spoke he squinted fiercely with each word as if he were constantly fighting a headache. Jake liked him immediately and was determined to earn his respect. Jacobsen, taking the lead, walked Jake around the perimeter and introduced him to the squad leaders and men who were not out on patrol.

The First Platoon was made up of three squads of riflemen, divided up into three fire teams of four men. In addition, there was a gun squad, made up of two gun teams of four men each. The headquarters group for First Platoon would be Jake, Staff Sergeant Jacobsen, Sergeant Hawkins, who doubled as the platoon guide, Doc Pony the corpsman, and Thomas Wormand the radioman, who, because he spent every free moment reading a book, was dubbed "the Professor."

Forty-four marines made up what was presently Alpha Company's First Platoon. Jacobsen was introducing Harry Bowman, or "Boston," as he was known, to Jake. Boston, the first squad leader (not surprisingly, from Boston), was a towheaded kid who looked like he belonged in a Bowery Boys movie—a strong Irish jaw and a shock of blond hair that hung down over his brow making an impish gleam in his eyes. Some guys you just like and others you know you can also trust and depend on. Jake instinctively knew that Harry Bowman could be counted on in both cases.

Sergeant Hawkins, the platoon guide for the time being, was also the second squad leader—a tall gawky Oklahoman with huge feet, reminding Jake of Disney's Goofy or maybe Ichabod Crane. Most men with the nickname "Hawk" would have merited it from their ability to hunt or perhaps from a beaked nose, but clearly Sergeant Alvin Hawkins took his nickname from his last name only because, with his gangly body and effervescent grin, it was difficult to take him seriously about anything.

The third squad was led by a black corporal, George Washington Carver Brown. "Sugar Bear" was a lot easier to handle and it certainly reflected this big marine's propensity to put away anything sweet. Sugar Bear was from northeast Washington, D.C., and had picked up the third squad with his promotion. Doc Pony, an overweight navy man who had volunteered to be with the marines, wore an old campaign hat with the brim tucked up George Custer—style. He carried a sawed-off shotgun as a sidearm in a cutaway holster. The Doc was flamboyant but, Jake would soon learn, had proven himself in the field. Thomas Wormand, the Professor, was short, bucktoothed, slight of build, and jowly with very thick glasses. The men in Alpha Company all agreed that the recruiter who signed up the Professor had grossly misrepresented his ability to see anything. Wormand had sat on the end of the bench and run the water buckets his entire life. Now, humping the platoon commander's radio, he had found a home and acceptance among the grunts in Vietnam.

Jake walked to the crest of Hill 30 and looked north to the DMZ. The sun baked down on his closely shorn head as he thought about this new family he had. For the next year, he knew, they would eat, sleep, live, and die together. Some, like himself, were still more civilian than military. He had to prove himself and earn the loyalty and right to lead that didn't come with his rank. Jake scanned the skyline before him. Vietnam was raw reddish-earth pockmarks amidst the incredibly green and thick jungle. To the north and east lay Con Thien. In another time it had been known as the Hill of Angels. To the south and west stood the Rockpile and the jagged trackless mountain peaks of Laos and Co Ka Leuye Mountain. Farther south the sprawling combat base called Vandegrift reached out with uneven tentacles into rolling mountains that were capped by circles of impending destruction called fire-support bases. He would soon learn the names—Cates, Snapper, Henderson, Tun Tavern, and Shiloh. Deep to the west was the Laotion border and Route 922. Just to the north and east of the border lay the Ashau Valley.

A few days later Jake was watching rivulets of water make canyons in the dirt outside his hootch. He had been trying to write Karen every day but somehow he never managed to do so. Letters and care packages began to arrive from home, each one a desperately needed reminder of his stateside family. He was developing friendships, both professionally and personally, with the other platoon commanders. In particular, he liked Bo Lawler, the Second Platoon leader. Bo was from Vicksburg,

Mississippi, and, in Jake's opinion, born about a hundred years too late. Bo had never really left the Civil War in the past. Jake could close his eyes and see him sitting on the veranda of a big Southern plantation like those that still existed in Natchez, Mississippi. Jeremy Motley, the Third Platoon commander, was far different from either Jake or Bo. He was old for his position and rank, but a good guy. He just had that easygoing attitude that made everyone feel at ease and yet he seemed to possess the maturity that came with his added age.

On his third day with Alpha Company, Jake and First Platoon were placed on the point of a company attack for a one-day operation designed to sweep a ridge line into a South Vietnamese Army blocking force. It was clear that Lieutenant Wolf wanted to find out right away just how well Jake could function in the field and in particular how well he could read a map. The North Vietnamese chose to avoid a confrontation and, other than an occasional sniper round, there was little activity. Jake did manage to acquire an unbearable sunburn and he didn't move as quickly as Wolf would have liked him to, but it was apparent he enjoyed the leadership and was willing to make decisions. Wolf decided that, if he lived, experience would sharpen his map-reading skills.

Day ran into day. Jake was becoming immune to the brutal heat and humidity. The sweat never stopped; wetness became a way of life, a way of life that gradually replaced the old. He was slowly getting to know each one of his men. Patrol followed patrol out of the perimeter and hunter-killer teams piggybacked with static ambushes became a daily routine. Then came Jake's birthday, in more ways than one.

Six weeks into his tour, Jake was preparing to take out another patrol. This time it was only about a kilometer or kilometer and a half away from Hill 30 toward the DMZ. They were to set in along the Song Cam Lo. Jake had issued a warning order earlier that day that since it was a one-night operation no packs would be taken.

"Listen, Harry," Jake said to Harry Bowman; he couldn't yet get used to calling him Boston. "You take the point with the first fire team. I'll move just behind your team and before the second fire team. The third team will follow on behind the other just about five meters." In the early dusk, the men assigned to listening posts were just getting into position. Jake called out on the PRC-25 radio to let them know he was coming through. By the time they reached the base of Hill 30 it was nearly dark. Under a heavy cloud cover it was difficult to see your hand in front of your face. But on this night, there were mixed clouds occasionally interfering with a very bright moon. Boston, on the point, moved just ahead of the first fire team as he had been instructed. He moved with the silence and wariness that was creating a reputation for his ability literally to smell the gooks.

Tactical silence was being maintained throughout the movement to the ambush site. It took about two hours to move one kilometer. Jake was grateful for the splotchy moonlight that allowed for an occasional compass check. At about 2100 hours they approached the Cam Lo River just outside the village of Cam Lo. The small column had spread out approximately twenty-five meters when it came to a halt. The Professor kept himself and the radio glued to Jake. Boston had made his way back through the darkness to let Jake know what the ambush site looked like. They were just in the middle of a one-hundred-meter bend in the Song Cam Lo. Two or three hundred meters to the east lay Cam Lo Village. To the west the river ran on until separated from Route 9, the road that ran south to Vandegrift Combat Base. To the north and beyond lay Leatherneck Square and the DMZ.

"Boston," Jake whispered, "set the men in at two-meter intervals just back in the elephant grass along the river." A worn path lay along the lip of the riverbank. Two feet into the grass put them about eight feet from the kill zone.

"Set them in a partial arc," he continued. "Put two claymore antipersonnel mines in the middle of the kill zone and every other man on automatic."

"Okay, lieutenant," Boston replied. "Let's get some."

Jake set the night up into three watches, from eight to twelve and midnight to four, then four to eight. Realizing they would run out only one-half of the last watch, he radioed a situation report to the command post and settled in for the rest of the night. The crickets hummed, a separate army of mosquitoes bit, a tiger screamed from across the valley, but the night itself was uneventful. Jake was beginning to wonder if he would ever see real action. What had happened to create the endless casualties he observed his first few days at Quang Tri? Not that he wanted to become one of those casualties, but so far this had not been what he had expected. He wiped some more bug juice on his face in the endless battle against the mosquitoes and lay back, listening to the music made by the river as it headed east. About five in the morning he removed one jungle boot that was bothering him. He had mentally decided that if there were any "tax collectors" trying to coerce the South Vietnamese villagers to give to the war effort, they would, in all probability, have made their way out before now.

He was tired and Karen was whispering in his ear that she wanted him to make love to her. She had just reached over in bed and grasped his shoulder to pull him to her. He smelled the fragrance that was her and felt the softness of her skin . . . then, for some unexplainable reason she shoved him hard. Only it wasn't Karen; it was the Professor and it wasn't his bed at home, it was a riverbank in South Vietnam. The danger could literally be felt. The air was thick with it. Jake, startled, could see three North Vietnam Army tax collectors to his left, just out of the kill zone he had set up in the ambush. It was almost light as he reached for his M-1 carbine. He liked this weapon with the small-caliber round. Sergeant Jacobsen had asked him if he would like to carry it. The M-1 carbine hadn't been a platoon commander's weapon since the Korean War, but he thought it was pretty nifty and it gave him something to hump other than his .45.

The first North Vietnamese soldier tensed up visibly and stopped. He supported what looked like a brand-new AK-47 assault rifle by its sling. The advantage of surprise was gone. This stumpy apparition in the early twilight turned and seemed to look directly at Jake. Every third round in Jake's magazine was a tracer; and it was still dark enough to see the luminescent lines they left on their way toward the mortal enemy Jake had come thirteen thousand miles to face. When the first round went off the entire line erupted. Someone blew the claymores and, though the gooks were outside the kill zone, the force of the concussion created greater confusion. For a moment Jake locked eyes with this Asian man. Jake felt nothing. There was certainly no hate. He had felt more anger when he had been cut off by some jerk driver back in the States. He could see what must have been the third round enter the other man's chest but still he remained standing. Below a shock of black hair, the man still pointed his assault rifle directly at Jake. Again Jake fired and more rounds tore through the man's jacket, but he still stood with a look of disbelief on his face. Just as suddenly, his broad nose disappeared and the vision of a hole remained where his nose was, imprinting itself forever in Jake's mind as the man dropped to the ground. A second round from the Professor's .45 took the side of his head completely off.

The second NVA in line returned one burst of fire that tore through the hands of PFC O'Neil as he was raising his M-16 to a firing position. The smell of cordite and death filled the air; the peculiar stink of warm blood invaded Jake's senses. The third man had fallen back into the Song Cam Lo as the claymores erupted. Rounds continued to rip into the fallen bodies as Jake attempted to call for a cease-fire above the din. The firing, however, suddenly stopped of its own accord. The smoke of battle drifted up to a hazy sun, the birds began to sing, and the marines were raising hell.

"Shit, lieutenant," the Professor said. "We got some! Killed those mutherfuckers dead. Wow! Did you see the look on that son of a bitch's face when he bought the farm?"

A couple of marines began to move out of their positions to treasure hunt. Just as quickly Boston yelled at them to hold their ground.

"Listen, lieutenant," Boston said as he sidled up to Jake. "We've got to call this back in to the Skipper. He'll want to have intelligence examine any documents. And O'Neil is gonna need a medevac, but I think he can make it back up the hill; at least that's what the doc says."

Jake called in a situation report and related the contact, casualty, and kills. He was trying to suppress his sense of pride in the flush of adrenaline that came with his first contact. Wolf was pleased, but Jake knew he was lucky. He had taken too much for granted and almost made a fatal mistake. As it was, O'Neil was hurt and would be lost to them, probably for good. Lieutenant Wolf told him to send a fire team back with O'Neil and wait for someone from G-2 intelligence to show up. Jake signed off and set out to search the bodies.

He ordered Boston to station two marines on each end of the kill zone to seal off the area. Jake knew that there was little chance of further contact. He was just as positive they would find out that these guys were tax collectors who had waited too late to come out of the village. Old women were already moving along the river in the morning light to retrieve wood for the day. Jake also told Boston to check out the area where the third gooner had fallen into the river and see if they could see a blood trail or find the body. Then Jake turned to look at the kill; instinctively he felt he should not touch anything, but he couldn't help examining the remnants of his first firefight. Besides, there was a sense of macabre fascination that drew him to the bodies. He had been to only one funeral in his life and there seen his first dead body. In fact, it had been his next-door neighbor's dad. Both he and his next-door neighbor, still kids, had sat in the back of the funeral parlor eating Milk Bone dog biscuits in some childish protest against the incomprehensibility of death.

So he slowly walked over to the bodies, both of which lay across the trail, arms splayed out perpendicular to one another. They were no longer human; they were kills. The contents of one man's wallet included pictures of his family. This was the man he had looked at and seen so clearly, but now there was very little of that face left. Boston picked up the dead NVA's weapon, a new AK-47 with what appeared to be a patent-leather stock. Jake was only dimly aware that Boston was trying to get his attention.

"What did you say?" Jake asked.

"Look here, lieutenant," Boston urged, his finger resting against the safety of the weapon.

Jake had been shocked when the man failed to fire, even as he stared directly into the dark eyes of his enemy. Now Boston supplied the answer. The safety was so stiff it had apparently frozen. One significant detail had saved Jake's life and cost that man his. Jake made an indelible mental note about detail.

After the troops from G-2 arrived, Jake and the first squad from Alpha, First Battalion, Ninth Marines, made their way back to Hill 30. They were tired but proud. They had met the enemy on the field of battle and were victorious. They had a body count and only one wounded. Jake was blooded and had performed acceptably. They were very, very far away from the rational, comfortable, sane United States of

America, where others their age were watching television, going to movies, shacking up, eating pizza, and protesting what Jake and his men were doing this very day. Jake found his knees shaking, somewhat, on the way back. He would learn that this was something he would experience over and over after any contact, throughout his Vietnam experience. He was praying, and he was grateful and flushed with the enormity of it all.

8

ALPHA COMPANY STAYED ON HILL 30 for a month. Captain Wolf left on R and R just after Jake's first firefight; Jim Clahan became acting company commander until his return. They ran hunter-killer teams and static ambushes every night. Day followed day and night slid into night; time seemed to be a continuum with no beginning or end, only the constant reality of incredible heat and dust.

From Jake's first contact on his birthday until the day he left Hill 30 there was very little enemy activity. Alpha was hit by artillery on occasion, and every now and then some lone NVA patrol would lob mortar rounds their way but, by and large, it was relatively quiet. It was far from what Jake expected after his first few days at Quang Tri.

One event, however, did have an impact. Not long after the firefight on the Song Cam Lo, a small ceremony was held to honor the men who had fallen during the operation just prior to his arrival. He and Bo Lawler, the Second Platoon commander; Jeremiah Motley, the Third Platoon commander; as well as "Fast Eddie" Gustefsun, the Weapons Platoon commander, gathered at the top of the hill overlooking the command post. Outside Wolf's hootch were twenty-three M-16s in a line with bayonets stuck in the ground, a helmet over each stock.

A chaplain named Dowd had arrived from Dong Ha to perform the ceremony and to offer communion to those troops desiring to take it. Fast Eddie turned to Bo and said, "Can you believe this mutherfucker? He hasn't left the perimeter at Dong Ha long enough to take a shit, and now he's out here to tell us how brave us boys were."

Jerry intervened, saying, "Give him a break, Ed. He doesn't want to be here any more than we do, maybe less."

Bo, in his long Southern drawl, said, "Waall, ya'll should know he's just here to give us moral and spiritual support."

Fast Eddie popped up, "Look, the only spiritual support I need is in the traveling pack in the Skipper's tent. His name is Jack Daniels and his label is black."

Laughing, they moved down the hill toward the ceremony. But Jake wanted to speak to Chaplain Dowd. The ceremony was short and unexpectedly moving. Jake saw tears in the eyes of many of the men as they remembered fallen buddies. He hadn't been able to get much out of anybody about that operation. It was like being back home at school and talking about sex with the guys. The ones who weren't getting any were always the ones who talked the most. On the other hand, the ones who were probably the biggest movers generally said very little. This must have been a really bad operation. What little information he did get came only later, one night when he was shooting the bull with Boston. He told Jake of how they found the bodies of one of their patrols tied around trees; their genitals had been cut off and stuffed into their mouths. Each one had been executed by one round through the head. It took place in the Ashau Valley, a name that brought grimaces of recognition to the faces of every marine in Alpha Company.

After the ceremony, as the troops were relieving men in the perimeter, Jake made his way over to the chaplain.

Dowd was a small man, extremely thin, with the haggard look of someone who had carried an incredible burden for a very long time.

"Pardon me, chaplain. Do you have a minute?" Jake said, stopping him midstep.

"Sure, lieutenant, what have you got?"

Dowd was a Lutheran minister who was ministering in the last place he ever wanted to be. He was sick and tired of being away from his family and sick and tired of death and these boys who never seemed to understand anything. Besides that, he wasn't even sure he believed in God anymore. Maybe he never did. Surely a rational God would not call people to serve in such a place or even allow such a situation to exist. It was to Dowd's spiritual vacuum that Jake brought his questions, pouring out so quickly they surprised him.

"Chaplain, I was just wondering if you could help me. I'm lonely and I miss my wife and baby," he said. "I have the responsibility of leading these guys, and it seems like I have so many unanswered questions about myself that it's difficult to know how to respond to their needs."

"What's your name, son?"

"Jake, Jake Adams," he responded.

"Well, Jake, I'll tell you, it never gets any easier. First tour, second tour, it just doesn't get any easier. Listen, boy, listen and you can hear it. Jehovah Jirah, El Shaddai. The voice of God calling for new souls to come home. And over here God doesn't have to wait, because every day the people who organized this little dance of death send more and more souls God's way. No, it never gets any easier." Dowd stood looking at him, using his left hand to pick at a spot of jungle rot on his face.

Jake's dad had given him a small New Testament, put out by the Gideons, one that he himself had carried during World War II. Jake had never been particularly religious; he had made a few attempts at going to church with Karen but that had primarily been to impress her parents, who were religious. Still, something had always pulled him in the direction of what he could identify as God. But this, this was not at all what he had expected from one of God's men. In fact, this was not what he expected from any man in a position of leadership. The chaplain asked if Jake would like to have chow with him, but Jake declined. He had heard enough. Maybe Fast Eddie was at least partially right. Spiritual power might be with Jack Daniels. It certainly wasn't with this chaplain.

Jake walked back toward his hootch, trying to understand what faith was. He fingered the .45 at his side and considered the death he was living with. At any moment it could all be over for any one of them. He had already heard scuttlebutt about John Baker, one of his basic-school classmates. The word was, he was being extracted from a hot landing zone and was about one hundred and fifty feet up when the jungle penetrator he was hooked to snapped. Jake wondered what John was thinking in those last few seconds. He wondered if he had time even to realize he was about to die. And Jake thought about the possibility that God was, even now, calling him home, as his mother used to say and as this chaplain put it in a grimmer way. What the hell does all of this mean? If there is a God, how does a man know for sure if it's God or someone else's drum he is marching to. And what about now? Oh, God, if you are there, say something to me, he prayed. Wham! Wham! Wham! Three mortar rounds landed almost simultaneously inside the perimeter. Pieces of dirt and shrapnel sang songs as they spun through the air. Someone on the left side of the perimeter was screaming for a corpsman. Jake dove into his fighting hole. These were only harassment rounds, weren't they? Or maybe the gooners took notice of their ceremony and decided to loft a few rounds in to mess it up. It was just a coincidence, Jake said to himself, as he huddled in his fighting hole, seeking cover. Some PFC from Weapons Platoon had bought a ticket home. The price was most of his left arm. Jake thought once more about what the chaplain had said. Jehovah's calling again. I wonder who will hear his voice next?

9

BO LAWLER HAD BEEN BORN IN HAT-
tiesburg, Mississippi. His mother and
father had roots that grew deep in the
South; Bo had grown up with the Old South and its way of life deeply
ingrained in his thinking. He was a big burly man with a dark mane of
hair that found no rest as it made its way down his back and worked its
way up again to his throat. He was just plain hairy, so much so that he
had to trim his chest hair at the neck. He would never have gone to
school at all if it had not been a legal requirement, and even that almost
wasn't sufficiently persuasive. He would have simply gone off hunting
and fishing and never come back. Bo's father, "Gripper" Lawler, drank
hard and Bo learned that habit along with his deep distrust of almost any
Yankee and all niggers. He grew up spending his summers walking the
great battlefields of the Civil War, with the Gripper explaining how
Gen'l Lee could have whupped them Yankees with enough men and
supplies.

Bo was both a natural leader and a natural goof-off. If there was a
short cut, he would take it. On the other hand, he was a decision maker.
He was nearly fearless and made quite a name for himself as a teenager

by jumping on the back of a twelve-point buck as it ran past his stand, and hanging on long enough to stab it to death. His roots went as deep as those of his parents and his grandparents. He grew up learning to distrust the people of Natchez because they conspired with the Yankees during the Civil War. In fact, until the day his mother died, she would not set foot in the city limits of Natchez, where all them ladies "laid with them Yankees." It was difficult for Jake to believe the depth of these feelings or that they still existed in the minds of people today.

Bo made it through the University of Mississippi just as he did everything else—barely. That, however, did not reflect on talent or ability, just on his attention span. There was really no other choice for him but the corps. Instead of a horse, he would ride airplanes; instead of Yankees, he would shoot gooks. His flying career came to an early end in Vietnam when he flew a CH-46 troop carrier into restricted airspace while chasing some NVA and then landed in the wrong LZ attempting to pick up some extra beer from the army. Instead of going into the bush as a forward air controller, Bo had volunteered to be a platoon commander, and since there was a shortage of officers in the First Battalion, Ninth Marines, the battalion commander agreed to take him. Besides, Bo was tired of those snot-nosed Yankees, smoking pot and trying to fly helicopters back in the squadron. He thought it would be a great chance to get out with the real Marine Corps and blow some slopes away.

Jake and Bo were becoming improbable but close friends. A marine paid a compliment to another by saying, "I would like to have him on my flank." Jake knew that he would always feel comfortable with Bo on his flank, regardless of his sometimes unpredictable behavior.

Bo stuck his head in Jake's hootch.

"Jake, come on, man, Wolf wants to see us. It sounds like another warning order. Maybe we're gonna finally get off this fuckin' hill."

It was about 1500 in the afternoon. Jerry Motley's platoon had patrol duty tonight and Jake, like the other platoon commanders, was running perimeter duty and setting out a couple of listening posts. He scrambled up the side of the hill and fell in step with Bo. As he did, he could see Jerry and Fast Eddie also walking toward Captain Wolf's tent.

Wayco Wolf was sitting on the edge of a field cot he had wangled out of the company first sergeant in Quang Tri. He had one boot off and was rubbing the bottom of his foot. The curls on top of his head were a little longer after his R and R. Wolf was examining three or four maps lying in the center of the cot. Jake reckoned that Bo was right, they were going somewhere.

"Well, it's what I've been waiting for ever since I got back," Wayco said. "The old man says we are going to move out to Vandegrift Combat Base down Route 9 on Monday. I don't know how long we will be there, but until we get further orders, we are going to run sparrow hawks and bald eagles in support of the rest of the regiment." Wolf turned toward Jake with a nod of recognition, saying, "We will disperse by platoons with First, then Bo and Second Platoon, and Jerry with Third. Fast Eddie will follow with Weapons. We'll saddle up at 0800 and transport by six-bys. Wolf stopped talking and looked at the map for a while and then back up at the gathered platoon commanders. "I'm not going to go into a complete five-paragraph order here," he said. "Just get your men ready. Let the top know if you need any special gear from the rear." Bo was looking at Jake, who happened to be looking at Fast Eddie, who was very methodically picking his nose. Jim Clahan, sitting outside the circle, shook his head. Vandegrift, he muttered, shit, that could be the first step to the Ashau Valley. Wolf looked over at him with an expression that was less than approving. "By the way," he said, "I've requested some extra special provisions paks, beer, and a hot meal on Sunday. The troops ought to like that."

"What about after Vandegrift, Skipper?" Ed broke in, saying out loud what Clahan had muttered beneath his breath. "What's happening after we pull that duty?"

Looking from Ed to Wolf, everyone focused their attention on the anticipated response. But before he could respond, Fast Eddie continued, "Sparrow hawks and bald eagles are shit duty. Basically, all we do is wait around in Vandegrift until someone really gets in a load of crap and then, depending on the size of the problem, we get heli-lifted into a hot LZ. A sparrow hawk is . . ."

Wolf interrupted, saying, "Eddie, none of us needs a lesson as to what type of mission a sparrow hawk or bald eagle is. The fact is, I don't know what will take place later. However, I have to be honest with you, there has been talk of going back down into the Ashau."

46

That statement was met with silence. As much as they wanted to "get some," none of them were real anxious to go back into the Ashau Valley; not even Jake, and he had never been there.

Clahan finally said it out loud: "I knew it!" With that he kicked an empty C-ration can across the floor of the tent area and got up. "Well, if that's it, Skipper, we all have a lot to do and we might as well get at it." Wolf allowed how that was it, and they all left to pass the word.

For the battalion, Operation Cameron Falls had lasted about one month. The intent had been the deployment of maneuverable battalions in western Quang Tri Province to reduce the enemy's threat from the west. In general, before and after Jake's arrival, the operation was against the 304th NVA Regiment. The First Battalion, Ninth Regiment in particular had faced the 57th NVA Regiment. At the operation's end just prior to the move to Vandegrift Combat Base, 97 soldiers had been killed, 11 marines had died, and 404 North Vietnamese were killed, while 37 were wounded. Thirteen hundred pounds of polished rice had been captured, one Russian truck destroyed, 190 mortar rounds captured, and 68,000 rounds of small-arms ammunition destroyed.

Vandegrift Combat Base lay about six clicks, about 1½ kilometers, south of the Rockpile on Route 9. It was a sprawling affair, four thousand meters in depth and five thousand meters wide. The Ninth Marines were to operate tactically, as needed, from Vandegrift south, southeast, and southwest. The First Battalion, Ninth Marine Regiment and Alpha Company rolled into Vandegrift on Monday, the first of January 1969. They took up a company position just about at the hub of the irregular wheel that was Vandegrift. A staff tent was erected with open sides, and an enclosed troop tent was erected about twenty-five meters away from it. Even though this was a forward combat base, there was still hot food here and even a makeshift slop chute or club of sorts. Wolf, Lieutenants Motley, Lawler, Gustefsun, Clahan, and Adams gathered at the slop chute the evening of their arrival at Vandegrift. Every day Vandegrift erupted periodically, spitting forth death for miles around its perimeter. Like clockwork through the day and night the North Vietnamese would loft answering rounds of 107 and 122 rockets into Vandegrift.

Captain Wolf pulled his special-occasion bottle of Jack Daniels from his pack as they all pulled up a chair around a small table. Glasses materialized from a gunnery sergeant who had apparently taken over operation of this primitive lash-up that passed for an officer's club. It wasn't much, just a wood frame with a tin roof and sandbag ticking hanging over the windowless panes. Small round tables made from communication-wire spools were adorned with a few wooden chairs that, at one time, had thatch seats. Wolf, standing by one of the little tables, gave up one of his sharklike grins and said, "Gentlemen, we're gathered here so that I can salute you and tell you that I have finally received my orders. I'll be rotating back to the world on the fifteenth. Believe it or not I'm going to the basic school at Quantico, where I can run through the woods and yell bang, bang at all those new lieutenants."

Everyone knew it was coming, but it was still a shock. Wolf had been like a rock, a professional who was respected not only by the younger officers and men but also by the older staff who knew that, in Wolf's heart, he was still one of them. The next question, of course, was who was going to be the new company commander? Lieutenant Clahan, one of only two black officers in the battalion, was senior to the others and in line for the job. But he was only two months away from rotating himself.

Wayco Wolf, after a couple of heavy shots of sour mash whiskey, became just a bit melancholy. He was reflecting on Crissman and all the others who had not made it back from so many patrols in the past two years. There were many of them, so many damn good people. Wolf had served two years in Vietnam, separated only by two short trips to Hawaii—not to see his wife, that was over by now, but just to lie on the beach, sink his manhood into a paid-for receptacle, and wish he were back in the bush with his men. After all, they were his real family, his only family. The blood, the sweat, the tears, the glory of it all. Son of a bitch, he actually loved it, he thought. If they would just let him stay, he might not ever go back. He chuckled to himself, knowing that in many ways he had succumbed to the bamboo complex. The lure of the East had taken part of his soul. He was more at home in Okinawa or Hong Kong or Japan than he was in the United States. Wayco looked up to find everyone staring at him. He had no idea how long he had been lost in reverie. Pulling up an empty chair he placed a full glass in front of it on the table. Hoisting his own glass in a toast, he rose, saying, "Gentlemen, I toast one of the best damn marines ever to wear the eagle, globe, and anchor, Lieutenant Barclay Crissman, who lived and died like a man."

"To Lieutenant Crissman!" Their voices joined in a ragged chorus, muffled by the walls of sandbags on the outside of the building. Jake was struck by the earnestness, the unguarded emotions displayed on each man's face. Then it hit him. Who, he wondered, would Jehovah call next?

They broke up, walking without speaking, back to the staff tent. Jerry Motley fell in beside Jake. As Jake had learned from quiet personal talks with him, he was nearly forty. He had signed an age waiver to get into the basic school at a time when most young men were grateful not to go at all or were trying to figure out ways to avoid serving in the military. He had two teenage sons who deeply admired a father who had walked away from running a successful auto-body repair shop to follow his dream and serve his country. Motley was stocky, short, and pug-faced with a pockmarked complexion that betrayed a lost battle with acne during his teen years. He had a good-natured personality that made everybody like him on first acquaintance. He simply never managed to rub anybody the wrong way. He loved his family and found his deep commitment to his responsibilities as an officer hampered only by the ache he felt at being cut off from his wife and children. He lived for the day when he would see his sons again; his sons lived for the day when they could hear their dad tell them what it was really like.

"Jake," Jerry asked, "what did you make of all that? Did you see Wolf's eyes? He was actually crying."

"I know," Jake said. "I wonder who is going to get the company."

"Yeah, I don't know about Clahan, and Fast Eddie would be unbelievable."

They both laughed at the absurd thought of Ed Gustefsun, company commander. They walked on down the hill and went behind the staff tent to a three-holer. Several marijuana "roaches" had been mashed into the plywood decking and the air was sweet with the stench of it.

"Hey, Jake, it looks like some of the troops were down here smoking some of that Vietnamese shit."

"Yeah, I still find it hard to take." Jake picked up an old *Playboy*. "It

49

looks like they were in here beating their meat at the same time." Jake paused for a few seconds, carefully selecting his next words. "How do you handle that part of it, Jerry?"

Jerry laughed. "You know, about every six weeks or so I wake up during the night or early in the morning, depending on the duty, to find my utilities stuck to my leg. It seems nature has a way of taking care of that, too."

"Yeah, I know what you mean," Jake responded.

It was funny. Jake had never liked sitting in an outhouse. Even here in Vietnam it still made him feel queasy. He would rather just take a dump in the woods. He always wondered what was going to crawl up his ass out of the dark recesses of the shitter. Once, when he was a boy scout, he made his first trip to summer camp and went three days without taking a shit because he was afraid to use the outhouse. It ruined his whole week; he was so miserable. Even here, with the possibility of a mortar round blowing up the whole damn shitter, he was still worried about what might crawl up his ass.

Here I am, he thought, the great war hero sitting on the shitter of life waiting to be called out to face something that surely couldn't be any more horrible than what was crawling around down in this hole.

Sergeant Hawkins threw open the door of the three-holer and said, "I thought I might find you two gentlemen here." He grinned at the dismay on their faces. "Pardon me! I don't want to interrupt your rest, but Captain Wolf wants to see all the platoon commanders."

10

THE BATTALION COMMANDER'S TENT stood on a rise just to the left of the Alpha Company front. Wayco Wolf was coming out of Colonel Dagomar's tent when Jake and Jerry came up the company street.

"Go on down to the staff tent," Wayco said. If you see the others, tell them to rally up there about 1900. We're going to take a little trip through the woods."

Fast Eddie, Jim Clahan, Bo Lawler, all three staff NCOs including Sergeant Hawkins, who had just been promoted, were already in the tent when Jake and Jerry arrived. Apparently they had been playing poker by the light of a dinky forty-watt lamp. Cards were strewn over the table and the yellowish light left pools of shadow that gave the impression you should whisper. Staff Sergeant Jacobsen had jury-rigged the lamp to a generator the army would discover missing the following day. Vandegrift had several army units and a company of South Korean tiger troops within the compound which often and inadvertently supplied the marines.

Captain Wolf showed up at exactly 1900, all business, and sat down on an empty ammo box vacated by Sergeant Hawkins. "Gentlemen, in three days, at 0800, we are going to move south-southeast overland toward Khe Sanh on a search-and-destroy mission. We'll hook up with elements of a doggie regiment that is sitting on the Khe Sanh airstrip wasting tons of ammunition in daily harassment and interdiction fire. Simply, our mission is to make contact with whatever lies between here and Khe Sanh." Wolf looked around at the circle of very worried faces flickering in the shadows of the dim lamp. "Gentlemen, this is Khe Sanh 1969, not 1968. We will not get caught up in a siege situation." Seeing Jake sitting back in a corner, he said, "Jake, we'll travel platoons in trace about fifteen meters apart. First Platoon will take the point, followed by Second, Third, and then Weapons. I want every man to carry one stick of C-4 plastique explosives and three heavy units of C-rations. Every man will carry a full complement of ammo, and each blooper carrier will hump six extra rounds." With that, Wolf got up and, sweeping the room with his right hand for emphasis, he said, "Well, let's do what we have to do and get this outfit tightened up; I want progress reports from each platoon commander daily." And he was gone.

The plan was to use Ca Lu, which was just a bend in the road about three clicks southeast of Vandegrift, as a line of departure. The next day was unbelievably hot. There had not been a great deal of heavy enemy activity since 1968, and apparently the North Vietnamese had pulled back and were using the Ho Chi Minh trail through Laos to bring supplies as far south as possible and then slip across the border into Vietnam and push still farther south.

Jake was filled with the kind of excitement that came along with any trial or challenge he had ever faced in his life. Only, this time, there was also a kind of enduring fear. Not the fear of failure, although in some sense that was there too, but the fear of dying, the fear that lingered in the heart of every man who had ever faced battle and had time to think about it. He spent time preparing his gear and making sure his men had everything they needed. Boston continued to carry an M-79 grenade launcher, even though he was now a squad leader. It fired a forty-milli-meter round of spin-armed grenade that was lofted or, as the troops said, "blooped" into an enemy position. Boston was one of the best at cranking out rounds from this breechloaded weapon.

On the day before they moved out, Jake met with his squad leaders: Boston, Hawkins, Sugar Bear, and Staff Sergeant Jacobsen. He was building solid relationships with each one of them but found himself becoming attached to some more than others. Boston was one. If Jake weren't careful, he would hang back from putting him on point because of the additional risk. On the other hand, Boston was one of the best out front.

Jake stood in the center of the staff tent looking at each man present. "Well," he said, "it looks like there is some bad shit coming down."

"Boston, first squad will take the point from Ca Lu. I'll move behind your squad."

He turned to the Professor who was holding an M-16: "Tom, you pack the PRC-25 in a pack and carry a .45 again. I don't want you carrying a rifle."

"Aw, come on, lieutenant, I feel better carrying a rifle."

"Look, Thomas, I want you there with that radio when I need it, not off shooting gooks somewhere."

Sergeant Hawkins, now acting platoon sergeant as well as second squad leader, and Staff Sergeant Jacobsen who had moved up to company gunny in a recent promotion, stood apart from the rest and looked at Jake with expectation.

"Hawk," Jake instructed, "keep the squads five to eight meters apart. I want each squad to carry one LAAW per fire team. I'm not expecting tanks but it won't hurt to have the added firepower. The M-60 humpers should carry two extra ammo boxes. We'll move in squad columns. That's about it. Any questions?"

Sugar Bear kicked a piece of rock across the dirt floor of the tent and asked quietly, "What about replacements, lieutenant? I need at least three new riflemen. I know Boston and Hawk are at least as bad off as I am."

"I don't know, Sugar Bear. The Skipper hasn't said anything about replacements. I'll see what I can find out. Anything else?"

That met with silence, so Jake concluded by saying as frankly as he could, "I want everybody ready, and be sure each troop is carrying a couple of smoke grenades, red and green."

Jake walked back up the hill toward Colonel Dagomar's tent. Captain Wolf was still inside, along with the other company commanders. Staff

Sergeant Jacobsen and Bo Lawler were moving in the same direction. It was completly dark now and although there were lights at various places within the compound, night security procedures were in effect.

Bo was yelling at Jake. Jake could barely make out his vague form in the darkness but there was no mistaking that Southern drawl.

"What you got, Bo?" Jake queried.

"Just come on over here, boy," Bo shot back. "You'll be glad you did."

Jake turned to Gunny Jacobsen and said, "Come on over here with me, Gunny, I may need a witness. Let's see what the good lieutenant is so excited about."

What Bo Lawler had was two bottles of Wayco Wolf's Jack Daniels black label. The three of them sat down in a little draw partway up the hill. Jake had never really been a big drinker but, as in high school, there was the added attraction of a touch of conspiracy involved and that was all it took. With each pull from the bottle, the stronger became the bonding among the conspirators.

Sam Jacobsen felt a little uneasy sitting there with two lieutenants drinking whiskey; not uneasy about the familiarity, but about their ability to handle it. But hell, he thought, I wouldn't pass this up for nothing.

"Sam," Jake said. "What do you think about all this shit? You've been here for two tours now. Why don't we just fly up to Hanoi and blow the crap out of all those little bastards and be done with it?"

"Damn, lieutenant, if I had the answer to that, I would be commandant and not sitting here in the bush drinking stolen hootch."

"Come on, Sam, you know what I mean. How many times are we going to take the same fucking piece of real estate, leave it, and go back and pay the same or greater price again? Bo, what about you, what do you figure?"

"Waall, I'll tell you, Jake. You ain't been here long enough to be thinkin' the things you're thinkin'. Plus, you shouldn't be puttin' those kinda thoughts in the head of the good sergeant here. All you damn Yankees been spendin' too much time thinkin' for years. We're here to do a job, boy, and when you put on them brown bars, you agreed to do it, period."

Sam Jacobsen, who had been listening to all of this in a near fog, was feeling quite mellow after he took another pull from the nearly empty bottle. Out of the corner of his eye he spied Wayco's jeep parked in front of the colonel's tent.

"Unhh, Gennelmen," he drawled, "how would you two upstandin' war heroes like to have a newly selected gunny sergeant as a driver and take a little spin in the Skipper's jeep at night in the middle of a goddamn war zone?"

Jake looked at Bo and then at the Gunny. All three of them, now feeling absolutely delighted with themselves, knew that this would be a really great adventure.

They crawled out of their comfortable ditch and, mutually supporting each other, made their way toward the jeep.

"Okay, Sam," Bo ordered. "You take the wheel and if you can make it, let's go all the way to Hanoi and ask Ho for an audience. Maybe he can answer some questions from our boot lieutenant here."

"All right, Bo."

"Knock that shit off," Jake interjected. "I'm not boot to you anyway, asshole. You might have been here a little longer than . . ."

"Gennelmen, gennelmen, please . . . let's take our ride."

"Okay, Gunny, let's hit it," Jake said as he and Bo scrambled into the back seat of the jeep.

They were about to finish the second fifth of Jack Black as the jeep spewed dirt and rock back up the road from whence they came. Vandegrift, even though a sprawling affair, was no place to be driving a jeep with its headlights on at night. Yet there they were, lights on, traveling too fast for the condition of the roads, and proud of it. They careened around the first turn in the road and headed up a steep grade toward the main gate. Beyond it the road was a continuation of Route 9 toward the Rockpile. The Gunny was shit-faced. He tried to maintain control of the vehicle but, as they rounded the second turn, much faster than anyone would have tried it, he just couldn't hold the wheel straight.

They left the road and were suddenly airborne. The drop, about twenty feet, had any of them been sober, would probably have killed them. As it was, Jake thought for a moment that he was back on the bobsleds at the Highlands Amusement Park in St. Louis. Bo didn't know or care where he was; however, he did let go with a respectable rebel yell that his grandfather would have been proud of. You would have thought that at least the headlights would be smashed out, since the jeep went in nose-first. However, not only did they not break, but they stayed on, casting pale circles around the nose of the jeep.

Sam Jacobsen flew over the hood and landed about ten feet in front of the jeep. Both Bo and Jake fell forward into the front seat and got tangled up with each other. Sobering up came real quick. Jake couldn't quite manage disentangling his legs from Bo's.

"Bo, Bo, come on. Help me get out of here."

Bo was laughing like a crazed hyena. "Holy shit, Jake, did you see that? That was terrific! Hey, Gunny, where the hell are you? Let's do that again."

"Come on, Bo, you are nuttier than a damn fruitcake, let's get out of here. Once the Skipper sees what we did to his jeep, he'll fucking court martial us."

They somehow extricated themselves from the jeep and found Gunny Jacobsen sitting up in the elephant grass.

The three of them made their way back to the staff and officers' tent. None of them were sober enough to do anything about the jeep. They just left it where it was. As Jake was about to doze off, however, the question did occur to him: Just what the hell was Wolf going to do when he discovered two bottles of his best whiskey missing. Shit, he thought, that's worse than losing the jeep.

Jake became aware that someone was leaning over him when that someone whispered loudly, "Lieutenant, wake up, sir."

He could make out a blur that could have been Sergeant Hawkins, against the dark backdrop of the well-weathered tent.

"What is it?"

"Sir, I just felt you would want to inspect the troops. I mean, before we rallied up to step off this morning."

Now definitely identifying Hawkins, Jake said, "Sure, sure, Hawk. I appreciate it. Thanks a lot. I'll just be a few minutes."

Sergeant Hawkins turned to go and, thinking the better of it, turned and said, "Lieutenant, you smell like shit."

Jake shook his head, trying to make some sense of why he had such terrible pain in his head. He was looking for his shaving kit and then began to remember fragments from the night before.

Oh, no, he thought. What in the world did we do with the jeep? In a panic he turned around looking for Gunny Jacobsen.

"Gunny," he yelled, "Gunny . . . Sam, where the hell are you?"

But Jacobsen's cot was empty.

Jake threw a towel around his waist and stumbled down to the showers the Seabees had built and took a "navy shower," one you use aboard ship to conserve water. All he could think about was that for the second time in less than two months, he had shot his career all to hell. His only consolation was that there was nothing he could do about it now. He made his way back to the staff tent and pulled on a relatively clean green T-shirt. After making sure his gear was together, he took a quick look around for the Gunny and then took off for the platoon area. As he approached, he could hear shouts coming from inside the main tent. He ripped back the flap and saw Boston standing just inside. He had just cold-cocked a PFC by the name of Pringale. Jake could see several black marines huddled in the left-hand corner of the tent. This kind of trouble had a peculiar odor to it. It was and yet it wasn't like the smell when the gooners were near. Jake could feel it and smell it. As he burst in, a deadly silence fell.

"What the hell is going on here?" Jake asked no one in particular. Before he could say another word someone walked up behind him and rabbit-punched him in the back of the neck. Jake could not believe this was happening. He turned instinctively to return the punch just as the whole tent erupted. Sam Jacobsen took one step through the hatchway to the tent and let a single round go from his .45 through the overhead. Inside the tent there was only silence and the heavy warmth of morning.

The Gunny took a sweeping glance around the room; picking out Jake, he asked, "Everything okay here, lieutenant?" Jake didn't have the slightest idea what the problem was or had been. He did know that sitting in a defensive perimeter for an extended period of time was getting on everybody's nerves and he didn't want to make an issue out of frayed nerves. Still, discipline required he not just walk away. That, he felt, could ultimately be fatal in the bush.

"Sam," he said, "it's okay. However, I still want to know what started this ruckus, once everyone has calmed down. I also want accountability from every NCO in this tent."

Then he turned and, making his way through the sweating bodies and dust-filled air, yelled back at the squad leaders to get their asses in gear and saddle up. "We've got exactly forty-five minutes to form up with the rest of the company," he said.

He had forgotten his main concern of the morning; that being what happened to Wayco's jeep and what was going to happen as a result.

Gunny Jacobsen strode up beside him and Jake, turning, asked, "Gunny, have you seen the Skipper this morning?"

"Sure did, sir. We had a little chow together just after dawn. Incidentally, he was really agitated about two missing bottles of booze."

"The whiskey?" Jake asked incredulously. "What about the jeep, didn't he have anything to say about the jeep?"

"Not much, actually," the Gunny replied with a grin. "He was only curious anyway. It seems he had a new army jeep available to him this morning, and he didn't know where that came from any more than he knew where the other one went. Besides, I think he likes this one better anyway. Anyway, we'll be gone before the doggies figure out where their jeep went, and Wayco won't need it after that anyway."

The morning wore on while preparations continued to move out to the bush. This was going to be a company-sized movement designed to join up with other elements of the First Battalion, Ninth Marines, during the two or three weeks required to make a sweep from Vandegrift Combat Base to the hill above Khe Sanh. Two map sheets were required, Thon Doc Kinh and Huong Hoa. Before they were finished, they would cover approximately thirty-six clicks on the ground, covering elevations from as little as one hundred feet to as great as one thousand feet or more. Resupply was to be by helicopter, as usual.

Company A formed up around the perimeter of the landing zone at Vandegrift. They would move southeast toward Ca Lu and then southwest toward Khe Sanh. The heat had set in early and was already tiring them. By now, Jake had acquired certain habits that made him more comfortable, as all bush marines had. He carried only three heavies, or meat units, from his C-rations. In place of the two or three other heavy units he carried books. Right now, he was deep into the trilogy of *Lord of the Rings* and *The Hobbit*. He found that when he was engrossed in a novel he could actually leave Vietnam for a while. He also had decided to carry a two-and-a-half-pound canvas water bag, plus two canteens on his web belt. It seemed he was always thirsty. In addition, he carried a small portable battery-powered radio, which he had gotten in trade a few days earlier from a lieutenant who was going back to Okinawa. It had cost him an NVA belt buckle but now he could listen to tunes from the armed-forces radio network, and that also had a way of taking him home.

Almost without his noticing it, he was becoming a veteran. His jungle boots had finally taken on the chalk-white coating of the bush. He was dropping the stateside fat he had accumulated and he was learning the basics of staying alive. He might just make it, as Captain Wolf had predicted nearly two months before.

This operation would be Wayco's last movement with Alpha Company, First Battalion. Jake knew from chats with him that his feelings were mixed. In many ways Wolf didn't want to leave the bush and the comraderie of the troops. On the other hand, if he had to leave, he didn't want to buy the farm now. Jake had been a little surprised to hear him say that, but even more surprised to hear him question the reason for the movement. It was true that the First Battalion had been in heavy contact off and on for months and it was difficult to get a rational explanation for why they were now going to make this trek down Route 9. At any rate, Jake felt, all they had to do was make their way down to the Khe Sanh airstrip and come back. Then, as far as Wayco was concerned, he could go back to the world. Then he could pull a tour there and come back if the war was still going on. After all, as Jake heard him say many times, "It might not be the best, but it damn sure is the only one we got."

11

ALPHA COMPANY HAD SADDLED UP and was waiting in formation at Vandegrift airstrip. There hadn't been any NVA rockets or incoming artillery in a couple of days. During the lull, Vandegrift spread its tentacles of destruction out into southern Quang Tri Province. Alpha Company would be just another one of them.

As he approached the company, Wayco yelled to the Gunny, "Saddle 'em up, Sam. Let's hit it."

He saw Jake Adams sitting beside the road with some of the men from his platoon. He recognized Hawkins and Boston and the black corporal, the one they called Sugar Bear. This lieutenant seemed like he might become a good one. Thank God, he thought; since Crissman was killed and Clahan seemed like he was more interested in promoting black power than the corps, he had become concerned. Bo Lawler was good in the bush but he was a little too loose, Wayco thought. Besides, he flew airplanes and you can never trust a flyer. And Fast Eddie, well, he was probably just plain nuts.

Wayco went up the Gunny and asked if he had checked out the platoon sergeants.

"Yes, sir," Jacobsen replied. "They are all ready to go. Lieutenant Clahan is going to stay back with the first sergeant and go into Quang Tri to pick up the company payroll." Wolf, who was straining to hear him over the helicopter activity, said that he knew that and had asked him to accompany the first sergeant. Turning to look back over the formation, he said, "Well, Sam, let's do it one more time." With that, he motioned for the platoon leaders to rally up, and the hundred and twelve men of Alpha Company, First Battalion, Ninth Marine Regiment came to life, forming up like a huge snake stretching out in the late-morning sun of Vietnam.

Ca Lu was only about three thousand meters outside Vandegrift, and it didn't take long for the column to reach its jumping-off point. Jake and First Platoon were on the point with Second, Third, and Weapons last.

The Professor moved behind Jake, who was following the first squad. Boston had taken his usual place just behind the first fire team and Hawkins was moving at the rear of the platoon. Captain Wolf took up a position just behind Third Platoon and moved with his headquarters group. They were making good time considering the heat, which was exceptional for January, and the hindrance of fully loaded packs. They made a southwest turn at Ca Lu and moved steadily along the Dakrong River.

From just above Vandegrift, Route 9 changed from a single-lane, hard-surface road, to a single-lane, loose-surface road. The troops called the hard-surface roads "red ball," from the color on the map sheets. They moved on past Khe Ca Lu, a small abandoned village about two clicks west of Ca Lu, and headed southwest on Route 9.

By now, they were far enough away from Vandegrift that the law of the bush was taking over. The men instinctively paced out a little farther apart and platoons were running about twenty meters apart. Movement was slowing to allow for greater security and the terrain was becoming increasingly elevated. Late on the first day, they reached Bong Kho, a destroyed village along Route 9, just north of the Song Quang Tri where it turns south and becomes the Dakrong. Just to the northeast was Dong

Chio Mountain, about seven hundred meters high. During the latter part of the day they moved skirmishers on the flanks, anticipating possible problems from the high ground.

The heat was beginning to take its toll when the captain sent word forward to halt and prepare to set in. Alpha Company formed a perimeter around Bong Kho, each platoon intersecting with the next, forming fields of fire between the M-60 machine guns. Jake set out his listening posts and sat back to prepare a little chow. Searching through his pack he selected one of the three heavies he was carrying: a can of ham and limas, or ham and mothers, as they were more often called. It wasn't long before Wayco made his rounds, inspecting the way each platoon had been set in. He asked Jake how he was doing, offered him a cigarette, and went on his way. Jake made a small elevated stove with three small rocks and placed a heat tab in between them using his "John Wayne" to ventilate the can. Then, lighting the heat tab, he put the can on top, the contents of which quickly came to a boil. The damn things never cooked evenly, he thought to himself. He fingered his "John Wayne" that hung on his dog-tag chain and marveled at how a little piece of metal alloy could be so useful. It was really just a small can opener but seemed to be so important to life in the bush. As he was thinking these things, Jerry Motley shuffled up and sat down beside him.

"How's it going, Jake?"

"Okay, man. It was a long day. I wish I felt better about where we are going."

"Yeah, me too," Jerry said. "Listen, Jake, I just wondered. Are you still writing your wife every day?"

"Yeah, I try, I don't always get it done, but I try," Jake responded. "The problem is, I miss her so badly it hurts to write because I start to think about things back in the world. I'm glad there's so little time to think when we're moving like this. Back in Vandegrift, there was too much time to think, period."

"Yeah, yeah, I know what you mean. Listen, Jake, I know this sounds like some pretty bad theater, but would you make sure Sally knows what happened here and how I felt, if I don't make it back?"

Jake looked up at his older counterpart, searching out his face for some sign of what brought on that request. Finally, he said, "Come on,

Jerry, don't be talking like that. We haven't even seen a fucking gook out here yet. What the hell are you thinking, anyway? If there's something you know that I don't, how about letting me in on it."

"I know that," Jerry said, "it's just that I want her to know. It's sorta like some kind of emotional insurance for me. I want to know that somebody out here will tell her like it is. Just tell me you'll write her or even go see her, if you get a chance. Please, Jake, I need to know that you will, it's important to me."

Silence stood between them. Once again Jake searched out the face of his new friend and could see that he was deeply in earnest. "Sure, sure . . . that's no problem, Jerry," he responded. "But, listen, you gotta learn to expect the right thing. I don't know exactly how to explain it, but I really believe that somehow we get what we expect, even out here. How many times have you heard about guys who just knew they were going to get it, and did? I don't believe in that premonition crap; I think they got just what they expected. They became accidents looking for a place to happen. You have to control your mental, Jerry. You know, I don't mean like superman or something. You don't just say, 'no gook in Nam can get me,' and then walk into a firefight. You have to use common sense—but you also have to have confidence you're gonna make it."

Now it was Jerry's turn to stare in silence. "Where did you pick up all of your philosophy, lieutenant?" he asked in a mockingly formal tone.

"I don't know," Jake replied. "I just know it in my guts. I also know the more I worry about losing what is at home, the more I lessen my chances. It's like being poor; when you haven't got anything there is just not much to worry about. But when you have a lot, all of a sudden your entire attitude changes and soon you start doing things that you normally wouldn't do and sometimes they are the wrong things." Jake found himself unconsciously scratching at the small cuts that were turning into jungle rot on his hands. "I also know," he continued, "I just can't worry so much. I've got to concentrate on what I need to do to survive. Besides, the more I concentrate on Karen, or Harmony, the more the pain. Why spend every day in pain? It's like being in jail here; I can go anywhere I want, here, and nowhere else. I love my family, you love your family. I tell Karen that in every letter. She doesn't understand why I am here and I guess maybe I don't either completely. She probably

63

even resents me being here in some weird way because I left her. I didn't want to leave her; I just wanted to do my duty the best way I could do it. Listen, Jerry, you son of a bitch. Look what you've done. Now you've got me thinking about it and that's just what I'm trying to tell you. It would drive you nuts. You have got to focus on staying alive."

It was getting dark and Hawk came up, interrupting the conversation to say it was time for the listening posts to go out and wondering if Jake wanted to tell them anything before they set in.

"No, Hawk," Jake responded. "Just make sure we get sit reps every hour. By the way, who you got going out?"

"Peters and Sump from Sugar Bear's squad, sir," Hawk answered.

"Okay, go ahead and send them out and then come on back. I want to discuss tomorrow's movement with you."

Jerry allowed how he ought to get back to his platoon, and Jake, now in heavy darkness, found the mosquitoes were taking over. He pulled a bottle of bug juice from his pack and was spreading it on any areas where his skin was exposed. There was a constant hum now from the mosquitoes. It was as if there was something else alive occupying the same space as he was. The bug juice smelled acrid and mixed with the dirt and sweat when it was spread on and burned like hell on the places that had already been itched raw.

Jake got up to check his lines and made his way along the perimeter. He stopped periodically to chat with troops in their fighting holes and then crossed over to Second Platoon to find Bo Lawler stretched out by a big banana tree eating a can of pound cake and peaches.

"What's happenin', man?" Jake asked.

"Not much," Bo replied, not bothering to look up.

Jake was anxious to hear what Bo thought of their little escapade back in Vandegrift, so he said, "Can you believe we got away with that crap back at Vandegrift? I thought for sure Wolf was going to string us both up. You know it was the Gunny that got everything squared away."

"Man, he is something else. It's no wonder he has made it through two tours in this asshole place. Streetwise is what Jacobsen is. Speaking of Jacobsen," Bo continued, "I hear you had a near riot in your troop tent this morning. What the hell was that all about?"

"You know, Bo, I never did find out. In fact, that's a good question.

I'm going to head back and see if the Gunny has learned anything. Catch ya later, hear."

Jake made his way slowly back, retracing his steps along his lines, reassuring the men and checking for firing stakes and intersecting lines of fire. He told one marine to put his cigarette out, knowing as soon as he was gone he would light up again. He found the Professor taking a sit rep from the listening post, and asked where the Gunny was.

"He's up with the Skipper in headquarters group, sir," the Professor responded. "Do you want me to get him on the hook?"

"No," Jake responded, "I'll talk to him in the morning." Jake sat down beside the Professor and told him to pass the word if anything came up on the company frequency. He was surprised at how tired he was and found himself drifting off into a semisleep without much difficulty.

About 0300 hours, the Professor shook Jake awake, saying that he could not get the listening post to respond to him and that they had missed their last sit rep. Jake, just coming to, said thickly, "Try it again, Tom."

The Professor whispered into the handset while at the same time poking his glasses up on his nose. "Alpha One, LP, Alpha One, LP, come in please . . ."

There was no response. Jake said, coming fully awake now, "Okay. Give me the hook, Tom." The Professor handed him the handset and settled back on his haunches to listen. Jake, whispering into the radio phone, said, "Alpha One, LP, Alpha One, LP, if you can hear this and cannot break radio silence squeeze your handset once for yes and twice for no, over."

Silence! Headquarters group monitoring the net came up and wanted to know if Jake wanted them to wake up the Skipper.

"No, not yet," Jake responded. "I'll get back to you in a few minutes."

Jake pulled out his .45 and began a field check. Hawkins, who was now wide awake and listening to the goings-on, asked what he was about to do.

"Well," Jake said. "There are one of three possibilities. One, they are asleep and not answering the calls and failing to make their sit reps. Two, they've been wasted and the gooners are about to make their way inside our lines. Three, their radio is busted and they can't make contact. Regardless, I've got to find out, so I'm going out there."

Sergeant Hawkins immediately said, "Shit, lieutenant, you can't do that. Hell, if the gooners are out there, they'll be between the LP and our lines. They'll be crawlin' right at you. If our guys aren't wasted then they're asleep and they might wake up and think you're a gook and blow your damn head off."

"Look, Hawk, if I'm not back in fifteen minutes or if you don't hear from me over the radio, get word to the Skipper ASAP. Otherwise, you don't do a damn thing. This is my problem, got it?"

Sergeant Hawkins tried to see Jake's face in the darkness but Jake was removing his 782 gear, preferring to stick his K-bar into the top of his boot. He jammed his .45 down the front of his utility trousers and moved up to the M-60 position that was directly opposite the coordinates of the LP. He had Hawk tell the men in their positions what he was doing and then crawled out in front of the lines.

Immediately he wondered what the hell he was doing. I don't have to do this. I'm not even sure it's correct. Fifty meters was a long way away. He knew that there would be trip flares and claymores rigged up, but they should be out in front of the LP. About ten meters out, he knew for sure he had made a mistake. Hell, I could have waited for light, he thought, a brief sensation of panic washing over him. But what if they were hurt? Besides, the security of the whole company was in question. He crawled as silently as he could through the elephant grass. The ground was flat and sandy with elephant grass in patches; it sloped upward until the bank of the river rose up to meet triple-canopy jungle and steep cliffs over the river. Jake wondered what would happen if Sump and Peters had set in at the wrong place. What would he do then? Fine time to think of that, lieutenant. He moved forward, certain his time was gone already. It seemed like an hour had gone by but in reality he had probably been out about five minutes.

Off in the distance the abrupt eerie cry of a tiger made the hair on the back of his head stand on end. Tigers, shit, what if I run into one of those? Tigers, hell, what if I run into some gooner? About thirty meters out, in unrelieved darkness, he got up on his knees in the higher elephant grass and began to make better time. He knew he should be approaching the position of the LP when he head a muffled groan just ahead. Jake dropped to his stomach and held his breath, straining to hear any further noise. The silence was broken only by the constant hum of mosquitoes. He slowly worked his way forward in the direction of the groan. It was hard to see; broken clouds allowed only infrequent moonlight to illuminate the landscape. Jake moved cautiously, pausing every few meters. He was about to get to his knees once again when he heard a snort, like a pig or some other kind of animal might make. Pausing, he once more moved forward; this time his hand landed on what was certainly a boot. No sooner had his hand hit the boot then its owner jerked it away, letting out a muffled cry. Jake knew immediately who they were and whispered urgently, "Shut up, you idiots, it's Lieutenant Adams."

Both Peters, a black private, and Sump, a new replacement, had fallen asleep. Jake had to wrestle Sump to the deck, and Peters got the full brunt of the butt of his .45 in the nose.

"Shut up, damn it," Jake said again. "It's me, Lieutenant Adams."

Peters was trying to stop the flow of blood from his nose and Sump was just realizing that he was not going to get his throat cut by some gooner. Jake called back in to the Professor and told him what had taken place. He knew the company commander "Six" would be monitoring the net, so that should take care of that concern. He turned to Peters and Sump and hissed, "If you two don't stay awake, I'm going to have your ass. You're damn lucky we aren't back in Vandegrift, because if we were I would have the Gunny dump both of you into the tactical wire." Still shaking with anger and relief, Jake began to make his way back into the lines, after alerting the Professor that he was on his way in. The clouds were thickening and the darkness was once more absolute and endless.

12

NOT LONG AFTER DAWN, ALPHA COM-
pany was up and facing another day's
march. Wolf had called the platoon
commanders together and was reviewing the day's planned movement.
They were to move northwest from Bong Kho, then southwest to cross
the Song Kao Quan and pick up Route 9, heading directly west to Po
Kang, about two thousand meters north of the airstrip at Khe Sanh.
They would set off in the reverse order of the previous day so that Jake
and First Platoon would be bringing up the rear. As they were about to
break up and go back to their platoons, Captain Wolf turned to Jake and
said, "Stick around a few minutes, will you? I want to talk with you."

Oh no, thought Jake, he found out about the jeep. Now I'm in for it.

Wolf, looking directly at him with those blue eyes squinting in the
sun, said coldly, "Listen, Jake, I think that stunt you pulled last night
was for the birds. I don't need any of this John Wayne bullshit around
here. Do you understand me, lieutenant?"

Jake was stunned. He began to protest, but Wolf kept going. "Look,
you go out there and buy the farm on some stupid-ass stunt like last
night and I have to replace another platoon commander for no real

purpose. You're here to lead troops, Jake. If you want to go to Forced Reconnaissance and run around in the boonies snooping and pooping, I'll put in for a change of orders for you. Is that clear?"

Jake, remembering the incident with Old Hatchet Face, felt it was not the time to say anything else, so he simply replied, "Yes, sir."

Wolf still staring at him, said, "All right, Jake, go on back to your platoon."

"Thank you, sir," Jake replied, and turned immediately to head back to First Platoon.

Peters was waiting for Jake as he approached the platoon that was now getting itself into marching order.

Peters stood up as Jake approached and said, "Sir, Private Peters requests permission to request mast with the company commander."

Jake had just about enough of this whole mess. It was clear Peters's nose was broken and it was also just as clear he was going to file a formal complaint with Captain Wolf. Jake didn't reply. He turned to Sergeant Hawkins who was standing idly by and said, "Hawk, make sure this piece of crap has a chance to request mast as soon as we are out of the bush."

"Yes, sir," Hawkins replied.

Peters screamed at Jake, who was walking away, "I want to request mast right now! I'm not going any farther in the bush with you."

Jake stopped in his tracks and turned around to see Sergeant Hawkins grabbing Peters by his flak jacket and, pushing his own elongated country nose against the nearly flat protuberance of Peters's, said firmly, "Private, you will go back to your squad and fire team. You will perform your duties as an individual combat marine as long as we are in the bush, and you will treat this lieutenant or any other officer with the respect of their rank. If you do not, I will see that you walk point from here to Khe Sanh. Do you read me, shithead?"

Hawkins had been reiterating each point by pecking his nose into Peters's face. They looked like a pair of ruffled grouse engrossed in their mysterious mating ritual. Peters said nothing. He dropped his head, grabbing his pack and weapon, which had fallen at his feet, and moved back toward Boston and first squad.

Jake looked at Sergeant Hawkins, who was breathing heavily with emotion. This, he thought, is a good man. I was afraid I lost someone irreplaceable when Jacobsen made Gunny. But Hawkins is gonna cut it.

If it were possible, this day was hotter than the day before. You could actually see the heat coming up in waves from the earth. It moved out in front of them as they struggled to keep up with the column. For some reason, they hadn't received a resupply, and water was running short. In some cases, food was already becoming a problem. Wayco wanted to cross the Song Kao Quan for sure that day. The problem was its depth and speed of the rapids. He had tried to pick what looked liked the best point to cross on the map. But the maps were seldom very accurate. Besides, the best crossing point for accessibility might not be the best for security. He moved his company in forty-five-minute intervals, trying to rest for fifteen minutes each hour. At different times during the day, they heard firing two or three ridge lines away. Wayco knew there should have been no friendly troop movement in those grids. He reported his progress and audio sightings back to the battalion.

They had moved up a ridge line that required pulling themselves up by vines at times. Even when resting, as they were now, they had to plant their boot heels in the dirt to keep from sliding down the mountain. Jake fired up his radio and could barely hear a static-coated "Age of Aquarius" fighting its way out over the Armed Forces Network. Everyone was exhausted. Between the heat and the elevation, it was slow going. It seemed as if they might not make contact with "Charlie" anyway. The long column moved laboriously, like a giant centipede trying to find its legs. Jake knew the front of the column was already moving. It was always a chase to keep up when you brought up the rear. He was listening to the final strains of "Ruby," as Kenny Rogers told her not to take her love to town, and beginning to feel sorry for himself, when he heard the whhummp! Everybody hit the deck. There were no secondary explosions, but Jake was certain it came from up front. He called the Professor up so he could monitor the net. The Skipper was already requesting a sit rep when Sergeant Chapman, the Third Platoon sergeant, came up on the radio. "Alpha Six, Alpha Six, this is Alpha Three Assist, over. Do you read me, over?"

"Go ahead, Assist. This is Alpha Six, over."

"Alpha Six. We have a gook claymore blown on the reverse slope of a hill at 02571438. We have two WIAs and one KIA. Alpha Three Actual is the KIA, over."

A moment of silence filled the net. Jake was not accepting what he had heard. He was sure there was a mistake. Captain Wolf came back up on the net and told Bo Lawler, who was moving behind Third Platoon, to move up and assess the situation and call in a medevac if the WIAs could not be handled by Doc Pony. He also told them to move out skirmishers left and right and hold their position until he could make his way up front.

Bobby Vinton was singing "Mr. Lonely," and Jake was thinking of Jerry Motley, thirty-eight years old, trying to fulfill a dream — remembering that just last evening he made a pledge to contact Sally and tell her how he had died and that he had loved her. He was Jerry's emotional insurance policy and now apparently he had to pay out.

Jake looked at his hands, covered with the scabs of jungle rot that never seemed to heal. How the hell was Jerry going to heal? What if that were me? How would Karen heal? How are any of us going to heal? This whole place is just like the jungle rot on my hands. It looks like it's healing, but it never does; it just scabs over, and mounds of pus collect underneath until you pull the scab off and start all over again. We just keep pulling the scab off and discovering new mounds of pus. Maybe they had made a mistake, he thought desperately. Maybe Jerry wasn't even dead. I just told him how to make it. He had to get his confession right. Where is that damn chaplain now? Where is God? Was Jerry Motley the next name that had come out of Jehovah's throat? The Professor was saying something, but Jake still had the earphone to the radio stuck in his ear and all he could hear were the Archies singing "Sugar, Sugar." He reached up and pulled out the earphone just in time to hear Wormand say that the Skipper wanted him up front.

"Okay, Tom. Send word back for Hawk to come up and take over until I get back."

He began to move forward in the column, up the incline, past the troops. They were tired and all wanted to know what was going on. You could see the fear in their eyes. It was as if they knew that a part of the body had died and were already in mourning.

It took nearly fifteen minutes to make his way to the head of the column. Two wounded marines sat on the deck by the side of the draw they had been standing in. Wayco, Bo, and Gunny Jacobsen were huddled around a poncho that covered a mound at their feet. You could see where the claymore had been hanging on a banana tree at the center of the trail. Gook claymores had small ball bearings, about a thousand, which were expelled out with tremendous force into anything in their path. The two marines on the ground didn't seem to be badly wounded. One had a couple of cuts in his neck and the other had taken a few pieces of shrapnel in his arm.

The trip wire had been strung along an old path in the jungle mulch. Jerry, it turned out, didn't trip the wire himself. Another troop, about six feet to his rear, must have hit it and Jerry was directly in front of the blast. There were large dark blotches in the poncho liner they had thrown across the body.

As Jake approached, Wayco said, "I don't want to stay on this trail much longer. I'm going to move the company up the top of this ridge and then down to the Song Kao Quan. Jake, I want you to keep one squad and a gun team out of your platoon for security until they can get a medevac chopper out here for the two WIAs and Lieutenant Motley. They won't be able to land because of the terrain, but it would take too much time to go back down or move up with them; so the bird will use a jungle penetrator to take them out. Sergeant Hawkins can take command of your platoon until you can rejoin us . . . now, let's take a look at the map so we're sure where we will rally up."

"Yes, sir," Jake replied, his ears hearing the words and his heart heavy with the loss. Actually, he was pondering over and over again John Donne's sermon about no man being an island, and that the death of any man diminishes me, the death of any man diminishes me . . .

Jake kept Doc Pony back to tend to the wounded. He was standing in a shaft of light filtering down through the double-canopy jungle listening to the birds beginning to chat again as the tail of Alpha Company disappeared up the trail. He arced one fire team to each side of the trail and set them in as best he could against the incline. They had to lean against the incline of the hill to keep from slipping. He sat down beside Jerry, reached over and inched the poncho liner back. Jerry Motley had been surprised in death. His eyes were still open; they gave no hint of his last thoughts other than surprise. By the look on his face he might have walked into his own birthday party rather than his death. The poncho liner came up farther and Jake was able to see the massive wounds. Motley's flak jacket had been torn apart; where it remained open, there was a sucking chest wound now beginning to clot around the edges. Jake dropped the liner back over his friend.

This had to be kept simple, he thought; love, loyalty, living, dying . . . there should not be gray areas here. It is, after all, quite simple; you survive or you don't. You act honorably or you don't. He thought back over what he had strained to understand in his college philosophy classes. What was the difference between pragmatism and relativism or collectivism? What the hell is truth anyway? I'm here fighting for the right reasons, right? Jerry just paid the ultimate price for the right reasons . . . right? He was wondering if Kant or Hegel ever had to worry about getting their asses shot off when they were trying to figure out whether or not you could prove existence, or whether there were any absolutes. I'll tell you one thing, he thought, the absolute truth is, Jerry is dead and he has no existence in this world. I wonder how long Karen would remember? Without thinking of what he was doing, he switched on Armed Forces Radio and heard the strident strains of "Little Deuce Coupe," hammered out by the Beach Boys. Shit, he thought, shit . . . shit . . . shit!

The Professor brought him back to the reality of the hill on which they were sitting by shaking his shoulder and relating to him that the chopper pilot was asking them to pop a green smoke to mark their position. The smoke cannister popped and the chopper came in at a right angle to their position. The rotors were battering down the trees and kicking up loose dirt and dust that hung there in the heat. Jake had Boston hook up the two WIAs on the jungle penetrator and the chopper lifted them out. He wanted to get the job done as quickly as possible because the smoke marked them and the Huey helicopter gunship for the gooks.

Finally they hooked the body of Lieutenant Jerry Motley to the penetrator. Jake turned and spoke quietly to the Professor: "Tell them to lift out, we're finished." He was half propped against a tree and watching the corrugated soles of Jerry's jungle boots fade away overhead when two splotches of blood hit his forehead and cheek. He brushed the blood away but he knew it was something he would never forget. He decided that dreams didn't die; only people did.

13

THE PROFESSOR GOT THE COMPANY commander on the hook and Jake reported the mission completed and moved out in their direction. Alpha had set in on a ridge line southeast of the abandoned Khe Sanh airstrip. The terrain and elevation to its approach were the most difficult Jake had experienced. The hill they had lost Jerry on was only the beginning. The final approach was nearly eight hundred meters straight up. Sure, he had run hunter-killer teams for a month back in April, but that was short-term movement and over less difficult terrain. This was incredible; the canopy ran from double to triple, and at times you simply had to pull yourself up the inclines. A "fuckin' new guy" in Harry's squad, Private Sweeney, kept bitching as the squad forced its way up. Movement through this was difficult even for the troops who were acclimatized, much more so for a twink like Sweeney.

They had moved only about three or four hundred meters when Sweeney sat down in the middle of the trail and refused to go any farther. Jake talked to him briefly but knew he was running out of daylight and desperately wanted to make the company perimeter before nightfall.

"Look," he said to Sweeney, "you see the top of that ridge directly in front of us?"

"Yeah, I see it," replied Sweeney.

"Well, that's where we are going. You can sit here in your own puddle of shit until the gooks come along to wipe your ass and carry you back to Hanoi, but we are going on."

He turned to Harry and said, "Okay, Boston. Let's get out of here."

Alpha Company sat on a ridge line noted on the map by Benchmark 471. They reached Alpha's perimeter by dusk. Because of the heat they had spread out more than Jake would have liked, coming into the perimeter at about five-minute intervals.

First Platoon had taken up a position at the center of the perimeter, along the forward crest of the ridge. Sergeant Hawkins had dug out a command post for Jake in the side of the hill and fortified it by placing what had been piles of old sandbags alongside new ones. They were tied in on their left with Second Platoon and on the right with Third. Hawk had done a good job interlocking fields of fire, positioning the M-60s on both sides. They didn't know how long they would be there—for sure a few days—so everyone dug good fighting holes and expected a resupply.

Hawkins had also prepared the LPs. They had to go out nearly one hundred meters down the side of the ridge to hit the tree lines. Bo had dropped by to see how it had gone, back on the hill.

"By the way," he said to Jake, "did you hear Clahan is coming out to take over Jerry's platoon until we can get a permanent replacement?"

"Well, that's all right," Jake said with a shrug.

"What do you mean, all right, Jake? The guy's a bro, he's a nigger. He's part of that yellow-towel brigade back in the Quang Tri. They are nothing but a bunch of rear pogues using their race to shield their yellow asses. The only difference is, he's an officer."

Jake was dead tired physically and mentally stressed out because of what had happened to Jerry. He liked Bo, but he had a hard time understanding or accepting his feelings about blacks.

"What about Sugar Bear, Bo? He's a great squad leader."

"Sure," Bo replied, "there are a few exceptions, but I'm telling you that Clahan is a damn delta blue gum."

Jake looked at Bo, not comprehending at all what he was talking about. "What the hell is a delta blue gum, anyway," he asked?

"Well, I'll tell you," Bo replied. "The real black ones with strong backs and dark-blue gums worked the fields. You know what I mean? On the other hand, the ones with lighter skin were house niggers."

Jake was tiring of the entire conversation. "Oh, come on, Bo. Knock that crap off. Clahan is out here getting shot at just like us . . . even the troops can't tell the difference between the color of cowardice and the color of bravery."

"Well, how about this, Jake. Remember Captain McCormack, the S-2 back in Quang Tri, the one they called Old Hatchet Face?"

Jake looked up at Bo, who was standing in the doorway of the CP. "Yeah, I remember him, Bo. What about it?"

"Well, a couple of weeks back, just before he was about to rotate home, a bunch of niggers in the yellow-towel brigade holed up in the armory and threatened to blow the place up if their demands weren't met. Old Hatchet Face went in, negotiated with them, and they left after they gave up their weapons. Apparently, not all of the black bastards felt that he had done the proper thing. The next night, McCormack was fragged in his rack. Ask your friend Clahan about that. Word has it he was a backroom leader for the whole group back there. They couldn't even find enough of McCormack to send back home. Sure, he was hard-nosed, but he was a good marine and nobody deserves that."

"Listen," Jake said, "you don't know who fragged McCormack and you don't know if Clahan was involved with those guys or not. I saw them running as a group and I didn't like the lack of discipline, but I know one thing for sure, we have to survive out here and we can't do it divided."

"Jake, that's just the way we felt down South a hundred and five years ago."

"Bo, let it die! Why are you still trying to fight the Civil War?"

Bo swirled around on Jake and growled, "I didn't fight it, but I would like to have tried. You know what my biggest dream is, Jake?"

"No," Jake replied, "I don't."

"Well, let me tell you then." Bo dropped to one knee, resting one elbow across the other knee. "I want to go home and go up northeast to Illinois. I've got two distant cousins buried in a Yankee prison where they died during the Civil War . . . I want to bring them back home and bury them in Southern soil where they belong."

Jake, now standing, looked down at Bo. One a remnant of the Old South, the other barely able to comprehend the depth of such feelings. There was simply nothing more to be said. Bo, rising, turned away and scuffled back toward his hootch as Jake watched. He wondered if some of what Bo said wasn't right. Time will tell, he thought, time will tell.

That night passed quietly. Jake woke up near dawn with the grungy feeling he got from having sperm stuck to his jungle utilities. The worst part was he couldn't even remember the dream . . . Jerry was right. Nature took care of the need! He hoped that the resupply would bring in a few pair of clean utilities. His waist size had gone down from 38 to 32.

Boston, Sugar Bear, and the Professor were all due to go on R and R in about two weeks. Jake hoped they would be finished with this operation before then, maybe in a stand-down period by the time their R and R was due. He was beginning to realize how important they were to him, his bush family. In fact, he loved them. A different love than he had for his stateside family, but deep nonetheless. It was love based on survival and mutual respect. And then it hit him. This survival instinct was really the only purpose they had as a unit. He had yet to figure out what they were doing tactically, and how it fit within a larger perspective. He hoped to hell somebody else did. But if the brass knew, why didn't they tell him? Even on a small-unit level it occurred to him that taking and retaking the same piece of ground over and over and paying higher and higher prices made no sense. Yet he had never questioned anything; he had decided that was the mark of the professional. He and his men were good at what they did. But he wondered how long this war could be continued to be fought without a dramatic objective that united more than just the men in his unit in their struggle to survive. He knew that back home in the world, any support at all was falling apart for lack of an emotional objective. He read the newspaper clippings his dad sent. What were the reasons for all of this? He made a mental note to ask some of the guys how they felt about it; then wondered if it betrayed his own commitment simply to ask them.

He slid off the earth bench at the rear of his hootch, which he had carved into the side of the mountain, and pulled the nearly dry utility trousers away from his leg, wincing as some of his leg hair came with them. He scrunched over to clear the exit of the hootch and found the Professor and Hawk smoking after a breakfast of K-rats eggs and C-rat beef and potatoes. The heat continued to come; even this early it pounded, making him want to retreat back to his hootch.

"Hey, lieutenant. Want some stew?" the Professor asked. "I put in some river snails we scrapped off the bottom of the big rocks this morning. They're chewy, but it's great stuff."

Gunny Jacobsen was sitting outside of Captain Wolf's hootch as Jake walked up to it, a helmet full of water on the ground next to him.

"How you doin', lieutenant? It's good to see you."

"Hey, Sam, it's good to see you, too."

"Sorry about Lieutenant Motley. I know you guys were close."

"Yeah, thanks, Sam. Say, are we going to get any choppers in with some replacements and chow and maybe a few pair of utilities?"

"Yes, sir," the Gunny replied as he continued to shave in his helmet. "The battalion commander says that we should get a resupply about 1400 hours today."

Jake, turning back toward his platoon area, said, "Thanks Gunny. I'll spread the word to the troops. Catch you later, hear."

"See ya, lieutenant," the Gunny responded, not taking his eyes away from the small metal mirror he was using for his morning shave.

Four hours later, as the helicopter blades beat at the superheated air, alerting everyone to their approach, Jake found himself thinking about the food and clean clothes that they might be carrying. What didn't occur to him at that moment was that on board would also be new candidates who might also hear the call from Jehovah's throat.

Alexander Scott was five-feet, eleven inches of packed muscle. He once placed as third runner-up in the Mr. Universe contest when he was in college. Since high school, he had made a way for himself and built a reputation by rebuilding his body. By the time he entered college he had his picture in *Muscle Magazine* and was looked on as a comer for future contests. Scott had been born in Dumfries, Virginia, a blink on Route 1 between Washington, D.C., and Richmond. His mother had married a marine sergeant and he grew up "falling out" for breakfast and hearing about the exploits of Chesty Puller until he felt he knew Chesty better than his own father. Life had been moving from camp to camp. Dumfries was always home, however, because invariably his father would be rotated back to Quantico, or worse yet, Headquarters, Marine Corps. He had grown up, for all practical purposes, without a father. The few times there was contact, it was without emotion because a marine didn't love outwardly. In order to prove to his dad he was a man, he began to lift weights. Eventually, this became a passion and a way to gain recognition. Alex was physically square. His body was square, his jaw was square, even his biceps and calf muscles appeared to be square. Every place else was angular. He was a hunk.

He was numbed by the rhythm of the rotor blades; the noise was so loud that it first dominated everything else, then became an unnoticed but omnipresent background. You soon learned to notice a change in air speed or some quick movement from the crew chief or assistant gunner, an indication that something was about to happen.

Alex was thinking how ironic it was that he was on his way in a resupply chopper to join Alpha, First Battalion, Ninth Marine Regiment, on some forsaken hill in Vietnam, especially since he had sworn he would never follow in the steps of his father. Reflecting back, he was still amazed at how such a thing could have happened. It began amazingly when he had been proselytized by members of Bill Bright's Campus Crusade for Christ on the campus of George Mason University. Alex, for his part, had never heard anything like what these young people were telling him. Like many of his friends, he laughed at them at first, that is, until he met Betsy. Betsy was different. Their relationship grew slowly. He asked her out initially because she was attractive and he knew she would be another notch on his sexual gun. Since getting to college, his confidence, good looks, and physique had made him very popular. Alex had begun to assume he would get whatever he wanted.

Not so with Betsy. Petite, blonde, blue-eyed, and principled. The more she withstood his onslaught, the more he wanted her. Besides, he thought, she is different. There was something about her that was compelling and radiant. It went far beyond her physical beauty. Alex had barely been near a church, much less in one. Betsy had grown up in the church and, moreover, belonged to some kind of emotional roller-coaster denomination that babbled in strange tongues. Yet, every time he made a move, she refused and would always be sure to point out that it was her relationship with God that forbid her to sin. Alex was falling in love. Not just because she said no, but because he was impressed with her commitment. He found himself being dragged to prayer meetings with her. He would suffer through what he classified as evenings of hypocrisy (that's what his dad had told him all Christians were) and then take Betsy home and go drink a few beers at the Heidelburg. He even went to church on campus just to prove his love, but all the while he was quite unconsciously beginning to listen more and more to what these people were saying.

He still wasn't sure exactly how it happened. But he was sure of one thing. If he were not a Christian, Betsy would never have considered marrying him. She had already told him that. So he decided he would become one. What the hell, he had thought, what have I got to lose? So, one Sunday morning he walked down the aisle as the preacher asked if anyone wanted to accept Christ as their personal savior. People rejoiced and cried. The pastor was certainly very pleased. And Alex, well, Alex figured that he had always had to pay a price for everything he had ever gotten, and in his mind this just happened to be the price for Betsy.

The crew chief was trying to get Alex's attention as the big CH-46 reduced its air speed. The back of the helicopter was filled with C-rations and mail. There were three other replacements in the front, a corporal and two PFCs who were just as green as Scott. The chopper also carried as many cannisters of fresh water as it could. The crew chief leaned close to Alex's ear and yelled that they were approaching Alpha's position. Alex made the thumbs-up sign and fell back into his reverie.

Betsy was certainly not a hypocrite. Of one thing he had been certain, and that was that she believed all the things she had been sharing with him about God. She had introduced him to other people who didn't seem always to be looking for the selfish end of a relationship, like everyone he had ever met. These people didn't seem overly impressed with his biceps but they did seem to take a genuine interest in him. It wasn't long before he felt comfortable hugging other men and talking about love without sex being what he really meant. Then one Wednesday, at one of the prayer meetings, Alex met God. At least that's what he had been describing to people ever since.

His life had completely changed. For one thing, Betsy would seriously consider him as a suitor, for now she could not complain about being "unequally yoked." Second, after much prayer and counsel with Betsy, he had decided after briefly considering the professional ministry that he could become a positive influence by becoming an officer and allowing his life to speak for itself.

So here was Alex Scott about to land in the middle of a war. He had his Bible and his U.S. .45 automatic. He had worked it out in the scripture so that there was nothing in conflict between these two tools. In truth, Alex felt that the United States faced a great disaster, not just because of the war in Vietnam, but because of an insidious moral flabbiness that had spread through a country deluded by liberal theology. He believed that no true Christian had a right to be a conscientious objector, much less escape to Canada, as so many of his peers were doing. War never changes, he had decided; it is always bloody and always terrible. But now an age of apostasy had been born and this whole conflict was doomed to failure unless a spiritual revival occurred. Alex was convinced that it was in the power of those who really believed to win the war; to uphold the nation and preserve its greatness. Just as he had done with pumping iron or anything else that mattered to him, Alex had made a total commitment.

The CH-46 circled in a landing pattern over the landing zone. Alex could see the lush green of the jungle pockmarked by the tons of TNT that had exploded throughout the countryside. It was really beautiful here despite the heat. If you didn't know that there was a war going on, you might want to visit, just to explore the mystery of such an alien place. But a war there was. Alex could see a small group of marines gathered around the LZ. He wondered what kind of people he was about to meet. He wondered if there were any Christians here. God, he prayed, I know you have brought me here, please help me to do thy will and not be afraid. Help me, Lord, to uplift and glorify thee in all that I do. In Jesus' name, amen. He took a deep breath and the big bird touched down harder than it should have on Hill 471.

Fast Eddie, Bo, and Jake had gathered at Wayco's hootch. All three platoon sergeants had taken a few troops to meet the resupply chopper and make sure they weren't cheated out of their gear. There was ammo to be passed out, new LAAW antitank weapons, grenades, C-4, a few pairs of utility trousers, fresh water in spent howitzer cannisters, and SP paks with beer, soda, candy, and cigars. It was important to get the resupply, but it was vital to get the beer.

14

THAT AFTERNOON, SHORTLY BEFORE the resupply, Wayco had been assigning patrol routes to his lieutenants. They were all sitting in a circle on the ground outside his hootch. Jake and Bo were sharing a cigarette and the others who had been listening attentively were now just sitting around shooting the breeze. It looked like they were going to spend a few days on this hill. The Second Battalion had replaced them back in Leatherneck Square and the Third Battalion was back at Vandegrift Combat Base. Like Boston, Wayco could smell the gooks. He knew they were here and he knew his men were going to find them. He was wondering why he didn't ask to be reassigned rather than come out on this operation with less than a month left in-country. He supposed it was because of some misspent sense of loyalty. In reality he had no family other than these marines. He couldn't bring himself to leave them early. He also wondered if he really weren't crazy. But now his mind was fixed on Lieutenant Clahan; Wolf hoped he was on the bird coming in. If Clahan was indeed going to take over the company when he left, this would be a good opportunity to start on the transition. He wasn't sure about Clahan. He had performed well in the bush, but you couldn't really be sure what was ticking just beneath the surface of that guy. Wayco was sure he had left most of his prejudice back in the States. There was no room for that kind of shit out here. But he knew everyone didn't think the way he did, including some of the blacks. He was also convinced that some of them used the racial excuse to cover up cowardice. This crap of calling this a white man's war was bullshit. White men were getting killed as well, and any black man in the bush knew it. It was the rear areas where you had real problems. There was too much free time and not enough discipline. Anyone with a bad attitude could find someone to encourage it and a reason to bitch. Color was just another rallying point against discipline and in support of fear. It wasn't that there weren't injustices. He had been around a long time; he knew there were problems. But a professional left all that shit in the rear, along with the four-holers. He remembered that the same problems had come up in Korea, but there was something different here. Something he couldn't quite get a handle on. It wasn't the discipline in the corps; that was as good as it had ever been. Maybe it was just the fact, Wolf concluded, that we took some draftees in; anyone knows one rotten apple can screw up the whole fucking barrel. Wolf got up, his legs cramped from squatting down, and saw that Bo, Jake, and Fast Eddie were still sitting around shooting the crap. Wayco told them to rejoin their platoons. He yelled for the Gunny, only to be told by his radioman that Gunny Jacobsen had gone up to the LZ to make sure the platoon sergeants didn't shoot each other over the beer.

Wayco trudged up to the LZ. Clahan was not on the chopper but a new brown bar was, along with three FNGs. The Gunny had everything under control. He sent two of the twinks to Third Platoon to replace those who were lost on the trail when Lieutenant Motley got killed, and the third to Jake's First Platoon. All the gear was split up and there was enough beer and soda to give every troop his choice of two cans... warm soda, or warm beer. There were also several 105 cannisters full of fresh water, which promised a cut in the water runs down the hill.

Alexander Scott, by way of George Mason University, by way of the basic school, by way of a personal meeting with Jesus Christ, reported into his first command in Vietnam. He was visibly impressive and he had the attention of the troops immediately. He had been forced to cut the sleeves of his utility shirts because his biceps were so large he couldn't roll them up. He had maintained his flexibility and quickness, unlike so many body builders. The word went out quick that you didn't want to mess around with this dude.

Wayco, in his usual way, wanted to test him early and had put Third Platoon on patrol duty the day after Alex got in the bush. There had been little contact in the first three days they had occupied Hill 471. There had not even been any night probes. The second night a trip flare was set off that erupted final protective fire from Second Platoon. Everybody was reporting seeing gooks in the wire, but Bo could only find two dead rock apes, which had apparently tripped the flare. Yet merely firing the final protective line seemed to release some of the tension that always built up in a defensive perimeter.

On the fourth night of occupation, several mortar tubes popped off in the distance, the rounds falling short of the perimeter. So the days passed in the heat: patrols going on all day, LPs being set out at night, and little else to break the monotony. Alex had quickly been given the nickname, "the Preacher." He handled himself adequately in the bush and learned quickly. He also had the charisma that made him a natural leader for his men. The other officers liked him, even if they joked about his religious mania. None of them, however, failed to take him seriously.

On the fifth night, several rocket-propelled grenades slammed into the compound. One dud fell not ten feet from Jake's hootch. Then someone discovered that the water that had come in the 105 cannisters had mosquito larvae in it, resulting in several cases of malaria. Doc Pony swore up and down to Wayco that everybody was taking their quinine pills, but it was clear many were not.

A company of army doggies had set up just south of the Khe Sanh airstrip and they reconned by fire every night. It irritated the marines that the army fired more rounds just in reconnaisance than they had been issued. Fox, Second Battalion, Twelfth Marines, fired harassment and interdiction rounds daily in support of Alpha Company. On the sixth day, a short round from Fox company took the top half of a lance corporal with it when it screamed through the perimeter. His legs were still propped up in his fighting hole when Fast Eddie got to him. The morale of the troops took another dip.

From the left side of Hill 471 a finger-shaped ridge moved into a small saddle, then turned left into another small ridge with a bomb crater just to its right. A hedgerow of small trees connected the bomb crater to a swath of elephant grass and on into the main tree line. It had been a standard route for several patrols moving off into the boonies. First squad of the Weapons Platoon was mounting a patrol with that finger as a kickoff point. Jake was sitting in his hootch talking to the Professor when the first shots were heard. To a bush marine, there is instant identification of any enemy round. It sounds different; these were AK-47 rounds. Wayco got on the company net, trying to find out what the hell was going on. The squad wasn't more than two hundred meters outside the perimeter, but they were masked from view by a clump of trees and the natural contour lines of the terrain.

Jake, standing in front of his bunker, looked through his field glasses and scanned the tree line for movement. He could see the smoke coming out of the trees and hear the difference between the 5.56-millimeter M-16s and the 7.62 AK-47s. Every troop hit his fighting hole. Wayco couldn't get any response out of Corporal Drummond, Fast Eddie's first squad leader. It was Drummond who was leading the squad-sized patrol, so Wayco told Fast Eddie to take his second squad and move down the finger to see what was happening in a sort of squad-sized sparrow hawk. Eddie, moving in line with his squad, inched cautiously down the finger and across the saddle. The firing had stopped, or at least was sporadic, and there was no answer on the radio. Fast Eddie and his second squad were moving around the side of the bomb crater and approaching a small clearing just short of the tree line.

Ed could see Drummond lying in the middle of the clearing. Doc Santini was straddled across his body; it looked like he had been trying to apply a compress bandage when he was shot. Eddie got Wayco on the net and told him what he saw. Wayco told him to form skirmishers and move out across the clearing and pull his troops back, along with any dead or wounded.

Wayco was shouting into the handset, looking at it as if he were trying to see Fast Eddie's face. "Listen, Ed," he said. "I'm going to send Jake's platoon down in support. Wait until you know he is coming up the saddle before you make your sweep. I'm gonna fix the coordinates of the tree line; be ready to fall back hard if I tell you we've got some heavy rain coming in."

Jake had already picked up Boston and Sugar Bear and was moving toward the short end of the finger. They were in line and working their way up the forward slope of the saddle when he grabbed the Professor by the arm and told him to tell Fast Eddie he could move out.

Ed had gotten about one-third of the way across the clearing when the AK-50 opened up. The patches of elephant grass were nearly waist-high and everyone dove for cover in it. Jake and his two squads were just on the rim of the bomb crater and they went over the side. Small-arms fire began pouring in from the tree line; two more marines in Eddie's squad were hit going down. Calls for corpsmen floated over the clearing in and out of the staccato of rifle fire. Ed was smack in the middle of a clump of elephant grass, not able to see anything, but rounds kept cracking overhead or spitting up the dirt all around him. Then an eerie, sudden silence fell over the small battlefield. Ed got on the net and told Wayco he suspected they were being sucked in.

"I can't see a damn thing, Six. Put some firepower on that clearing so I can try to get to Drummond and the rest."

"Okay, Ed. I'm going to start with M-60s," Wayco replied.

Jake moved his men back up over the top of the crater and to the right of the tree line. He put everyone in line and got suppressing fire pumped out in the direction of the clump of trees. At about the same time, the first of the M-60s began tearing up the tree line. The "crumps" of supporting mortar fire came in groups of three. Ed, and his remaining men, the equivalent of a fire team, moved forward on their bellies. Doc Pony moved forward as well, to see if he could be of any help. While the troops were working their way forward, Jake got Wayco on the radio: "Six," Jake said, as he hunched himself down in the elephant grass, "hold off on the tubes and let me see if I can't move through Fast Eddie's position."

Wayco, considering Jake's request, finally responded, "What about Ed's feeling that he is being sucked in?"

"I don't feel the same way," Jake said. "The small-arms fire has stopped and I think the mortars have driven the little people back down the hill."

"All right," Wayco responded, "but I'll set a TOT on the tree line in case you have to get out in a hurry."

With that, Jake turned to Sugar Bear and told him to remain in position and keep firing until he gave him word to stop.

"C'mon, Boston, let's cut to the right out of the line of fire and try a single envelopment of the tree line."

Sugar Bear's fire team continued to lay down suppressing fire until Jake got into position. Then, in assault position, they began inching forward and hosing down the trees with heavy fire. At that exact moment, he had Sugar Bear's fire team move forward, hitting the tree line from the front in a double envelopment. There was no further returned fire.

Drummond was dead, shot three times, any one of which was enough to buy a body bag. Santini, the corpsman, had apparently taken a round through the neck while trying to treat Drummond. Three other marines were wounded. Ed retrieved the wounded and dead and began the trek back toward the perimeter.

Jake went on through the trees. The sound of battle had ceased but the silence of the jungle and the smell of cordite filled the air. Jake and Sugar Bear reached the tree line; midpoint at the same time. There were two dead NVA lying there and several blood trails leading off down the hill. One man, very large for a Vietnamese, lay across an AK-50 machine gun with a cylindrical feeder. Another, his head canted downhill, apparently had been hit while retreating. Jake walked partway down the reverse slope of the hill and decided to send Sugar Bear and one fire team in pursuit about one hundred meters or so on down the trail. He picked up the dead NVA's helmet, which had fallen a few meters away from the body. He thought it would make a good souvenir. A piece of shrapnel from one of the mortar rounds had apparently smashed through the back of the helmet, ripping a three-inch hole in the back of the gooner's head. Bits of his brains dripped out on the jungle floor as Jake picked up the helmet. There was an inscription crudely scraped in Vietnamese on the inside of the helmet. Later, one of the Kit Carson scouts would translate it for Jake. It said, "This helmet is unvulnerable."

The Professor came up and told him Wayco wanted him on the hook. Jake took the handset and said, "Alpha six, this is Alpha One actual."

"Alpha One actual, pull your team back in and mop that mess up. We have indication from G-2 there is heavy movement to your front."

"Roger." Jake told the Professor to bring Sugar Bear back in ASAP. As Jake walked back through the clump of trees, he noticed that the ears had been cut off the dead NVA. He made a mental note to find out who was doing that shit and get it stopped.

Back inside the perimeter, Wayco gathered the platoon commanders around him. Apparently, Clahan had stayed in the rear on some special assignment the battalion commander had given him. Wayco mentally counted them off; Fast Eddie, Jake, Bo Lawler, and the new brown bar, Alex Scott, the one they were now calling the Preacher. Wayco had requested the medevac choppers while the dead and wounded were being brought in. By the time Fast Eddie was entering the perimeter, the first bird was touching down in the landing zone.

Right before he had brought Jake back in, Colonel Dagomar had told Wayco that it looked like they were directly in the way of a fairly large enemy troop movement. Intelligence didn't know exactly how big, but the Colonel wanted Wayco to pound the entire ridge line with artillery and fixed wing jets and then follow up with a platoon-sized reconnaisance. Wayco thought hard about which platoon to send out. The new guy, Scott, was too green for this, he felt. Bo and Fast Eddie had taken their turns. Jake was blooded and was doing a good job. Besides, he had a good sergeant in Hawkins and some very good squad leaders. So, he decided, it would be Jake and First Platoon.

It was that warning order that Wayco had been giving the platoon commanders during the debriefing after the morning's contact. The last duty Wolf would perform that day would be to write letters home to the families of the dead marines—Drummond and Pevos, the private killed by friendly fire, and the corpsman, Santini. That was the part of all his responsibility that he hated the most. He always used Clahan for that type of thing because he seemed particularly good at it. Wayco just never seemed to know what to say. They bought it and that was it, he always thought. But how in the hell can you put that in a letter home?

Extra precautions were taken. The troops knew it was time to fortify their fighting positions, and the holes were dug deeper. You couldn't worry about the one that fell in the same hole with you, but you sure didn't want to buy it because you weren't dug in deep enough.

Jake had discovered something today. In the first firefight he had back in Cam Lo, some time after the fighting had ended, his legs began to shake. It lasted for about ten minutes and he thought that it was a result of it being the first time in combat and the extra adrenaline. Then the same thing happened, only not as bad, back on the trail when Jerry bought it. Today, his legs shook again; he went off by himself so the troops couldn't see until it went away. He couldn't stop it by sheer will power but he really wasn't too concerned, because it always happened when the action was over. Yet it was there. He wondered about it for a few minutes, worried a little, and then just sluffed it off.

Although the night went by without incident, the firefight of the morning and the colonel's indication that there might be a large NVA force in the area kept everyone on edge. Jake was up every few hours to check his lines and make sure the LPs were reporting in. It appeared that total blackout was observed and that even the habitual smokers abstained or went underground. Dawn was brilliant. The sun exploded over the ridge line that would be the day's objective. Jake was already at work checking and double-checking the coordinates that Wayco had given him the day before. He was going to take the same route out that Ed had used: down the finger, up and around the bomb crater, through the clearing and the clump of trees; then down the finger into the tree line and up the ridge that the sun was now drying of dew. He looked at his movement pattern as he had written it down; R.09, U.1.1, R.0.8, U.1.5, R.0.7, U.2.5, R.0.3, U.2.8, R.0.6, U.3.2. The weather was holding and along with it the heat. All afternoon the day before, he had watched the sky guys pounding the shit out of the hazy ridge line that he now had to reach. He couldn't understand how anything could withstand such a beating. He could see whole lines of huge trees shudder and fall under the onslaught. Both Bo and Eddie had told him that it didn't make any difference; the A-frame bunkers the gooks built could take a direct hit. But Jake found it hard to believe.

He had written Karen the night before. He couldn't sleep; despite his resolve to write every day it didn't always get done. He always carried the Third Marine Division (rein), FMF, stationery they had given him back in Quang Tri; he was looking at it now. Dirty, still damp, and smeared where the black government ballpoint pen clotted on the paper, his scratchings revealing that he had occasionally smoked. He feared she could sense he was changing. He, the fanatical athlete with a pure-minded approach to fitness. That would blow her mind for sure, he thought. He tried not to write lugubrious, self-pitying letters that would betray the confusion in which he lived. But after a while, what was left to say? He carried every one of her letters in his pack; when he had time he read them over and over and over again. He would read them and fantasize: What was she doing on her secretarial job? He tried hard to remember his daughter's face; even the pictures Karen sent didn't seem to help. This was his baby but he really didn't know her. Karen had told him in her last letter that her sister had moved in with her. Jake was glad of that. He knew it would offer her company and help, but the ordinary sane world reflected in her letters made him realize that she could never understand what he faced and felt every day, every hour, every moment. Gradually his letters had become almost impersonal chronologies of movements. Sometimes Jake wrote about Boston and Sugar Bear and the new guy, Alex, and once he had a few lines about Jerry Motley's death because she had known the Motleys during basic school. He wondered if writing about death would worry her. In some confused way, he hoped it would. Then he would swing around the other way and hope it wouldn't. Anyway, wasn't she supposed to endure the separation stoically in public and cry herself to sleep at night? He was sure that Karen was facing struggles and challenges of her own. It was just that it was so difficult to relate to what was going on back in the world. It was just that he missed her so much.

15

THE DEW WAS BURNED AWAY. IT WAS hot. Everything was hot. The ground was hot, the trees and leaves were hot, and the air was hot to breathe. The heat and the mosquitoes were part of life. At least the little bastards were not as bad up here as they were down in the low country, Jake consoled himself. The platoon would travel light because they planned to be back that day. Jake knew he would put Boston and his squad on the point. He was keyed up and more than a little apprehensive, maybe even scared. It was a deadly treasure hunt, a poisonous mystery shared by the members of his platoon, his "Nam" family.

Every rifleman has read that part of the Marine Rifle Squad manual, FMFM 6-5, that says, "the offensive mission of the squad is to attack." Movement-to-contact is the first phase of the attack. Movement-to-contact is a tactical movement to gain or reestablish contact with the enemy. It ends only when the unit is forced to open fire upon the enemy or when the unit goes into an assembly area to prepare for combat. Movement-to-contact is what it is all about.

At 0800 hours they were due to leave the perimeter. Replacements from Weapons Platoon took their position in the perimeter. Jake checked with his squad leaders before they moved out. Hawkins had everything squared away. It had taken him time to get used to this new lieutenant. Hawkins was not yet convinced he was one of the few who were going to make it with the troops. He knew all the book crap; he had gotten some in-field experience. But Hawkins was from the old school. He grew up breaking horses almost from the time he could walk. He enlisted in the Marine Corps as an alternative to going to jail for blowing up the local police station as a kid's prank when he was in high school. He stayed in because the discipline appealed to him. He knew that an unbroken colt was no good to anyone. The Marine Corps had broken him in, but he was not altogether sure just how reliable Adams was.

Jake walked over to Hawkins and asked if the troops were ready.

"Yes, sir. We're all carrying light packs; a couple of C-rat units and three grenades, two extra magazines, and about ten extra rounds for the bloopers."

"Put Boston up front. I'll hang in with the Professor behind first squad, then put Corporal Dragin and second squad in line, with Sugar Bear and third squad bringing up the rear. You hang around back there with them, Hawk."

"Okay, lieutenant. Sir, I think we should move slow and take our time, especially on the approach to the clump of trees where Fast Eddie hit the shit yesterday."

Jake held his ego in tow, wanting to say, I know that, sergeant. But instead he said, "Thanks, Hawk, that's good advice. We're not going to set any speed records getting there. Bring 'em up on line and let's move it out."

The approach to the saddle was made easily. It was a beautiful, cloudless day; if it weren't for the heat they might have been taking a stroll through the woods. The trip around the bomb crater was uneventful except for the sight of a body spread-eagled at the bottom of the crater. It was one of the dead gooners from yesterday's firefight. He had been crucified with bamboo shoots stuck through his hands. Apparently, some troop's idea of a not-so-subtle comment to the NVA. Jake said nothing and declined to call it back to Wayco, even after Hawkins asked him about it. They just moved on. Jake had Hawkins put them in squad wedges to cross the clearing to the trees. Again, no contact and no movement. They continued on through the trees in line and approached the finger leading to the next ridge line and halted. Jake reported in to Wayco and moved out again. They proceeded down the saddle and up the reverse slope of the next hill. Near the top, a small clearing opened up just inside the tree line.

There were two Kit Carson scouts, with the company. The oldest of the two, Kim, was walking with Jake and the Professor. As they approached the clearing, Jake could see Kim tense up. What they had walked into was a company-sized field kitchen. Like some sort of mirage, an old iron stove stood there in the middle of triple-canopy jungle. Jake radioed a report to Wayco and pressed on through the staging area, down the forward slope of the hill that led on into a draw between the two ridge lines. In the dead, fetid air they had to use machetes to hack their way through the thick undergrowth. Only twenty meters in they ran into a store of B-4 rockets. Twenty-five meters farther brought them to stacks of sixty-one mortar rounds. Kim was becoming increasingly agitated. As they moved farther down the ravine the triple canopy cut out more and more of the light and fresh air. It was becoming almost spooky. Jake had gone ahead next to Boston because progress was so slow and new, unsettling surprises kept popping up. He spoke quietly on the PRC-25 to Wayco, asking if they shouldn't blow the rockets and the mortars. Wayco gave him a flat negative with no explanation. Jake wondered why they were humping all of the damn C-4 explosives.

The first round came cracking through the banana trees, forcing Boston and the first fire team to the deck. Automatic weapons instantly opened up directly to their front and began tearing down the meager protection of the banana trees. Wayco was on the net calling for a report but Jake couldn't see anything. He grabbed the Professor and made his way up to Boston's position.

FMFM 6-5 sternly lays down the law: When a scouting fire team is fired upon they should immediately take cover, locate targets, and return fire. Boston frantically tried all these things at once, but the triple canopy made it impossible to identify the enemy, much less return fire. Then, according to the book, the fire-team leader is to locate the enemy, determine the extent of his position, the types of positions, the number of the enemy, and the nature of the terrain. Jake and his men were in the bottom of an extended draw, virtually unable to breathe in the triple canopy that trapped and intensified the unbearable heat. Jake questioned Boston and asked his advice, but Boston had nothing more to offer.

"Shit, Boston," Jake said, and then snapped at the Professor, "Get Captain Wolf on the hook."

Jake described the situation; Wayco said to try to turn around and go back up the draw.

"There's some fixed wing coming in, Alpha Actual, and we want to drop a five-hundred pounder on that field kitchen that you passed on your way to your present position."

Jake rogered that and turned to move his way back up the column. He told Boston to hold his position and the Professor to get Hawk to move to Boston's position. As he made his way back through the semidark draw, trying to move as quickly as possible, he began to realize what a shit sandwich they were in. He couldn't move left, he couldn't move right. He was obstructed by an enemy he couldn't see at the front and he had to turn and see if he could move back up the forward slope of the finger they had just descended, and about twenty-five meters of that was without cover. Jake was getting nervous and wondering why the hell he had been given orders to come down in this damn draw in the first place. He passed Hawkins midway, told him what he was going to do, and instructed him to form the last squad into a vee-formation for rear security and wait for the column to move.

Sugar Bear was now the point squad and fire team. Jake began movement immediately, and they had slogged their way about fifty meters back up the finger when automatic fire from farther up the hill sent them all back to the deck again. Once more Jake could not identify the exact enemy position or numbers. One thing was sure, he knew he was in a world of shit, sitting here in this low ground with the enemy on the high ground at least one hundred and eighty degrees. He was back on the hook with Wayco.

"Six, this is Alpha Actual. We're taking small arms and automatic weapons from the vicinity of the field kitchen directly to our front about one hundred and fifty meters back up the finger at coordinates 162430."

"Roger, Alpha Actual, hold one," Wayco replied.

Jake wondered what the hell was going on. Wayco had been in contact with the flight leader on the first wave of F-111s that now arrived over the target. He told Jake the frequency the sky guys were on and told him to monitor the transmissions.

"Blue Seven, Blue Seven, this is Chicken Sniffer. Do you read me?"

"Chicken Sniffer, Chicken Sniffer. This is Blue Seven. Go ahead."

"Blue Seven, I would like you to make a visual recon of the area where Chicken Sniffer One has made contact with the little people at coordinates 01598241. Do you copy?"

"Uh, roger. We copy and will do. Ten four."

Jake could see the jets screaming in for a look and was comforted by them just being there. They came in low, and perpendicular to his position, not more than a couple of hundred meters off the deck.

"Chicken Sniffer One, Chicken Sniffer One. This is Blue Seven Leader, over."

Jake grabbed the handset from the Professor and said, "Go ahead, Blue Seven Leader."

"Chicken Sniffer, to your immediate rear you have a large body of little people and a multi-unit A-frame bunker complex. It looks like they have dug in for the party. Directly to your front you have a smaller group that seem to be reinforcing their positions and number as we speak, do you read me, Chicken Sniffer One?"

"Roger that," Wayco cut in. "Blue Seven, can you make passes perpendicular to Chicken Sniffer One's position and take out the hostiles?"

"Roger, Chicken Sniffer, we will commence our first pass as soon as Chicken Sniffer One marks his position with smoke at both ends. Ten four."

"Did you read that, Chicken Sniffer One?" Wayco asked.

Jake replied, "Six, I read you and will comply, but I am not happy about marking myself out. Ten four."

"I roger your concern. Now mark 'em, One."

Jake turned to the Professor and had him tell Hawk to drop a red smoke at his end of the column and pulled a yellow for their position. Then he got Blue Seven Leader on the hook and told him, "Blue Seven, we are marking coordinates 03859231 with a ringo and coordinates 127592243 with a yankee. Do you copy, Blue Seven?"

"I roger you, dig in, Chicken Sniffer One, over."

"Roger the dig-in, Blue Seven. Get some!"

The first wave came in low, screaming with their twenty-millimeter cannons tearing up the tree line. They sounded like enraged giants bellowing at some unseen antagonist. With each screaming pass, another section of the jungle just seemed to disappear. A half-dozen passes rained twenty-millimeter fire as the prep. Next, two passes with daisy chains ripping up the deck on each end of the column sent marines even further to ground. Finally, a wave brought tidings of napalm to the overheated air of the jungle. The earth shook and trembled with the explosions and Alpha, First Battalion, knew gut-wrenching fear. Boston found cover underneath a berm at the base of the draw. Everyone had gone to ground including the gooks.

Hawk was royally pissed. *What the hell are these guys doing? We need to fight our way out before they blow us away,* he thought.

"Chicken Sniffer, this is Blue Seven. Do you read me?"

"I read you, Blue Seven. Go ahead," Wayco replied.

"We have a problem here, Chicken Sniffer. This terrain is too elevated for us to do much perpendicular for Chicken Sniffer One. I am requesting permission to make our passes directly over and parallel to Chicken Sniffer One, ten four."

Jake couldn't believe what he was hearing. Surely this asshole wasn't serious. He wanted to fly right over the top and drop his napalm on these gooners, but what would happen if his pinpoint-precision bombing was anything less than pinpoint?

"Chicken Sniffer One, did you copy Blue Seven?" Jake heard in the receiver. He rogered he had and told Wayco he would rather try to move back up the finger again.

"Wait one, Chicken Sniffer One," Wayco replied. Wayco turned to Gunny Jacobsen and said, "What do you think, Gunny?"

The Gunny, absently pulling at his crotch like a left fielder, paused for a moment and then said, "Well, sir, we don't really know how big this unit is the lieutenant is facing down there. We don't know what the bunker complex is hiding; and we can't see a damn thing." Now pulling on one of his oversized ears, Jacobsen said, "What we do know is that they have been building up this whole area, moving down the Ho Chi Minh Trail to build up Base Camp 911. We can't get to him quick enough to help if he really hits the shit, so I think we should move a couple of squads out to pinch off the gooners to his front if we have time, give the lieutenant a crack at making it back up the draw, and if that doesn't work, give Blue Seven a shot at the overhead."

Wayco stood pondering the Gunny's comments with the handset hooked in the crick of his neck and his shoulder. Finally he said, "Thanks a lot, Gunny. I know why you're still alive after all three tours. You can think."

When Wayco finally got to Jake, Jake was beginning to wonder if he was ever going to get any instruction. "Alpha Actual," Wayco said, "Blue Seven will soon have a fuel problem and will have to release his ordnance before returning to his nest. You've got one crack at that draw. I want to be kept informed, but have at it. Do you copy?"

"Ten four, I copy, Six, out," Jake replied.

Turning to Sugar Bear, Jake told him to bring up a gun team and a couple of bloopers. "Look," he said, "I want your squad to lead off in fire team and squad wedges. Guide on the trail we hacked out on the way down here, right up the center of the draw." Jake made his point by gesticulating up the hill.

He got Hawk on the line and told him what they were going to do. They were going to have to maneuver in a wedge line with each squad as an assault team in general support. Both Dragin and Boston would have to engage targets of opportunity during the movement and, it was hoped, consolidate on the objective. If the first squad could make it to a point where the trail widened out, he wanted Dragin to lay out a base of fire into the tree line, where they had discovered the field kitchen.

They had now been out six hours since leaving the line of departure, and it looked like they were going to be out a little longer. Sugar Bear moved up the trail as far as he could; his line of sight was no more than five or ten meters ahead. He told Hickman, his first fire team leader to form a wedge and start up the hill. Kim, the Kit Carson scout, told Sugar Bear he was some kinda nuts: "You bullshit marine, you betta not go upa that fuckin' hill."

Sugar Bear moved out. The slope of the draw was bad enough. After about twenty-five meters the draw began to widen out with less incline, when PFC Henry lost the front of his forehead to an AK round. He slumped to the middle of the trail as a hail of small-arms rounds began to spit through the trees. PFC Geights went down when his left kneecap disintegrated, pulverized by the force of a bullet.

Brisbane and Picks went to ground, but not before they had both taken less serious wounds. Sugar Bear was yelling for Doc Pony and Jake was trying to make his way up the draw. He took a casualty report from Sugar Bear and realized that he now faced a greater problem than he had before, because now he would have to carry his wounded with him. He felt that an assault by the gooks would be just as difficult for them because of the terrain, but he was still boxed in. Above all, he needed time to get a medevac in; and with the terrain the way it was, the NVA could easily blow the choppers out of the sky.

He explained the entire situation to Wayco and much to the consternation of Sergeant Hawkins recommended that they give Blue Seven his shot.

"Okay, Chicken Sniffer One . . . go to ground as deep as you can get. Do you roger?"

Jake confirmed that he did and then without thinking said to the Professor, "That guy has got to be shittin' me. Go to ground, hell, I'm gonna try to get to China." The Professor, whose eyes were normally large, now looked as if his eyes might bulge right out of his head. Jake looked at him rather strangely and then turned to Hawkins and told him to get the troops dug in as best he could.

The first wave of fixed-wing aircraft screamed in at what seemed to Jake like fifty feet. Once again it was the twenty-millimeter cannons that offered the greeting. He knew that if he lived through this he would never forget the sound they made as they went directly overhead. In one sense he was gaining a new respect for the enemy, who faced that sound and destruction daily. Next came the daisy chains. The marines on the ground could actually read the stenciled lettering, "no step," on the aircraft as they roared overhead, tearing up swathes at each end of the column, trying to create more room for Jake and his men. Next came the napalm. Cannisters came dropping out of the sky that seemed to set the entire jungle on fire. They rolled and roared and tore great gaping holes in the earth and trees. Surely no one could live through this.

One aircraft seemed to be having a problem; Jake couldn't quite make out what was happening. He saw it disappear in the distance and then, what was apparently the same plane, turn for another pass, but it was shaking left to right like it was trying to do a roll. Then Jake realized in terror what this nut was going to do. The napalm pod must have failed to release on one end of the cannister: This guy was going to pass over them and shake his plane from side to side, hoping it would fall off at the appropriate spot. The pilot knew he couldn't go back to the ship with the loose cannister half secured, so he decided to give it another try, without considering that he was running over friendlies instead of flying in perpendicular to them. Even as Jake grabbed the handset from the Professor's pack he knew it was too late. It was premonition time; he knew what was going to happen, just as if he had written the script. As the jet passed overhead there was a tremendous explosion. For a second Jake thought that the plane had blown up, but in the next second he could identify the vapor trail coming out of the smoke.

Then it began to rain fire. The pod had either blown before or just after release, and napalm jelly was raining down all over them. As it hit the trees and the overgrowth it stuck, then dripped off like wet gobs of burning molasses. Men were catching on fire as it stuck to their clothing and burned through to their flesh. Jake heard Hawkins scream over the radio, "Let's get the hell out of here, for God's sake move out." Jake knew the entire unit was close to panic. There was no direction to go; they were burning up where they stood. The recent lack of rain had dried the vegetation out, so small fires were starting wherever the napalm hit. Now they were in danger of either burning up or being asphyxiated by the increasing heat and smoke.

Wayco, monitoring the net, told Hawk to get off and put Jake on. Jake was already listening and told Wayco to go ahead.

"All right, Alpha One. Here's what you are going to do. Take these coordinates and shoot an azimuth from where you are. They will set you on a straight line with us. I know how bad the terrain is, but use machetes and cut your way out if you have to. You'll have to move slowly anyway, and that means you can travel with the wounded. And, Alpha

One, you obviously may have to fight your way out as well. At the first opportunity we will put a five-hundred pounder on your present position, so get moving."

Wayco really didn't need to supply him with an incentive to get out, but if he'd wanted to, he'd certainly done a good job of it.

"I roger that, Six. I'll get back in route, out," Jake replied.

Jake turned to Corporal Dragin, who had taken over Hawkins's squad, and told him to bring all the machetes to the middle of the column. They would start to cut their way out in a line exactly perpendicular to their present position. Dragin, who typified the don't-give-a-shit competence of many bush marines, looked at Jake in disbelief, debating whether to tell him just how fucked up he thought this whole mess was. They stood staring at each other until the corporal, who should have been a sergeant by time and grade and competence but deserved to be a private by his history of insubordination, just shook his head and walked away. "If I ever get the chance," he muttered, "I'll never give these assholes the opportunity to get me killed again."

The departure from the draw was on hands and knees through the mulch and jungle for most of the first fifty meters. The men were scared and desperately wanted out. They had yet to see more than a shadow of the enemy but were carrying out one dead and three wounded. At least a dozen others had been burned in different degrees by their own napalm. Suddenly a clearing opened up. In the middle they could see the biggest A-frame bunker that any of them had yet encountered. Having crawled and clawed their way largely on their bellies, they had bunched up. The entire column was not more than twenty meters long. Hawkins was trying to spread them out. Jake was in the clearing with Dragin's squad and Kim, the Kit Carson scout. It seemed as if they had been magically transported to a different part of the world. The sky had opened up, the sun and clouds were visible; it was as if they had found an enchanted part of the jungle. Kim reached up and began to peel off the aluminum foil he had used to cover up the flash suppressor on his M-16. He figured it would keep the rust off. Jake, seeing him do that, knew they were in trouble. The palm fronds on the roof of the bunker were still green and clearly had been recently cut.

Jake moved them around the edge of the clearing, keeping away from the bunker itself. He radioed Wayco, describing what they had walked into and asked if he should send a tunnel rat inside. Wayco, obviously feeling that all of them needed to get out of the area and not sure of what they would find, told them to keep moving. He took the coordinates from Jake and decided to put one of the five-hundred pounders right on top of that big bunker. Kim could not take his eyes off the bunker. As they went forward, he turned so his back was never to the bunker itself. This was a large compound. There was no way of knowing exactly how big a unit this area was being shored up to support. Jake wanted to get attention for his wounded, but most of all he wanted to get clear of all this mess.

The platoon kept moving and spread out again. Jake, moving with the point-fire team, fell to the ground as a burst of automatic fire and the whump of a concussion grenade came from the rear of the column. Hawk came up on the net almost immediately.

"What happened, Assist?" Jake asked.

"Well," Hawk replied, "as we were passing the A-frame back here, a little person opened up with a burst. Boston put a blooper in his pants. He has some leg wounds, but not particularly serious. What should we do with him?"

"Wait one, Assist," Jake replied.

Jake contacted Wayco, who had heard the conversation anyway, and Wayco told him to bring the wounded gooner in for G-2 to question.

"Hawk, did you copy that?" Jake asked.

"Roger that, Actual, I copied, but none of the grunts back here are going to want to hump the little bastard. He's not hurt bad but he can't walk. We've got to make it up the ridge line in front of us even to get a medevac in, and we have our own guys to carry."

Jake listened and felt the exhaustion in Hawk's voice. "Just hump him out along with our own, Assist. Let's move." Wayco interrupted to tell them to go to ground because they were about to drop the first big one. The column went down again on the shouted commands of Jake and Hawk. The jungle suddenly seemed to be totally still, as if anticipating what was about to happen. It was like being in the eye of a hurricane. There was deafening quietness and then the earth shook, the trees shook, while every man in the column tried to retract himself into his helmet.

Pieces of shrapnel and trees and dirt and rock hailed through the air and peppered the column. Then, once again, everything was still. No one moved; time seemed to have stopped. Jake vaguely noticed that the Professor was pulling at his trouser leg.

"Lieutenant, lieutenant. Sergeant Hawkins wants you."

Jake took the handset, wondering if someone else had been injured by the bomb. "What's up, Assist?" he asked.

"One Actual, I have to report a KIA as a result of the big one the sky guys just dropped." Jake said, "oh no," out loud so that the Professor's eyes began to bulge again.

"Actual, the little person we had taken with us apparently either took a hit or succumbed to his wounds. Over."

Jake thought for a moment, relieved that there had been no further casualties to his own men but realizing that in all probability somebody had wasted this guy because they didn't want to carry him up the hill. He was irritated because, as Wayco had said, valuable information might be available to intelligence. Still, he could understand it, in light of what they had just been through. Without commenting, he just said into the handset, "Roger that, Assist. Let's get up the ridge."

By now it was 1700 hours; they had started out nine hours ago. Now as the squads trudged back up the ridge line they stopped at the first flat area and medevaced the dead and wounded out. Moving slowly, they made their way back to Hill 471 before nightfall as originally planned. Bo, the Preacher, and Fast Eddie were standing by Wayco's hootch when Jake walked up for the debriefing. Maybe it was just his imagination, but he thought he could see a new kind of respect in their eyes that wasn't there before. Now he had not only been blooded but tested; apparently he had passed. He couldn't help asking himself a question, an afterthought: What for? Just what the hell was that all about? Three months ago, I was in college, playing football and wrestling . . . at least there I had an objective; I knew whether I had won or lost. I'm here and I don't think I understand. Back in the draw I prayed again. What was that all about? And what about the North Vietnamese we wasted just because somebody didn't want to hump him up the hill? The longer I'm here, the more I learn but the less I understand.

Jake was debriefed by Wayco and Colonel Dagomar, who had flown out in his little two-seater helicopter called a Loach. He took some heat for losing the prisoner but, since it was impossible to prove he didn't buy it from friendly fire, the matter was dropped. In the end, he got a "good job" from the colonel, who mentioned something about a Bronze Star. Jake walked away feeling soiled, and he knew it was a feeling caused by more than the filth that covered his body.

Wayco had hinted that the company might stay there a few more days but that the Third Battalion, Ninth Marine Regiment, was due to replace them in position. Then they would go back to Vandegrift to await further orders. They would probably run sparrow hawks and bald eagles again. As he was leaving Wolf's hootch, Wayco reminded him that Corporals Bowman and Brown were due to go on R and R in a week. Jake slowly drifted back to his own hootch, thanking God he had not lost more men and that he had made it out alive and unhurt.

They stayed on Hill 471 for four more boring days. The Preacher took his platoon out on patrols. Fast Eddie and Bo took their turns, but apparently the NVA had decided that this was not going to be the time or place for a major confrontation. A few mortars came in nightly. A couple of gooks were sighted on the far ridge. One actually stood up and traded shots with a Huey gunship. Jake watched him disintegrate as the gunship casually spiraled a cluster of miniballs from its galley gun in his direction. They got more SPs and beer and cigarettes. Then around noon on the fifth day a couple of CH-46s and a big CH-53 came in and lifted them out; it was as if they had never been there at all. Elements of the Third Battalion, Ninth Marine Regiment flew in; the drama ended on 471 for Alpha, First Battalion, Ninth Marine Regiment, and commenced for someone else. As they skimmed over the treetops, the jungle sped by like an old-time movie shot in green and white. Cocooned in the nose of the helicopter, Jake once again dared to allow himself the opportunity to ask, why.

Alpha had been away from Vandegrift about two weeks. On their return they assumed the very positions they were in when they left. Lieutenant Clahan was back from Quang Tri. The top was there with mail and pay for the troops. Wayco had made up his mind he was goddamn well not going back to the bush. He also decided that Clahan, with almost ninety days left, could take over the company. He made up his mind to recommend that to the colonel as soon as possible. Wolf didn't give a shit what the troops thought; he knew Clahan walked a thin line with the racial crap, but he was convinced that he was a good marine. He would do the job right, given the chance, and he was going to get the chance. He chuckled a bit when he thought about what Bo Lawler's reaction would be to Clahan's getting the top job. He knew there was a big operation brewing; what they had just done was merely a probe to find out what kind of activity was taking place in the Ashau Valley. So he knew one thing for sure, he was not going back down there this trip.

PART TWO

DIALOGUES OF
THE DEAD

O God of battles, steel my soldiers' hearts,
Possess them not with fear. Take from them now
The sense of reck'ning, if the opposed numbers
Pluck their hearts from them.

SHAKESPEARE, THE LIFE OF KING HENRY V

Let every nation know, whether it wishes us well or ill, that we shall pay any price, bear any burden, meet any hardship, support any friend, oppose any foe to assure the survival and the success of liberty.

JOHN F. KENNEDY, 31 MAY, 1961

If we have to fight, we will fight. You will kill ten of our men, and we will kill one of yours, and in the end it will be you who will tire of it.

HO CHI MINH TO JEAN SAIMTERRY

I predict that you will sink step by step into a bottomless military and political quagmire, however much you spend in man and money.

CHARLES DE GAULLE TO JOHN F. KENNEDY

16

ALPHA COMPANY WAS LICKING ITS wounds. Other than the one NVA Jake saw disappear in the smoke when the Huey locked and loaded on him, and the other gook who expired suddenly by the big A-frame bunker, there were no bodies for a body count. The air support had to have taken a toll; surely they had blown a few away down in the draw. The colonel reported a body count of seventy-five. "Guestimating," he said, "the effect of aircraft ordnance." The colonel obviously had command instincts.

Alpha Company had three dead and twenty-seven wounded—four seriously enough to be medevaced back to Okinawa or on to Japan. The others were suffering from varying degrees of burns. At least half the company was down with malaria contracted from the contaminated water cannisters. Alpha would need time to heal and get new replacements.

Jake had a bout with malaria and amoebic dysentery. His left knee had gotten infected and was swollen nearly double its normal size. Even though Doc Pony was giving him quinine and penicillin, he was feeling terrible. Karen's letters came weekly, telling him about what was happening at home. It was really just like being in prison, he thought.

111

Thirteen thousand miles away from home and no phone or car to close the distance. He was afraid that if he went on thinking about it too much he would go nuts. You were almost forced to forget at times, to deaden the pain of separation, he reflected. Jake was becoming at one with his men, and with his company. The purpose was not to win the war. Who the hell knew what that meant strategically, anyway. The purpose was to survive. What it was all about was written on the helmets of almost all the marines: 365 days left, 158 days left, one week; I'm a short-timer. Don't smoke; it's hazardous to your health. Can't dance; you owe it to yourself. You owe it to yourself; you owe it to yourself! A whole new method of communication, helmet covers. Jake retreated to his books and was lost in the middle of J. R. R. Tolkien's *The Hobbit*. While his knee healed and malaria shook his body intermittently and he crapped his brains out at other times, for a while he could be Bilbo Baggins in search of something truly worthwhile and important. But when he put down the book he found himself in Vietnam still.

Showers were the item of the moment at Vandegrift Combat Base. Jake was trying to cope with the boredom of a forward rear area once again. But weighing that against what they had left behind, he decided maybe it wasn't so bad after all. As Wayco had reminded him, Boston and Sugar Bear were due to get some rest and relaxation and, as it turned out, Corporal Dragin would be accompanying them.

Aaron Dragin was a rear-echelon pogue; he had been back in Quang Tri for the last four months and, like Wilbur Akins, had managed to work his way into a soft billet. When Captain McCormack was killed, he got kicked out by the new G-2 and sent back into the bush. Dragin was slight of build; he wore a bush hat tilted back over a pockmarked face with piercing black eyes that always appeared to be in some degree of dilation. Dragin could be very good, Jake thought, but he was one of these guys who always seemed to be walking on the edge. If everyone was dirty, Dragin was dirtier. If everyone had shabby and tattered uniforms, Dragin's was shabbier. He laughed like everyone else but his laugh was cold; it lacked warmth, suggesting something that had absolutely nothing to do with humor. Dragin was streetwise, more than smart enough to stay alive. The last thing he had done before he left the rear was arrange an R and R he hadn't earned. And that was why he was going to be the third party on a trip that included Sugar Bear and Boston. The Professor would lose his turn for several months until someone figured out he had been overlooked. He would never know what had actually happened. The three of them got together, Bear, Boston and Dragin, and decided that they would take their vacation from war in Manila and then swing down to Olongopo City; people said it made Tijuana look like a nursery school. Sodom and Gomorrah would be shrinking violets next to the tantalizing offerings and temptations of Olongopo.

They would have seven days. Seven days to become human beings again; seven days to feel clean sheets and taste real food; seven days of not having to live in fear at the pop of a mortar tube or the whistling of a rocket. Seven days to find physical solace in the warm flesh of a Philippine prostitute. Seven days to wonder how their brothers were doing back in the bush.

The three marines from Alpha Company landed in Manila and made straight away for the Savoy Hotel. They had five months of pay to spend and at least that much pent-up frustration and desire. A trip to a local haberdashery produced civilian clothes. Duded up, cocky and jaunty, like all men who have faced and passed the ultimate test, they began to look for someone who would appreciate sacrifice as they journeyed through Manila. Each man bought two pairs of double-knit trousers and several ultra-long—collared shirts.

Dragin was seriously considering not going back. He thought about his promise to himself back in the draw when the lieutenant had sent him to round up the machetes. Why should I give these assholes another chance to blow me away? Back in Quang Tri I could get all the dope I wanted for arranging the right R and R for the right person. I had influence and position—and now look at me, he thought bitterly. Shit, there are people running away to keep from coming over here at all; why can't I do it after getting here? He decided he would keep his distance from Boston and Sugar Bear. Besides, he knew they didn't give a shit about him. Most of the troops knew what he was doing back in Quang Tri. But he also knew that as long as he didn't screw up in the bush he would get by.

They spent two days making the rounds of the bars in Manila. On the first night they found a repository for the quick-ended sex that comes from months of abstention and the accompanying short fuse. They went as a trio to one house that specialized in blow jobs, and for five bucks watched each other get their socks blown off. Twice, they visited the Soldiers and Sailors Club in Manila with its huge open porches and ate breakfasts of steak and eggs. They spent one entire evening obliterating the salad bar, until they were asked, not so politely, if they hadn't had enough. It was a search for satiation. Dragin urged them to hurry up and get to Olongopo where, he promised Boston and Sugar Bear, everything a man could want could be purchased within five feet of the main gate at Subic Bay. He was a veteran of Olongopo, having docked there with the Seventh Fleet before going to Vietnam.

The trio rode overland silently in a Jeepney, the Philippine answer to a taxicab, with its garish adornments of paint and horns and decorations limited only by the imagination of the driver. They drank in the pungent odors of the countryside, remarked on how closely the terrain resembled Vietnam and, since the two countries shared the same rainy seasons and monsoons, how similar the climate was. They devoured great meals of fried rice and greasy pork *adobo,* with lighter *pancite* noodles and *lumpia* as an accompaniment. The roads were mostly unpaved dirt and rock; by the time the three hours of travel was over they were ready for a rest.

Olongopo City was nestled in a valley that rolled down from the mountains to form the main gate at the U.S. Naval Base Subic Bay. It was estimated that sixty thousand people crammed themselves into this small city. It was truly an experience, a combination of the very old and the very new, incorporating abject poverty and great wealth. Physically, it was one main street stretching from the main gate at Subic Bay for about one mile; bar after bar lined both sides. The streets were dirt, the walks concrete or slat board. Each bar had its gun-toting bouncer stationed at the door.

The main street made a T at the fringe of the jungle, veering left and right, lined by even more bars and gin houses. The Cave, Pauline's, The Door, Angeles Club, gift shops sporting thousands of items carved from monkey pod and nara wood. There were dinner sets, crucifixes everywhere, paintings by very good copiers; vendors selling monkey meat and baluts. Only the very drunk sailor or marine could master the balut, a fertilized chicken egg or duck egg buried in the ground until feathers began to form. Once it was resurrected, a hole was punched in one end of the egg. Only the very resolute could swallow the entire contents,—egg, bones, and feathers. The smell was an added obstacle.

The odors of the market mixed with the sour smells of urine and feces, which floated into the open *binjo* ditches at the sides of the road. It was a bazaar of the absurd, wide open twenty-four hours a day to accommodate the men at the base and the sailors on leave from the Seventh Fleet. The ubiquitous bar girls, some young, too young, and some too old, but all wearing great sheets of caked makeup and sickening perfume—such was the uniform of the day for the whores who haunted the streets and the bars.

Boston and Sugar Bear were enthralled. They carried with them everything they owned: for Harry, that meant one less set of civilian clothes than Dragin or Bear. He had persuaded the Jeepney driver to let him try to ride a water buffalo at Castillios and had succeeded only in ending up on his face in a rice paddy. It provided great entertainment for the farmers. The three marines had been drinking for four days by then and had two days left before they would have to head back to Manila. That meant little to them at the moment, for they were off on another adventure and wanted to make every second count. Boston was having a great time.

They stormed into Olongopo with all cylinders hammering. The Jeepney pushed through the foul, wet sludge of the street, which never quite dried out, even in the parchest seasons. The driver guided them to the Paradise Hotel, newly built on a back street of Olongopo. It was small but new. In fact, it was out of character with its surroundings, like a tuxedo in the middle of a desert. They checked in and took a shower again. That is, Boston and Sugar Bear took showers and Dragin said he didn't need one. Then they hit the streets.

"Let's go on over to the main street," Dragin suggested. "Naw," Sugar Bear responded, "let's see some of the sights here first." The three of them shuffled along, heading down to the Olongopo River that separated the town from the base at Subic Bay. The sailors called it "shit river" because of the raw sewage that made up most of its flow. It was great sport to stand and watch the Filipino boys and girls sitting on *banca* boats and begging beneath the causeway. Sugar Bear threw a quarter into the river and several of the smaller children dived into the slime to recover the treasure. The very poor of Olongopo lived here. These houses were perched on stilts above tons of garbage that rotted daily in the tropical sun. Nowhere else in the world was this smell to be found. Continuing on past the armed-forces police shack near the main gate and getting the once-over from the Olongopo Police, they moved on into town. It was a night of monkey meat eaten off of sticks hawked from the streets. At least it was supposed to be monkey meat; Boston swore he had eaten dog before and this, he claimed, tasted just like it. Little wooden elephants were purchased and larger Marine Corps emblems made of monkey pod found their way into straw bags provided by the vendors. They consumed unknown but vast quantities of San Miguel beer and dared the street thieves to steal from them.

Darkness overcame them as they continued their shambling progress from bar to bar. A ritualistic procession to drunkenness. Dragin was mixing his beer with pot and coke, both of which could be purchased in the street. Boston and Sugar Bear were content to smoke cigarettes and concentrate on the women. They warned Dragin that if he blew himself away, they were going to dump him. Boston, becoming very melancholy, turned to Sugar Bear and said, "What do you think Lieutenant Adams is doing right now?" Sugar Bear looked up at him out of his San Miguel and said, "Why don't you shut up? We're going back there soon enough." Dragin had had enough. He got up and announced, "I'm going to the head." He disappeared in the dark and smoke of The Cave. Unlike the bar girls in Okinawa, those here would leave you alone as long as you were buying drinks—unless you invited them to stay. Sugar Bear was admiring the dark-skinned Filipino girls, whose complexions reminded him of the chocolate-colored skin that Esther would rub against him back in the world. Esther, with softer curls in her hair than that of his sisters, and an odor of musk that brought an erection almost immediately. He loved Esther; he had fathered a son by her in high school. That was one of the reasons he had joined the corps; to find out for himself if she was to be the one . . . he knew now that he would go back to Esther. He also knew he was going to take her off the block and show her the world. He was thinking that he was comfortable here. He didn't see the contempt in the eyes of the women here that he had seen in those of women in other places.

The brothers had told him he was fighting the white man's war, that he should disobey orders and create problems. But he knew the truth of the bush: There were good marines and bad marines . . . some were white and some were black. In the bush it didn't matter. What mattered was survival. The rules weren't white, they were colorless, they dictated survival. You followed them or you died or, worse yet, you got your balls shot off, or your arms or legs didn't make the trip home with you. If you disobeyed them, you got chewed up statistically as just another nigger who used his color to hide his cowardice. He knew he had some of the feelings that Lieutenant Lawler had and couldn't hide them; but, hell, even the lieutenant had to survive and he had never used color as a reason to put someone on the point. Sugar Bear, he just wanted to make it home and do something with his life. He wanted to smell Esther again and feel the softness of her lips and the flex of her abdominal muscles as she enveloped him inside her. Yes, he loved her and would marry her when he got back. He had confidence; he knew he was good and could even make a place for himself in this corps. White or black didn't matter; the bush had shown him the equality of death.

A rather small Filipino girl came up to the table where Boston and Sugar Bear were seated. Their backs were against a wall and people were seated on either side. To their left, two sailors were hanging on a couple of the worst-looking skags Boston claimed he had ever seen. "But what the hell," he told Bear, "I mean, after all, they're squids. Fact is, those ladies are probably doing those guys a favor."

Sugar Bear rolled his eyes and the little girl in front of the table asked if they wanted a good time. Bear looked at Boston and rolled his eyes again, wondering exactly what she meant.

"Well," Boston said, "let's ask her. How much would a good time cost and where would we have to go?"

"You would go nowhere, marine. Just sit right where you are and for ten pesos you can have a great time."

She was slight and not very clean and as she spoke she smiled, revealing a gap in her front teeth. One soiled shoulder strap on her skimpy dress was about ready to give way. Maybe she was fourteen or fifteen years old going on forty underneath all the makeup and eyeliner. Almost as a lark both Boston and Sugar Bear put their money on the table, only to have it and the girl disappear as if by magic.

Boston looked at Sugar Bear and said with some embarrassment, "What happened to her? Where did she go with our money?" The band was loud and the crowd was noisy and smoke filled the air, mingling in and out of a general state of confusion.

Bear smiled and said nothing in response to Boston's query. Boston was ready to get up and search for the thief when something in the expression on Bear's face betrayed knowledge he clearly didn't have.

"Bear, what the hell is the matter with you? This little lady just stole twenty pesos and took us . . ." With that, he felt a pull on the zipper of his pants. Then the same surprised look he had seen on Sugar Bear's face crossed his own. This girl was going to give him head right here in a busy nightclub. "Psst, psst." He could hear the familiar hail of the Filipino; her job done, she was motioning him to provide her with some table napkins. A couple passing by saw only her hand as it reached up between Boston and Sugar Bear and disappeared again. Boston was thinking that this was truly an example of free enterprise. She beat the competition at White Rock Beach by going directly to the customer. They didn't have to go to her. She cut down the price because she had no overhead to share with the other girls and she was completely mobile. Free enterprise, he thought, the idea that made America great, alive and working here in Olongopo City, the Republic of the Philippines. Boston ordered another San Miguel, because neither one of them felt they were prepared to get up yet. Dragin had not returned.

A couple more San Miguels bit the dust. The locals called it "tiger piss." Sugar Bear finally went to see if Dragin had passed out in the head, but failed to find him there or anywhere in the place. Leaving The Cave, Sugar Bear and Boston went down the main street where the noise of one band overlapped the next, each trying to win the award for the highest decibels ever put out by a live group. The night sounds of the city were mixed in with a wave of festive music washing over the sadness that was the reality of Olongopo. They had left Vietnam for the fantasy of a week of R and R, but maybe the fantasy was back in the jungle and the reality here in Olongopo. Life-and-death decisions were being made here, too. On the left-hand side of the street was a steel cage, six feet by six feet. There must have been a dozen young people and urchins of the street caught for attempting to pick someone's pocket by the Olongopo Police, incarcerated there to spend the night as a general rule, or until someone thought to let them out the next day. That way, they became a public spectacle; people would see them and learn to avoid them in the future. They often fought each other inside the cage; more than once, when the cage was opened, one or more of the occupants was found dead.

Boston and Bear passed the cage and rolled down the street, one periodically holding onto the other for support, vaguely looking for Dragin. They passed Pauline's, one of the most popular bars in Olongopo, with its crocodile pit in front. Boston even bought one of the baby ducks the Filipino children were selling to feed to the old crock. But it was evident the creature was so sated from previous ducks that he couldn't care less about another.

The remainder of the night was spent overdosing on San Miguel beer and, even worse, San Miguel gin, sex, and perfect renditions of the Temptations singing "Cloud Nine," "Runaway Child Running Wild," Bob Dylan's "The Times They Are a Changin'." Unconsciously they made their way back to the Paradise Hotel, and without saying anything to each other they both knew they were ready to go back. Bitch about it they would, but by rejoining their unit in the bush there would come the cleansing of the return. Just as they had needed to take R and R, they needed to go back. Sobering up somewhat, they set about finding Dragin in earnest. These were strange times. People were simply not acting in rational ways. What was the truth? What was the purpose? What was right? Sugar Bear once heard Jake say to Boston that it was as if Jehovah were calling different people home. Who, he wondered, had been called home while they were gone? Who would be called home when they returned? Boston and Sugar Bear were rushing to find out.

Dragin had decided he wasn't going back. He left The Cave and walked through Olongopo thinking about Nam. He had it made back in Quang Tri. All he had to worry about was incoming and doing his time. Now he was out in the fucking bush. And not just out in the bush, but out in the bush with the First Battalion and a Medal of Honor company commander in Wolf, a black with a point to make in Clahan, and a gung-ho platoon commander in Adams. Sure as shit, one of them would get him killed. Besides, good reefer was harder to get out in the boonies. He had heard the stories. People were protesting back in the world. Things were not going well politically; now there were rumors that U.S. combat forces might be pulled out. Who wants to get killed at all, much less for a cause we might walk out on. Damn, he thought, I'm mixed up. I don't want to get a bad-conduct discharge, I don't want to go AWOL, I don't want to get killed. In fact, I don't like any of those choices. It's just so easy to float away on cloud nine and worry about it all later. In fact, the song said it, "you ain't got no responsibility." He knew this was it. Bear and Boston would be heading back in a Jeepney in the morning. He could take off for the barrios and hide out. But for how long? How obvious would an American be out here in Luzon? Tonight was not such a problem, but what about tomorrow and the next day and the day after that? He decided he would find himself a little bar girl to shack up with for the night and then get up early to meet Bear and Boston at the Paradise.

Paradise, right! he thought, right here in the middle of all of this garbage, paradise. What the hell, I might as well throw the dice again. Old Dragin has made it this far, I can pull four more months and a wake-up, even with the walking dead. How fucking bad can it really be? He lit up another joint.

While Dragin, Sugar Bear, and Boston were making their way across Luzon having gorged themselves on food, booze, and sex, Alpha Company, First Battalion, was setting in a defensive perimeter inside Vandegrift Combat Base. There was card-playing in the staff and officer's tent, hot chow and cold beer replacing the usual C-rats, and, as before, the North Vietnamese peppering the compound with 107 and 122 rockets daily. Scuttlebutt had it that some big operation was being planned. Replacement troops were due in.

Jake was getting over the malaria and dysentery. Wayco Wolf was heading back to Quang Tri. It had been formally announced that First Lieutenant James T. Clahan would be taking over the company. Bo Lawler showed no visible reaction. Alex Scott was holding Bible studies and prayer meetings with the few troops he could persuade to join him. So far, he had no luck with the staff or officers. Jake was more than a little curious about what made this big guy tick. He was obviously good at what he did. He handled himself well in the bush and seemed to have no trouble separating blowing someone's head off from his love for God. Jake made a mental note that he would have to ask him about that sometime.

No sparrow hawks or bald eagles were launched. Twice, the men were mustered down to the airstrip but never got off the ground. So the days ran one into another and the short-timers prepared to leave, while the others just drew another line through a date on the calendars they had engraved on their helmet covers. Jake hoped that Boston, Dragin, and Sugar Bear would make it back before they got into any real crap. Boston was indispensable as far as Jake was concerned. Sugar Bear had proven himself over and over, and Jake relied on him too. Dragin? Well, Jake was unsure of him but he knew Dragin could do the job if he could keep his head straight. He wondered what they were doing in the Philippines. Boy, he thought, I can't wait to see Karen on R and R. And as soon as the thought hit his mind he repressed it and began to concentrate on what he had to do to keep himself and his men alive.

The only casualty that occurred while Boston, Dragin, and Sugar Bear were on R and R took place during a rocket attack. Fast Eddie, ignoring the incoming rockets, had stood out in the middle of the company area, cursing at the NVA and the incoming rounds. Before the barrage was over he had taken shrapnel in his face, neck, and legs. Much to the dismay of the colonel and the departing Wolf, he had to be medevaced to Okinawa. That left the Preacher, Jake, and Bo Lawler, no Weapons Platoon commander, and Jim Clahan as the company commander with no executive officer. The company was up to about one hundred and thirty people. Jake, with fifty-eight men, had the biggest platoon. Almost at the precise moment Sugar Bear was thinking about Jake's comment to Boston concerning Jehovah's throat, Jake himself was wondering who might be called next.

17

J AMES T. CLAHAN, FIRST LIEUTENANT,
Alpha Company Commander, black,
relieving Wayco Wolf, captain, near-
legend, white. Jim Clahan sat in his hootch at Vandegrift Combat Base
and thought about his new command; he wondered how much his color
had to do with his selection as company commander. He was ambitious,
had the necessary drive and desire; he felt he was just as good or better
than any of the white boys. He could compete in their world. He had
excelled in all athletics in high school and made all-metro in basketball at
Spingarn High School in Washington, D.C. He went on to Howard
University and brought home the first bachelor's degree that a member
of his family had ever possessed. He went into the Platoon Leaders Class
Program in his sophomore year and at graduation, along with his degree
in sociology, he put on the brown bars of a second lieutenant, United
States Marine Corps.

James Clahan had been one of a handful of blacks in the basic school.
He felt he had to run faster, score higher, have shinier shoes and
brighter brass than any of the white guys. So he did. Still, he was
plagued with the doubt that everything he accomplished was half given

to him because he was black. He knew about quotas and he hated them. Sure, they gave the brothers a chance where there often had been none, but they also took away self-respect and dignity—and always introduced an element of doubt about what had or had not been earned. He felt he could see that in the eyes of the white guys he competed with. If he won, it was because there was an edge given to him. If he lost, it was because he just didn't measure up. Hell, he thought, I had even won the watermelon-eating contest at the graduation picnic because I was so damn competitive. He knew what sort of jokes that would bring on. And now, given command, he wondered how much of it had to do with the fact that the corps needed to be able to say there was a black company commander in-country. He knew Wayco worried about his loyalty; whether it was to the corps first, or to the brothers. He had spoken up in support of allowing black marines to pass the dap and carry their short-timer sticks, and it had marked him.

Yet there were some things that Wayco and the others just didn't understand. Nonetheless, here he was, a company commander; now he had white men reporting to him and working for him. He was the boss. Clahan knew he was a professional, that he could separate himself from his roots; he had to. He knew he would make the proper military decision in the bush. It was true that he could not, and would not, leave his blackness behind, but he knew Wayco would never have allowed him to take the company if he didn't feel he could pack the gear. Maybe a couple of hundred years of rejections had taken ther toll. Maybe that's where this "nigger" feeling of not measuring up came from. He wondered if the others were ever worried about their ability to do the job they were in. I simply have to do well. There is no other alternative. I will do whatever it takes. With that, Jim Clahan pulled his stationery from his pack to write home of the good news.

The triumphant trio, Dragin, Boston, and Sugar Bear, came rolling into camp in a doggie jeep. Jake was glad to see them—and the troops were anxious to hear about their exploits. Colonel Dagomar had called a staff meeting of all the company commanders and executive officers in the battalion for 1600 hours. This must be it, Jake thought. The scuttlebutt for two weeks was that there was a big operation being planned and that it was going to be different from anything else before. Clahan had appointed Jake as acting executive officer, as well as First Platoon commander, so Jake was going with him to the staff briefing.

Jake had seen Dagomar before and had been amazed at the way Dagomar was always clean and wearing a fresh uniform in the middle of the bush. But today, unbelievably, he was dressed in starched jungle utilities. Balding on top, with a long, sometimes mournful-looking face, he could have passed for a college professor. Jake instinctively did not like him, although he could not define exactly why. The colonel had a high forehead and a rather pointed nose which, combined with his attitude and swagger, gave him the appearance of a sanctimonious, sour individual who might be waiting for a vacancy in the Trinity. Jake had respect for rank and seldom made snap judgments; but there was just something about this guy.

It also bothered Jake that Clahan had taken on a different attitude since being appointed company commander. He seemed aloof, distant. Jake wondered if he just needed somebody to talk to. He hoped Clahan was smart enough to use Gunny Jacobsen and his knowledge and experience. Not that he was worried about Clahan; he had performed okay before, and there was no reason to expect anything else now. But something was getting at him; Clahan was not the same person as before. Jake wondered briefly if perhaps he was bothered by the fact that Clahan was black. He even asked himself if thinking about Clahan's color made him prejudiced. He didn't think he was prejudiced, but the thought made him uncomfortable. The truth was, he reasoned, that back in the draw on Hill 471 he felt confidence in Wolf's direction. He was not sure about Clahan. That wasn't prejudice, that was fact, and confidence wasn't a function of color. It had to be earned.

Colonel Dagomar paced back and forth on the small raised platform at the front of the briefing tent. There were holes in the sides of the tent from pieces of shrapnel that had ripped through during previous rocket attacks. Sunlight played through the holes, illuminating wisps of dust that floated around inside the tent.

Dagomar began speaking in a voice that cracked like an adolescent's. "Gentlemen," he began, "in three days we will step off on an operation that will be different from any other the Third Marine Division has embarked on in Vietnam." He paused, gauging the effect of his words

124

on the packed tent. Jake was aware that similar meetings were going on in the Second and Third battalions, so that this was to be a regimental-scale operation. The colonel stood to the right of an easel that held a large map mounted on some type of corkboard. He looked around the room, apparently trying to add broad emphasis to his presentation. He continued: "We will, of course, be using mobile Marine Corps units against what we believe is a sizable enemy resistance. The battalions will be under the protection of artillery fire; the rifle companies will operate independently for extended periods of time on what we will refer to as 'saturation sweeps.' As you can see by your maps, what makes this operation decidedly different is the remoteness of the area of operation from friendly tactical artillery support and resupply, as well as the known enemy antiaircraft capability in the Ashau Valley."

The colonel paused, measuring his audience in the afternoon heat. The beating of rotor blades continued almost nonstop in the distance.

"Gentlemen, Route 922, heading from Laos to the Ashau Valley, has been reopened by the NVA. Antiaircraft activity has become evident all along that road network. Several antiaircraft weapons, 127-millimeter, 25-millimeter, and 37-millimeter, have been identified. We have already lost an A-6 aircraft. Truck traffic had doubled; it's up to one thousand a day. Visual reconnaissance has sighted large enemy forces. In every attempt at additional visual reconnaissance we are now taking small-arms fire. Intelligence has indicated probable movement of the enemy back into the Dakrong area. Our commitment will be to the mountains west of Hue and southwest of Quang Tri. From there, the enemy could mount attacks as far south as Da Nang.

"In addition," the colonel continued, now using his pointer on the map, "the topography is rugged; triple-canopy mountains with sharp ravines descending to lowlands covered with high elephant grass. High hill masses on the Laotion border frame the western and southern boundaries of the area of the operation. On the west, as you can see, Co Ka Leuye, a razorback ridge approximately 1,400 meters high and 3,500 meters long, looms along the entire area of operation. In the south is a series of ridge lines rising out of the Dakrong Valley and running north and south to the borders, reaching a height of 1,000 meters."

The colonel paused to let the impact of all this sink in. Marines were looking intently at their maps, trying to tie in what he had said with the flat contour lines in front of them. Dagomar continued on: "South of the border of Laos, the ridge lines in the southwest drop off into an east-west valley, while those to the southeast rise to a mountainous area. At the southeast corner of the area of operation is Tam Boi. Mark it on your maps, gentlemen. It is a mountain 1,224 meters high. Just inside the eastern edge of the area of operation is Co A Wong, or Tiger Mountain, 1,228 meters high. Tiger Mountain, as you see it, sits at the head of and dominates observation of the Ashau Valley. On the other side of Tiger Mountain are the headwaters of the Dakrong River.

"We have reason to believe that a base camp, one we will designate as Base Camp 911, is being constructed on the border of Laos along Route 922. It may be the biggest base camp ever constructed by the NVA. Route 922 approaches the RVN border at an angle south from southwest through the Laotion Valley south of the border, and then curves, running generally parallel and south of the border until it reaches a point four or five hundred meters west of Tam Boi. There, it crosses the border and wanders around Tiger Mountain and finally turns east and south into the Ashau Valley. There it becomes Route 548. Gentlemen, we intend to destroy this base camp and stop the flow of enemy logistics down the Ho Chi Minh Trail. Are there any questions?"

The colonel continued to pace back and forth; as he did so, small puffs of dust popped up between the boards of the platform, dulling the shine on his jungle boots. Silence followed each footstep. A captain sitting next to Jake leaned over and said, "What are we supposed to say, anyway? People only ask questions in situations like this in the movies."

Jim Clahan wanted to ask a ton of questions, but he had too many to pick just one. Jake wanted to ask a question, but only if he wouldn't look like an ass, so he said nothing since he was the junior officer present. He wondered what everyone else was thinking. The thought popped into his head that this had the potential to be some real bad shit. The colonel finally broke the silence. "Well, if there are no questions, I'm going to turn this over to Major Bedendorf, the battalion G-2, to explain the basis for your five-paragraph orders. I don't think I need to tell you the importance of this operation and its potential effect on the outcome of the war. We have never attempted anything like this before and we want to kick ass and take names."

Bedendorf paused, facing the assembled officers of the First Battalion with his hands on his hips. The heat was stifling and everyone was anxious to be dismissed. Small drops of sweat made their way down the major's temples. "Good luck," he began. "I think we are about to make history."

This would be the last month and a half in Vietnam for Jake. He obviously couldn't know it now but, while the first four months brought the questions that still had not been resolved with rational answers, the next two months would change his life completely. And, interestingly enough, as he sat anticipating what Major Bedendorf would say, he knew what was going to go down. It was Jehovah's throat once again whispering in the wind, calling from the cosmos, circumventing time and unifying the spirit of those who had walked distant battlefields past. It was the voice that beckoned men to their destiny, called the agnostic, the atheist, the seeking, the religious to face themselves, death, and God. It was the part that is man claiming to be God, looking for control, and the part that is spirit, seeking to find God and looking for the answer.

Basically, what Major Bedendorf began saying was that I Corps Tactical Zone, Quang Tri the NVA had created a staging and infiltrating complex astride Route 922, fed war stores through Thua Thien and Quang Nam via Routes 548 and 547, through the Ashau Valley to the southeast. With Third Armored Marine Air Force thwarting enemy communications in west and north Quang Tri, the Ashau artery assumed greater importance. Bedendorf, a wiry bantam rooster of a man, was saying that the battalion would move with two rifle companies on parallel ridge lines for mutual support, with one company in trace of each lead company. In this way, the momentum would never be lost. When the lead company was heavily engaged, the rear elements of the trace company could take the dead and wounded and move through the lead company to the attack. The entire regiment would sweep down the Dakrong River in such a way, en route through the Ashau Valley.

Even as the briefings went on, scuttlebutt was spread through the regiment down to the battalion, down to the companies, and on down to

127

the platoons and squads and fire teams. The whispering in the wind became a hurricane that no one could avoid hearing. The men were mentally preparing themselves; the inanimate organizational scheme of platoon, company, and battalion came alive with a purpose of its own.

Boston regarded all this with his usual black humor; and it was still merely a rumor. He knew it would happen, though. Ever since they had been down in the Dakrong the last time, he knew they would go back. He had really hoped to be gone. He didn't want to go back.

Dragin was ready. He was glad he had come back. He would do his time and get out. Later, he thought, there would be time to figure out the rest of the heavy bullshit; now was the time for survival in the bush and that meant keeping your shit together.

But Gunny Sergeant Samuel Jacobsen did not want to go back to the Dakrong. It was a place that almost screamed death. He was sure it would take all the experience of three tours in-country to walk back out of this one. It was as it had always been: the new troops asked questions about what it would be like. The old salts laughed and nervously made it worse than it had ever been before and, in general, tried to scare the crap out of the twinks. Sugar Bear and Hawk were tightening up even before the word became official. It was an unusual thing in the marine corps. History dictated that the last private in line should be the first to know of any major changes, even before others in the chain of command. "The word" had a life of its own and it traveled faster than a laser beam through every command. Even though the orders had not been given, the troops were nearly ready.

Jim Clahan had gathered his platoon commanders plus Gunny Jacobsen, Hawk, and Sergeants Wayne and DeJesus, the Second and Third Platoon sergeants. They gathered in the staff and officer's tent and sat on folding chairs or on the sides of field cots. Most of them had their shirts open with the tails hanging out of their trousers. They each wore one dog tag strung around their neck and the other through one boot lace for identification; in case either the leg or head was lost the remains could still be identified.

Jim Clahan and Jake had left the regimental briefing area and walked together down the hill before they told the Gunny to get everybody together. They walked in uneasy silence. Now, as Clahan looked around the tent, seeking any challenges to his leadership, he knew intuitively that he had Jake's support. The Gunny was all pro and Alex Scott was a thoroughbred straining at the gate. Clahan knew it didn't make any difference to either of them who the company commander was. The Preacher's chain of command ended with God. But in Bo Lawler's eyes, just for a moment, he thought he saw the old flicker of recognition. You're here because you are black, so let's get on with it. Just screw up one time, nigger, and you're done. What the hell am I doing to myself, Clahan thought. He shook his head to get his thought back to the meeting. Leadership comes from me, he told himself. I do not need some white boy's approval. I will be the best and then no one can say a thing.

The schedule and details of the attack had been set. There would be three waves of vertical assaults to establish three separate fire-support bases for the operation. The first would be made by the Second Battalion at grid square 1428, 188 kilometers south of fire-support base Shiloh. This new base would be called Razor. It was going to be farther south than the Ninth Marines had ever been before; yet it was only halfway into the new area of operation. The Third Battalion would secure the second fire-support base, located 6,000 meters southeast of Razor. It was 1,100 meters long. Located in grid square 1813, it would be called Cunningham. Cunningham would be the hub of activity during the main attack. The First Battalion would secure the third fire-support base. In grid square YD 1180, four miles southwest of Cunningham on Hill 406, would sit fire-support base Erskine. The farthest point south into the new A.O. belonged to the First Battalion, and the first wave of that assault belonged to First Platoon. Jake, Boston, Sugar Bear, Dragin, Hawk, Doc Pony, and the Professor, all of them were about to cross over the line.

Company Commander Clahan was finishing his briefing. Situation, mission, execution, administration and logistics, command and communication. The same format for a five-paragraph order that historically preceded marines into combat. They were as ready as they could be. Each one had found his own way of accepting what faced him. Some based on authority, some on loyalty, some on patriotism, others in futility, but all were resigned to whatever fate would bring.

Back in the world, Kent State had raised to the forefront the flag of revolution as national guardsmen fired at and killed protesting students. A rallying point was established for every discontent. In Haight Ashbury the hippies protested and the Fifth Dimension brought in "The Age of Aquarius." Young men were finding support for fleeing to Canada to avoid the draft. Judy Collins was singing of ice-cream castles in the air and the many things she would have done if clouds hadn't gotten in her way. And a generation was being split apart, warped and changed forever because of clouds of war.

Parade magazine published pictures in its "Intelligence" section of an assault on Hill 689, showing half-buried marines. And every mother wondered whether those exposed legs attached to a pair of jungle boots belonged to her son. *Parade* stated that the marines were the most elite fighting force that America had ever put together and were being needlessly sacrificed in questionable missions.

In Quang Tri Province of Vietnam, the Third Marine Division, Ninth Marine Regiment, was about to move once again back into the Dakrong River Valley.

In the United States a civil war erupted once more; it divided father and son, mother and daughter, brother and sister, husband and wife. The Vietnam War had become a war of ideas manufactured by politicians, carried on by an unknowing military, and attacked by an angry press seeking to confirm its own prejudices. All would find what they wanted in the killing fields of Vietnam.

18

I T WAS THE DAY FOLLOWING THE COL-
onel's warning order and Clahan's five-
paragraph order. The First Battalion
was preparing to move out, but the exact time of departure was still
unknown. Jake was walking along the boardwalk up toward Clahan's
tent when he was stopped by what he heard emanating from Alex Scott's
hootch . . .

"O God," Scott prayed, "help me to serve you in this hour of trial and
act honorably as a Christian solider. You have told me in Psalm 144
through your servant David, blessed be the Lord my strength, which
teacheth my hands to war, and my fingers to fight." Jake, embarrassed at
his own eavesdropping, stooped to dig an imaginary clod from the heel
of his jungle boot. "O God, you teacheth my hand war so that a bow of
steel is broken by my arms. Though a host should encamp against me,
my heart shall not fear . . ."

Jake pushed aside the canvas flap of the hootch: "Hey, Preacher, I
have never heard anything like that, even in the few times I've actually
been in a church. What were you talking about, Alex?"

Scott pushed his weight up off his knees, using the side of his field cot as a lever. He wasn't sure whether he was being ragged or not.

"Jake, are you serious? Do you really want to know what I was talking about?"

"Sure, Preacher," Jake responded. "To tell you the truth, I believe in God, but I sure have a lot of questions that I would like answered. You're too damn big to argue with, Alex, and even though many of the guys make jokes about it, I know most of them respect your faith and commitment. Hell, I respect it! Anyway, here's a question I've been wanting to ask you for a long time. How do you justify killing in light of the Bible?"

Alex stared at Jake, still searching his face for any evidence of mockery. He was not prepared to cast his pearls before swine and he would not hesitate to give him, as he called it, the left foot of fellowship if Jake wasn't sincere. But he didn't see that in Jake's face; it wasn't there.

"Listen, Jake. No one has the right either to shirk military service or to be a so-called conscientious objector on the basis of morality, and certainly not on the principle of religious freedom or Christianity. From the standpoint of the word of God, there is no such thing as a conscientious objector. Thou shalt not kill is literally, in the Hebrew, thou shalt not murder. This commandment refers to homicide, which has nothing to do with warfare. What Calley did, as an example, was murder. But it would be murder back in the states, the same as it is murder here. I know we've got troops collecting ears, and doing things that border on barbarism. However, there is barbarism back in the world."

Scott halted abruptly, as if he had said too much or been too revealing. He turned, looking at Jake again with a long deliberate stare, as if measuring him somehow. "I'm not going to go off the deep end with you, Jake, but you asked. The ultimate solution to any problem, personal or a nation's, is personal faith in God. In Ecclesiastes, God said there was a time for war and a time for peace. There will always be war, in spite of man's efforts for peace. Jesus said, "And when ye shall hear of wars and rumors of wars, be ye not troubled; for such things must needs be . . ." Man relies on his own systems to solve his problems, just like you and I do, problems such as poverty, war, and environment—when he should rely on personal salvation and then turn his problems, personal and national, over to God. This is God's plan for the human race.

Jake stood there dumbfounded. Alex was saying that God apparently had a plan for the whole human race, and Alex was having trouble figuring out the five-paragraph order for this one frigging operation.

"Alex, you're presupposing that this war is approved by God. I think I came over here believing something. I instinctively know I must believe in the righteousness of our purpose. I must follow orders. I don't question the system. To me that is what a professional does. I just haven't made the spiritual connection that you apparently have. I know this; I want to survive; I think right now that's the main purpose of everyone here, with the possible exception of some of the lifers who want to win medals and further their careers." Jake looked off into the distance through the window flap in Alex's tent. "It may not be a very good war but, as Wayco used to say, it's the only war we've got."

Alex stood looking at Jake as the distant helicopters churned up the superheated air around Vandegrift. He stared a moment longer and then bore into Jake. "No one can afford to leave Jesus Christ out of their personal or national life. Do you know Christ as your personal savior, Jake?"

Jake took two steps back and said, "Whoa, boy, I don't think I'm ready to become another notch on your evangelical gun just yet. I know you're sincere, Alex, and I appreciate what you have shared with me; just give me a little space."

"Jake," Alex shot back, "neither one of us has any space. Tomorrow you may get your head blown off and I just want to impress upon . . ."

"Listen to me, Alex," Jake broke in. "I want to continue our talk when we get a chance, but I've got to go up and see Clahan. All of the Ninth Marines and their support units are already linked up from Vandegrift south. We are going to leapfrog into the new area of operation. Jim has our jump-off time."

"Jake, please think about what I said," Alex persisted.

"Alex," Jake said, shaking his head, "I see why they call you the Preacher," and he turned to leave.

Alex followed him outside the tent and as Jake walked up the dusty walk to the company commander's hootch, he yelled after him, "Hey, Jake, remember when you're right with God, even if you lose you win."

Jake turned and yelled back, "I hope the damn gooks aren't as persistent as you, Preacher, or we're in for a world of shit."

The sides of his hootch were rolled up and Jake could see Clahan working on his gear as he approached. He walked in, saying, "What's up, Jim?"

Clahan looked up from his gear and said, "Jake, I want you to refer to me as Skipper from now on, okay?"

Jake was taken aback but said, "Okay, Skipper," trying to remove any sarcasm from the word, "I just thought that was reserved for the rank of captain."

"I've been selected and I am the company commander," Clahan responded. "Okay, okay, Skipper," Jake retorted, this time laying heavy on the word. "Now what's this about the jump off? When do we go?"

Clahan stood up, adjusting his crotch with his left hand. "All the chopper activity you've been hearing this morning is the Second Battalion lifting off into Tun Tavern fire-support base. That's at grid square 6532. It's a fire-support base that hasn't been used since December of 1968. From there they will move to FSB Razor tomorrow, the twenty-first of January. They have until the twenty-third to secure it. On the twenty-fourth, the Third Battalion goes into Cunningham, and then sometime after Cunningham is secured, we will get the word to make a vertical assault into FSB Erskine. Once we're in place, the battalion will be in position to cross the Dakrong River. So we know we've got a couple of days; we could have as long as a week. There it is." Clahan turned back to his gear, and Jake, still wondering at the formality, turned and left.

He made his way back down the path, part dirt, part boardwalk, to the staff tent. There he found Bo and Hawk and a couple of the troops shooting the breeze. Hawkins was asking Bo how he ended up with the grunts. Boston had a couple of the guys from his squad with him and they were all just rapping. Bo was waxing eloquent: "Well, I'll tell ya, Sergeant Hawkins, before I got in-country, I was flying in and out of Cubi Point in the Philippines. Off duty a bunch of us guys used to go up to the Cubi Point Officers' Club and do carrier landings in a contraption they had up there. If you missed the tail hook you ended up at the swimming pool. I always ended up in the pool. In November, I just happened to be there for the Marine Corps birthday ball and there was this big celebration. Admiral Muse was there and Colonel Keith and all the troops from the security detachment. Nancy Wilson was the entertainment and the corps was trying to do a good show for all the squids on the base. Well, you know, if you've ever been to Cubi, there's this sort of flying bridge out over the dance floor, just as you come in the door. I know this sounds a little silly now, but I missed that damn tail hook so many times, and we were about sixteen sheets to the wind and, well, I saw that five-tiered birthday cake down there and I just couldn't resist it. I made a perfect three-point landing right in the middle of the Marine Corps birthday cake." Bo, pausing for reflection, looked down at his boots. "That, incidentally, led to my first letter of reprimand and the request that if I wanted to stay in the corps, I was coming over here to visit you guys."

The silence was finally broken by Boston, who said, "No shit, lieutenant, you really dove into the damn cake? Right there in front of the admiral and the colonel and God and everybody?"

"No shit, Boston, I really did," Bo answered "But I'll tell you this, if I had to do it over again . . . I would wait until the crowd was bigger."

Everybody was laughing. PFC Pringale said, "You owe it to yourself, lieutenant."

"Can't dance," the Professor said as he walked away, shaking his head. "One thing is for damn sure," Corporal Dragin observed, "if that had been one of us enlisted slobs, we would still be in the brig."

Jake had heard enough. "Okay, okay, we've all got lots to do before we lift off. Hawk, I need to see you. Bo, grab Alex, Clahan wants to see you. Incidentally, he wants to be called Skipper now."

"Well, no shit," Bo said. "So the boy is boss."

Jake swung around and said, "That's enough of that bullshit, Bo. I'm the exec now and I won't put up with that crap from you or anybody else, kidding or not. We either maintain discipline and respect for rank or we have nothing out here."

"Holy cow, Mr. Executive Officer," Bo shot back, "forgive us our indiscretions. Let us not tamper with the leadership."

"Shut the fuck up, Bo, there are troops here." Jake turned immediately to Hawk and told him to break up the gathering and get the troops ready for field inspection. "I want every squad leader accountable for the T.O. of his fire teams. I trust none of you has forgotten that we are about to lift off on an operation. Bo, don't forget," Jake reminded him, "get Alex and go see the Skipper."

"Aye, Aye, sir, Aye, Aye, sir," Bo said, saluting smartly and turning about in his jungle boots, kicking up dust and rocks as he went. Jake picked up a loose can of cheese and crackers and hurled it after him.

Sergeant Hawkins looked up at Jake and inquired after him, "In all that college you have, lieutenant, did you ever read anything about Sisyphus?"

Jake thought a moment and replied, "Well, Hawk, I think he was the guy in Greek mythology who was stuck on an island or something with nothing to do but push this boulder up a hill. I'm not sure, but I think that was it, wasn't it? In fact," Jake continued, "if I remember right, he never got to the top of the hill."

"That's pretty much it, lieutenant, except that it was in the task he had that he maintained his sanity . . . I was just thinking, after nearly two tours here, that that is what we're like. Just like that fellow Sisyphus. We just keep pushing the damn rock up the hill and never seem to get to the top. But if it weren't for at least having the rock to push, we might all go nuts, you know what I mean?"

Jake pondered what Hawk had just said and then said, "Yeah, I think so, but then you've spent more time in-country than me, but I'm sure beginning to have a few questions I didn't have before I got here. Anyway, Hawk, we're gonna have to begin pushing the rock again soon, so let's make sure we're up to snuff, Okay?"

In the next few days the weather turned back. It was raining daily, as if the monsoons from down south had decided to move north. The sun was nearly invisible and the fog kept most of I Corps tactical zone socked in. It was depressing. As bad as the dust was when it was dry, the mud may have been worse. The water ran and the mud found its way into your socks and shoes and crotch. It became impossible to keep the rust off a weapon because you simply couldn't keep it dry. In the bush, the ground sucked up the jungle so that everything was just one wet sloggy mess. The wet loam smelled ancient and was a reminder of that part of each of us that is earth, and beckoned you to return from whence you came. It was alien yet familiar; miserable yet exciting. Still, if it would only dry off, just for a little while. The colonel was becoming unhappy with the weather; yet on further reflection he felt it might be an advantage. The North Vietnamese would not expect them to mount a helicopter assault at all, much less in this kind of weather—and stuck thirty miles away from the nearest supply point.

Jake had his talk with Lieutenant Clahan on the twentieth of January. The go-ahead was given on the twenty-first and the Second Battalion had made its approach to FSB Razor. Operation Dewey Canyon had commenced. Elements of the Ninth Marines and their supporting units had linked up at Vandegrift and moved south. Razor resulted in no contact. The die was cast. Three days later on the twenty-fourth, the Third Battalion took fire-support base Cunningham with very little resistance. All that remained was for the First Battalion to take Erskine and the Ninth Marines would then be in place to thrust through to Laos. There was some concern about the lack of resistance encountered in taking the first two fire-support bases. Maybe the gooks just didn't care as long as the Marines didn't go any farther south; maybe they just didn't expect a push farther south at all and didn't want to rock the boat.

Colonel Dagomar decided to wait a few days after Razor and Cunningham had been secured to see if the weather would break. Three more days went by and, on the fourth day, the twenty-seventh of January, a discussion took place about how far south they would go, given the chopper pilots' limited ability to fly in under a heavy cloud cover. Six more days passed and, if anything, it was more miserable, raining every day, with huge mists rising up to meet the sky somewhere out of sight. It was gray everywhere. One more day went by and the decision was made that tomorrow, on the second of February, the First Battalion would lift off for Erskine, come hell or high water.

19

ONCE AGAIN, AS WITH SO MANY SPAR-
row hawks and bald eagles before, they
were soon lined up along the landing
strip at Vandegrift. The weather still had not broken. Everything was
wet; ubiquitous mist rose out of the ground and hung over the jungle
like a great gray shroud. They had formed into heli-teams and were
moving by CH-46 helicopters, the troop-carrying workhorses of the
marine air wing. It appeared to be impossible not to break down the
tactical integrity of the platoons. Each marine weighed an average of 240
pounds with full combat gear, so movement to the landing site had to be
largely by squad.

What was to be fire-support base Erskine rose out of the jungle in the
northwest corner of grid square 1810. At the bottom or base of the
extremely steep sides of this huge saddlelike formation ran the Dakrong
River. The landing site itself was nearly dead center on the ridge line,
with room for only one bird at a time.

Jake would be in the first wave on the first chopper into Erskine. He
chose Boston's squad to accompany him in. He just didn't want to break
up a winning combination; at least that was how he rationalized his

decision. One gun team would ride with the first two squads and they would come in numerical sequence. That meant that Sugar Bear would ride in the second bird and Dragin would be in the third with Hawk. The choppers were gathered like a gaggle of geese on the landing zone. Orders were being screamed in order to be heard, and marines everywhere were shielding their eyes from the dirt being kicked up by the rotors, in spite of the dampness.

The flight commander gave the sign for the first team to move forward, and Jake motioned to Boston to bring them on up. They loaded in the back end of the forty-six, and roughly seven men filed to each side, where they sat on canvas stretched between aluminum poles anchored into the bulkheads of the helicopter. Up front the crew chief, in his flight suit and helmet, leaned over and yelled into Jake's ear that they were ready to take off. Jake gave him the high sign and the forty-six began to lift off over Vandegrift. On the right side, a fifty-caliber machine gun was mounted out over the landing skids. The smells were of wet canvas, dirt, and fear. Below them Vietnam sped by with foliage fading from blue to yellow and back to lush green. It was beautiful, really; in another place or another time, it would have been quite romantic in its mystery and beauty.

They were in the air some twenty-five minutes when the crew chief went forward to say something to the pilot. Turning around, he motioned to Jake that they were approaching the landing site. The marines, as a group, were looking out the little portals in the sides of the forty-six, trying to get a glimpse of their immediate future. The helicopter turned into its approach pattern and Boston readied his men. They were going to form a hasty perimeter, gauging the amount of resistance before the second flight came in. The pilot went in quickly, and as he did so, small-arms rounds began to snap in the air. The big, somewhat ungainly bird hit the deck in a stop-and-go maneuver, dumping its fifteen combat-loaded marines out the back end. A fifty-caliber tore into the side of the helicopter as it made its way up. Jake yelled at Boston to get the men in ten-meter intervals around the small landing site along the military crest of the hill. It was difficult to tell where the hostile rounds were coming from. It was not oppressive fire, but the fifty-cal was doing damage and it appeared to be coming from about two hundred meters off the north side of Erskine. Jake called in one wave of fixed wing, which dropped "daisy chains."

Taking a moment to look at his new home, Jake could see the long, saddlelike finger stretching north and south, with east-west sides dropping off immediately about two or three hundred meters. He could see how it was chosen as a fire-support base. The second helicopter interrupted his thoughts as it pounded its way into Erskine. Touch-and-go again was the method chosen to disgorge the troops. Sugar Bear stepped out onto the apron of the helicopter as the fifty-cal opened up again. Jake assimilated his second squad into the perimeter, widening its diameter as he went. Small-arms fire picked up and marines fired back sporadically, putting down suppressive fire when a target was identified. The third chopper came in and spit out Dragin, Hawk, and the rest of Jake's platoon. Monitoring the net, Jake heard the pilot radio back that while enemy fire was still being taken, there appeared to be no casualties and the landing zone seemed secure.

The first helicopter carrying elements of the Second Platoon approached the landing site. Jake didn't know if Bo was on this bird or not. He stood just inside the landing site, looking up as the bird made its descent. Still about fifty meters up, the helicopter lurched as the distinct rattle of the fifty-cal was heard. The rear rotor flew apart, separating itself from the main body of the chopper, which hovered for a few moments before slamming into the deck. Jake, still looking up into the main rotors, seemed snake-charmed by the whirling blades. Marines were now returning fire, while each passing blade flailed at the air as the wounded bird struggled to remain upright. If it tipped his way, Jake knew he would be sliced up; if it went the other way, one of the others would surely suffer the same fate. Still Jake could not move. A small incline on the right side of the hill ultimately made the decision by pulling the weight of the helicopter down to its final resting place. It slid about fifteen meters down the hill, where it landed atop a stack of sixty-millimeter mortars. The blades splintered and bent as they beat at the ground, and then the powerful rotors turned no more.

The spell was broken and Jake yelled at Hawk to help him as he scrambled down the incline and jumped up on the glass bubble of the cockpit. The chopper was burning and the rear access was jammed shut, so they had to get the men out the front. The first man they were able to extract was the crew chief. Next came the pilot, already in shock. He jumped out of the cockpit and ran around the small crater at the bottom of the hill. "Where are they?" he yelled. "Where the hell are all the fucking gooks?" As he tried to get his .38 out of his shoulder holster, Jake jumped him and they both rolled, falling back into the crater. Jake punched him in the face one time, yelling at Boston to tie him up, if necessary, but to keep him down in the hole. Jake prepared to remount what now looked like the body of a huge grasshopper all askew on the side of the mountain. As he did so, the first of the sixty-millimeter mortars cooked off underneath the belly of the fallen aircraft. The explosion blew Jake and Hawk clear, but they could no longer get near to the wreckage because of the heat. It seared the skin and made it nearly impossible to breathe. Several marines could be heard still inside the chopper, screaming for help. They couldn't get out the rear and now they could no longer make their way forward. The crew compartment was becoming a giant pressure cooker. Jake stood at the side of the hill hearing the death calls of those he was called to lead, members of his bush family. The roar of the fire, fed by the hydraulic system of the aircraft, competed with the calls for help that became screams and then agonizing shrieks as the men inside realized that death was inevitable. A second round cooked off and the rear apron blew off the bird. From the middle of the inferno, one marine made his way out. Only his facial features betrayed that he had been black. Walking like a child leaving a cold shower he stumbled with arms outstretched from his body, hair gone, eyebrows gone, skin pigmentation burned away and slick all over with precious body fluids seeping out. Another marine ran forward and threw a poncho liner over him as he continued his zombielike walk up the hill. The next bird that came in would medevac him out, but Jake had learned to recognize the look of death; it was in this young man's eyes.

Rounds continue to cook off. If there was any good luck in this it was that the doomed chopper went down the right side of the hill, because the LZ could still be used. As it turned out, Bo was on the next bird. Several more waves of fixed wing continued to drop daisy chains, finally knocking out the fifty-cal. But there was something about this hill. It seemed evil or jinxed, and the troops began to talk.

20

TRIPLE CONCERTINA WIRE WAS wrapped around the perimeter at drops of about fifty and one-hundred meters down the side of the mountain. The big guns—105s and 155s, the hardware of Fox Company, Second Battalion, Twelfth Marines—were heli-lifted to the landing zone. Room was made in the middle of the saddle for four hundred harassment and interdiction rounds of 105-millimeter casings, and the smaller craters at the north and south ends of the finger accommodated several hundred beehive rounds for the 105 howitzers and a couple of hundred rounds of high explosive for the 155 howitzer. It appeared that Fox, Second Battalion, would not have any problem carrying out its immediate mission of harassment and interdiction fire. Jake and his platoon had the south end of the finger that made up Erskine; they were linked with Bo on the left and the Preacher on the right. Bravo and Charlie companies comprised the rest of the perimeter. Alpha Company sat on the south end, wrapping around, as part of the east and west perimeter of Erskine.

The sides of the finger on the east and west were so steep that Jake had to cut a gouge in the forward slope in order to be able to walk his lines.

He had one gun team on each side of the perimeter, tied into gun teams of Bo and the Preacher. Fields of fire were being established and marked off for each emplacement. Everyone knew what position to be in, should the need to fire the final protective line occur. Such a measure would be taken for maximum suppressing fire in the event of a major assault or if the perimeter lines were compromised.

Late in the day, a Catholic chaplain named Laporte arrived in the perimeter, asking about the dead and wounded. Any walking wounded had already been medevaced. No one had yet approached the downed chopper because of smoldering rounds still cooking off. It was dusk and the wreckage still smoked, but Laporte wanted to try to find the dead. Jake wondered about this chaplain. The others he had met would rather sit in ripe shit than come this far into the bush with the troops. Yet here was a man ready to go down into the wreckage of a downed forty-six with sixty-millimeter rounds cooking off underneath, just to see if he could give the last rites to the dead. Jake decided to go along. Navy Chaplain Commander Laporte was a big man with a reputation already building. He had been awarded the Silver Star for bravery in Leatherneck Square.

"Come on, chaplain, I'll go down with you. They screwed up the boarding manifests so badly I still don't know who is missing and who was medevaced. I need to find out myself."

They half walked, half slid down the fifteen meters to the fallen bird. White ash coated everything and continued to wisp upward in curls of black smoke. The chaplain waded into the wreckage like it was his backyard. Since everything was still extremely hot he carried a stick to probe the ash and debris. The smell was the thing. It was indescribable, induplicable, and devastating. It was as if burning flesh had imprinted itself permanently into memory. Sweet, pungent, and acrid all at once. It filled the air and meshed with the cloth of clothing, sticking to hair and filling nostrils to the exclusion of all else.

Jake watched the chaplain kneel amidst the clutter, probing with his stick, pulling up a half-burned wallet and a set of dog tags. He turned and tossed them from the end of his stick back to Jake. Near what was left of the cockpit were the remains of two bodies. One lay across what had been the door into the cockpit area. Apparently, a piece of the aluminum tubing that once had held the canvas seating split apart in one of the explosions and a portion had been driven through the side of this man's head. And there it stayed; like a skate key, it protruded from both sides of the skull. Jake, following behind, decided that these were no longer people; his conscious mind was bailing out so that he would not relate his own frail existence to these dead. Another marine lay along the length of the floor. One knee was bent, the other leg completely gone. The right arm reached out for something no longer there. Wide vacant eyes, lips curled and crisped back against gums revealing teeth in a wide grisly grin. Flanagan, Pringale, Sharp, and Norton were still missing. Jake couldn't tell who this was, but it was familiar; this face that half laughed, half screamed, rebuking them for being there too late.

Chaplain Laporte was praying; Jake could see tears running down his face, leaving meandering tracks in the soot and dirt. Jake was drawing into himself again. He knew he could feel nothing if he so desired, he just had to will it. Later, the last chopper in took what was left of the men along with Chaplain Laporte back to Vandegrift. Jake was impressed with this big chaplain. Maybe what the Preacher said was true; maybe there were some sincere Christians who weren't gutless or shallow. And then he remembered the dead and Jehovah's throat and who had just been called. He had listed the names on the paper as he loaded the remains of the men on the medevac. Just names, nothing else. Doing a job for some reason, personal or otherwise. They were his family now. He lived with them. Yet he knew if you took any one of those kids out of the muddy, water-filled bunkers, removed his helmet, flak jacket, and field uniform, took away his rifle, cleaned him up and put a sport shirt, slacks, and loafers on him, you would have a nineteen-year-old kid who was playing on last year's school football team or cruising through Steak N' Shake or downing "sliders" at the nearest White Castle. He once heard Walt Disney say that the youth of America were our greatest national asset. Now he could see nothing but the death mask on the young marine rebuking him in death.

Oh shit, oh God, oh something, reverberated inside his head. What was happening? Off in the distance the little men in skull caps and brown shorts observed their objective with Oriental calm. They had purpose. They knew what was happening. They had no questions. Their reasons were rooted deep in their history and lay in the soil toiled in and returned to, as generations had before them. They would prevail, they knew. There was no question, they had been told. They sat eating rice and fish, wearing the rubber-soled shoes the marines called gook boots, preparing their satchel charges the way they had before Jake had even read in the basic-school cruise book that the challenge lay to the south and the east. And now here it was; the south and the east.

21

MAJOR RICHARD GERSON WAS THE OF-
ficer in charge of recruiting in Indianapolis, Indiana. He had been there
since the middle of 1968 and had walked up the steps of seventy-eight
homes to tell someone inside that their loved one was badly wounded or
dead and not coming home. He had endured being spit on, hit,
screamed at, and, on one occasion, propositioned by a less-than-remorse-
ful wife, and even thrown out of some homes. He had called for medical
aid when shattered relatives collapsed in front of him. He hated his job
from the beginning and he liked it less now.

Dick Gerson was a poster-board marine. Six feet, one inch tall, broad
shoulders, square jaw, flattop overlooking a rather long forehead and
Roman nose. As a flyer, he was filling an unusual type of billet. But
there were many unusual circumstances in the corps these days. He had
gradually started to drink more, especially after every house call. He
was beginning to ask himself if he still had control of how much and
how often he was drinking and in the asking realized he was losing
control.

They always traveled in pairs now, in case back-up support was necessary. In the beginning they didn't do that, but, after the first time some marine's father tried to punch out the local I and I officer, the order came down to travel in pairs. He could understand the strain. Often he was aware that someone was looking out the window or through the shades as he approached a front door. By now he already knew what they were feeling and what they would say. He understood the sinking heart, the burn in the guts, and the desire to escape the reality. It was the haunting look in those faces that made him drink now. They would come to him in the night, brushing the inside of his mind like bat wings on the inside of a barn, accusing him of murdering their children or husbands. He knew he shouldn't let it bother him, but it did. He knew he wasn't responsible, but who was? He couldn't answer that question for them; hell, he couldn't even answer it for himself.

He was pondering all this for the thousandth time when the word came down about Private First Class Jonathon T. Pringale dying on fire-support base Erskine, Quang Tri Province, South Vietnam. God, so many times they were certain it wasn't their son inside and they couldn't even look in the casket. It was early afternoon on a Friday. He and Staff Sergeant Benson could make this call and be back before happy hour.

"Bill!" he yelled over the divider that separated their desks, "let's do this one today. It'll be the last for a while, I hope."

As they climbed into the well-worn, all-green Marine Corps sedan, Sergeant Benson turned to his boss and friend: "Major, do you ever just want to pack it in and not make another one of these calls?"

"Bill," Gerson replied, "there is not one of these damn trips I want to make. It might even be different if we were in the middle of what the public viewed as an honorable conflict. But, hell, I never know what reaction we will get anymore. It makes you almost afraid to walk the streets in your uniform." Pulling away from the building, he said, "Last year four lieutenants who had just graduated from the basic school were shot to death eating at a restaurant in Georgetown, in Washington, D.C. Just eating dinner, for Christ's sake. You know, it's bad enough to tell them their son or husband or father is dead, but to deliver the speech about serving their country proudly and doing it with honor is almost too much to take."

Bill Benson switched on the radio only to hear Jerry Vale "going out of his head." After a few minutes of silence he asked, "Don't you believe those things anymore, major?"

Without hesitation, he responded, "Look, Bill, I believe with all my heart. I'm a professional, just as you are, and you know it. I am not a rear pogue. I serve at the whim of the president, wherever that leads me. These young men have served their country with strength, humor, gentleness, dignity, and honor, and done it in one of the dirtiest, roughest periods in recent American history. What hurts almost unbearably is that the media has chosen to ignore that part of it. In fact, the country has chosen to ignore it as well. But these people we are talking about, these young men, can't forget, and I predict, Bill, they won't ever forget. They will remember. Oh, yes, they will remember."

They turned right and headed west on Interstate 70. Snow covered the fields that Jonathon T. Pringale walked through as a child; plowing in the spring beside his father and in the summer trying to heave bales of sweet hay that were really too heavy for him. The fields were still there, but where the farmhouse had been, tract development, boxlike houses similar to all others, stretched out in the distance, rising from the once-cultivated earth like some strange crop waiting to be harvested. House after house, driveway after driveway. Here middle-class America lived, worked, loved, played, dreamed . . . and waited for marines in dress blues to come to their home and tell them that part of their dream was dead. God, Major Gerson thought to himself, how I hate this.

The Pringales had moved into one of the little houses on the land they sold to the developer. It had been part of the deal. It brought with it running water and inside plumbing, and with what was left over they could live comfortably. The Pringale house sat in a cul-de-sac, brown on brown. Sergeant Benson was making his way around the car as the major got out. The driveway was short, not more than fifteen yards long. They began the walk. Outside to the left of the house in the cold, a woman was trying to wash mud off the brown stone of the house. In her middle fifties, she looked older. The face of a farm woman turned toward the two marines. Lines crossed her forehead and crow's-feet crinkled the corners of her eyes. She wore a kerkchief on her head in the babushka style as she sprayed the foundation of the house.

Myrtle Pringale had already turned to see why Patches, Johnny's last effort at animals, was barking. He didn't bark, really, he never could. When he was little, a collie had nearly bitten through his neck in a fight over a stray potato chip. Apparently, something had happaned to his vocal cords, because ever since then he could only squeak. He was squeaking now, and once again she wondered how such a big fight could have occurred over such a little chip. And, for Patches, the consequences would last a lifetime. Major Gerson and Staff Sergeant Benson, reacting to the squeaking dog, had seen Myrtle at the corner of the house. She was eyeing them now, as they made their way across the lawn. They both saw the pain in her face as she recognized who they were. The pain came with the intake of cold air that stabbed through her chest in confirmation of this moment, a moment that Mr. Pringale had confessed upon her almost daily since Johnny had left for boot camp at Parris Island. He had written letters to their congressman, slamming him for sending their son and not his own or any of the other congressmen's sons, for that matter. He had written the president, damning him for the war and the lousy politics that were killing off the youth of America. And most of all, every single day, he had confessed his worry to her. "He'll be killed, mother," he would say. "As sure as the whole damn war is a sickness of those lousy political whores in Washington, he'll be killed."

Early on, she had tried to allay his worries. But after thirty-two years of marriage, she knew he would expect the worst, and she tried to shut out the negative so it wouldn't affect her. Yet here it was. Once again he had asked for the worst and, in a strange way, would be relieved when the world and circumstances proved him right.

Myrtle Louise Pringale walked toward the fence around her small backyard. She was still holding the hose in her hand; it was spattering water and bits of dirt all over the brightly polished shoes of the two marines.

"Yes?" she inquired, with a tilt to her head and a questioning expression on her face, "can I help you?"

"Yes, ma'am. I'm Major Gerson and this is Sergeant Benson. Would you happen to be Mrs. Pringale?"

"Yes," she replied, "yes, I am."

"I wonder if we might be able to go inside and chat for a few minutes. I'm afraid we have some bad news," Gerson continued.

"I know, major, Johnny's dead, isn't he?"

A plump tear had already formed at the corner of her eye; as it moved downward, it was being diverted by the erosion of the crow's-feet at the corner of her eyes and now was running almost horizontally on her cheek. She was shivering, but not just from the dampness and cold. Once more Dick Gerson hated his job and was beginning to hate himself.

22

I T WAS SO QUIET. JAKE SAT ALONE outside his hootch at 0430 in the morning. Even in the night the heat and wet made their presence known. He absently picked the scabs off the jungle rot that spotted his hands and arms. He pulled gingerly at them to avoid tearing out the hairs that surrounded the sores.

The listening posts out, the trip flares and claymores set, Jake began the routine of walking his lines every four hours and conditioned the Professor to wake him at the appropriate times. He sat there next to a clump of bamboo by an old gook A-frame bunker, preferring to stay above ground but ready to use the A-frame when the mortars or rockets announced themselves. Fifteen meters above his hootch the huge barrel of a 155 howitzer, a great phallus, protruded out into the night. With regularity, the harassment and interdiction firing raised his entire hootch off the ground. The big gun fired a 155-millimeter shell and had an effective range of eleven thousand meters with a fifty-meter killing radius. Jake sat on his "rubber bitch," the inflatable rubber mattress he carried above his pack. It was the third one in as many months; the others had developed holes from shrapnel or rocks or just the wear and tear of movement.

The noises of the jungle were the only changes in the night. When the big gun spoke, the earth itself moved. When it ceased, the quiet was even more pronounced. As morning closed in, the things that moved through the jungle at night grew quiet, while the birds woke announcing the coming day. He could have been at camp, really. Last night, Boston, the Professor, Hawk, Sugar Bear, and several others had shared an evening meal together as the day grew dim. They made a mulligan stew out of combinations of C-rats, trading peaches and pound cake for pears or whatever. They put too many heat tabs under their stew and nearly asphyxiated themselves inside the hootch, trying to keep out of the rain. They were friends now. Jake had their respect and loyalty. They were family.

Nothing smells like wet 782 gear. Damp canvas webbing and soggy leather with the metal of U-rings and the clamps on the web belts that could almost be tasted in the mist. Even the smell bound them together. It was the fifth day on fire-support base Erskine, and still Jake could not eat without tasting burning flesh in his food. That smell, also, had imprinted itself in olfactory memory, and it too bound them together in the present and the future, for whenever a similar smell would be encountered it would bring them back to Erskine.

Jake's helmet topped a short pole stuck in the mud at his side; his flak jacket also dangled from the pole. Getting up, he slowly shrugged into the bulky jacket and put on his helmet before going to check his lines. It was still dark, but one could sense the coming of morning. Jake walked along behind fighting holes, chatting with and encouraging the troops. He finally reached the command hootch for Fox, Second Battalion, Twelfth Marines, and spoke for a while with its executive officer, Jerry Dollar. Jerry, a first lieutenant, had won the Silver Star at Camp Carroll when it had been overrun. He told Jake that he had just gotten a letter from home announcing the arrival of his new son. He was prematurely balding and, although tall, was built somewhat like a pear, not fat, just pudgy, so that his head looked too small for his body. Jake liked him because, unlike so many artillery officers, he seemed to have an appreciation of the ground troops. They spoke for a while and then, running out of things to say, the conversation just trailed off.

Jake moved on to one of his gun teams, picking his way in the semi-dark, and from there to a 106 recoilless-rifle position. He was comfortable with the firepower he had. He knew that his troops could put out awesome suppressing fire, if need be. The M-60s fired a 7.62 round with an effective range of 1,100 meters and could fire at a sustained rate of 100 rounds per minute or at a rapid rate of 200 rounds per minute. The 106 recoilless rifle was a crew-served weapon that was effective at point targets up to 1,365 meters and moving targets at 1,097 meters. The M-72 LAAWS could hit a point target at 325 meters and a moving target at 250 meters, penetrating eleven inches of armor.

It was nearly dawn now as he made his way back to his hootch; Jake could hear the approaching helicopter as it appeared out of the mist earlier than normal. Out of curiosity he looked to the landing zone and stood, mouth agape, as PFC Pringale walked off the apron of the chopper, looking like he knew what he was doing. Jake was refusing to accept what he was seeing. Pringale was dead. He had sent the report in himself. They had found the wallet half burned and the dog tags. Chaplain Laporte had taken it all back in the medevac chopper. Jake half walked, half jogged to the landing zone, grabbing Pringale by the shoulder to make sure his eyes were not deceiving him.

"What the hell is going on, Pringale? Where have you been? Damn it, you're supposed to be dead; killed in action. Do you know that?"

Pringale looked at Jake as if he had completely lost his mind. "Listen, lieutenant, I don't know what you're talking about. I was thrown clear of the chopper after the first round cooked off and I had some contusions and cuts. I couldn't breathe and I thought maybe my lungs had been burned or something, so I just got on the first medevac chopper that came in. They sent me back to C-med in Quang Tri and released me, and here I am."

Jake couldn't believe it. He told Pringale to join his squad and made his way over to Clahan's hootch just above the artillery battery.

"Jim, you in there?" he yelled. "Hey, Skipper, I need to talk to you."

Jim Clahan came out of his hootch wearing only his Jockey shorts, clutching a half-eaten can of scrambled eggs and bacon. Jake wondered fleetingly where in the hell he got Jockey shorts from. They certainly weren't regulation.

"What's going on, Jake?"

Jake told him about Pringale's return; Jake had no idea whether his parents had been notified. After thinking for a few minutes, Clahan said, "Well, look, Jake, there's not much we can do now. Just go on back and I'll notify battalion and leave it up to them. Damn, that's incredible, isn't it? There was so much shit going on that first day, it's a wonder that more screw-ups like that didn't occur. Those fuckers back at Vandegrift screwed up the loading manifest anyway. Nobody knew who was on what bird. Don't worry about it. I'll take care of it, Jake."

"All right. I just thought you ought to know."

Jake felt funny about the whole thing. He had a bad feeling deep in his gut. There was something ominous about the return of Pringale; it was as if he had returned from the dead. Mentally Jake had filed him away; such things were not supposed to happen. But, what the hell, he needed an extra man.

On the fifth, Golf, Second Battalion, Ninth Marines had taken the ridge line at Co Ka Leuye. There had been a scarcity of heavy-lift choppers, the marine CH-53s and the army CH-47s. As a result, none of the fire-support bases had received a full complement of artillery, and there was little artillery support between the first and the eighth of February. On the fourth, a water patrol from fire-support base Cunningham had been ambushed with two WIAs from Charlie Company and one from Delta, Second Battalion, Twelfth Marines. But from about the sixth of the month on, the Ninth Marines were in position and ready to go.

23

THE MONDAY AFTER THE FRIDAY VISIT to Mrs. Pringale, Major Richard Gerson received a wire that PFC Jonathon T. Pringale had been mistakenly listed as a KIA, and, in fact, was alive and with his company in Vietnam. He sat at his desk reading the message, especially the last part about his being with his company in Vietnam.

"Oh, shit," he yelled at Staff Sergeant Benson. "Bill, Bill, come on in here, will you? You are not going to believe this."

Benson came around the corner of the modular wall and leaned against the corner, only to have it shift under his weight. Straightening himself, he said, "What's up sir?"

"Bill, remember Mrs. Pringale last Friday out off of Interstate 70?"

"Sure, I'm processing the paperwork now for the funeral, once the body arrives."

"Well, you can stop," said the major in a tone of exasperation. "Pringale's alive. They screwed it up in MAC-V."

"Kid's alive!" The major was thinking out loud, "I wonder, I guess we should go out and tell the family. I don't know about this; I've never had to make a call to tell someone that their kid was alive."

"Why don't you just give her a call, major?"

"No, no. That wouldn't work. She would just think it was some kind of warped joke. Besides, we owe her a personal visit. In fact, we owe ourselves this one. Come on, let's go now."

They made the trip in silence, each one trying to anticipate how Mrs. Pringale would react. Even if the government messed it up in the first place, it was still good to be bringing a happy message for a change. They pulled into the short driveway and were out the doors of their sedan simultaneously. Mrs. Pringale was waiting at the door. She had had a rough couple of days. The news about Johnny was bad enough, but her husband had nearly buried her with their son. His I-told-you-so's were almost too much to take, as if he were accusing her of sending him in the first place. She wanted desperately to hold onto an honorable image of her son and his death. She wanted to believe there was a purpose, a significance, to his life, even as her husband denied her any comfort or support.

She was about to drive over to the church to do some work for the pastor. That had been routine for nearly eight years now and she saw no reason to change it. In fact, she needed to go, to do something that was part of her normal life. She had just opened the door when the green sedan pulled into the driveway. What could they possibly want now, she thought angrily. But years of country hospitality rooted in Midwestern tradition enabled her to smile and invite them in as they walked up the steps. They were smiling and it irritated her, but she managed to offer them a seat. Even before they were seated, however, she was saying that she didn't have much time, that she had to go to church to do some work for the pastor. The major waited politely until she was finished and then said, "Mrs. Pringale, your son is still alive. As far as we know, he was only slightly wounded and somehow an error was made that had him listed as being killed. We are deeply sorry that you were given incorrect information and that's why we wanted to come out here personally as soon as we could."

She could not comprehend what they had said. She had a funeral to make arrangements for. Myrtle Pringale wanted to make sure that a military burial could be arranged; Johnny would like that. In fact, she hoped today to get the pastor's approval for a small memorial service at the church.

"Mrs. Pringale, Mrs. Pringale..." Major Gerson tried again. "Mrs. Pringale, ma'am, did you hear what I said? Your son John is alive; in fact, he is not even badly wounded and is already back with his unit."

She looked vacantly into the face of this man she did not know. A face that she wished she had never seen, when his words finally reached her understanding.

"Oh, my God, oh, sweet Jesus, oh, father God, dear Lord, dear Lord, dear Lord." Her astonishment and joy literally precluded tears. She sat there across from these two men, rocking back and forth, clad in her cotton housedress with severe, manly shoes protruding from underneath a plain wool coat.

"Oh, thank you, sir, thank you."

"Ma'am," replied Gerson, "we simply are no more responsible for the bad news than we are for the good news."

But she was having none of it. It seemed to be the way of things. People associate the bearer of information with the information itself.

"Well, ma'am, if it's all right with you, we need to be getting along. If there is anything we can do, please give us a call. Incidentally, the request has been made to move your son out of the hostile zone and possibly back to the United States. As soon as we have confirmation, I'll be giving you a call."

They got up from the sagging couch in the Pringales' living room. There was an ancient musk there that seemed to be a part of all such homes. It was the distillation of family gatherings; the good times, the bad times, they were all there. Dick Gerson felt good for the first time in a long time. He was leaving a good memory behind. He even imagined that the musty smell was taking on a new aroma as they left the house. Myrtle Pringale was still standing at the front door as they drove away.

"Major," Sergeant Benson said, "I can tell you just from having to talk with him a couple of times on the phone how excited she must be to be able to tell that crusty old fart of a husband that he was wrong after all. I'll bet she can't wait."

"Yeah," Gerson replied, "she must be elated all the way around."

But Myrtle Pringale was not even thinking about having her son back. It was as if her long-dry breasts were able to suckle again. Her whole life had taken on a new meaning from the utterance of one sentence. Your son John is alive! He was reborn and she had been reborn vicariously. Oh, she thought, I'll be late. And as she had weekly for the last eight years, she got into her old Chevy and made her way to the church to help the pastor prepare for the Sunday services. Won't he be surprised, she thought. Well, maybe not, after all. He has such faith.

24

IT HAD TAKEN KOAN NEARLY THREE days from the time he had reached the base of fire-support base Erskine with his sapper team to move the final five hundred meters. He watched as the Americans flew in big guns and supplies. His job was to penetrate the perimeter of the hub of activity and neutralize as much materiel and personnel as possible. Nguyan Koan was a soldier of the 304th NVA Division, Twenty-ninth Regiment, Ninth Sapper Battalion. Day exploded across the jungle roof as if night were an enemy to be unmercifully vanquished. A time of sun in the middle of so much rain. Koan knew it would not last. It made no difference to him. He had a final one hundred and fifty to two hundred meters to travel. If it took three more days to move that distance, it didn't make much difference to him or his commanders. They would know when everything was in place and then they would move.

Koan sat silently on the ground, dressed in his green skull cap and shorts, while fire ants bit at his legs. He would not move. He was prepared for death, ready to wrap his body in high explosives and to vanquish the enemy through his total commitment. After hours and hours of scratching forward to claim inches and feet with his fingers and toes, he would push long hollow tubes of bamboo, through which explosives would be shoved, to blow up the triple concertina wire around Erskine. He would, on prearranged signals, blow his bangalore torpedoes and then compromise the perimeter with his body and life. He was the product of hardship, war, and suffering. The history of his people was a struggle against the Red River Valley Delta that is Hanoi and Haiphong. Thousands of years ago his ancestors settled there, facing irregular rains and periods of starving drought and raging flood. A people spawned into a life of cooperation, unity, and pride that would endure. They were a people that, when France was called Gaul and the Brits wore animal skins, had already embraced a high level of civilization. Now they were politically divided but spoke one language and were physically identical.

Koan's ancestors had built fantastic systems of dikes and hydraulic controls. Before the first Caesar, they had constructed fifteen hundred miles of dikes by hand and basket. They were united by close family relationships in hamlets and villages and entire regions. Their very prosperity had brought the Chinese hordes, and for one hundred years, four generations, outnumbered, their lands were laid to waste. Then came Kublai Khan, and he sent over a half million Mongols down upon the Red River Valley in 1284. The Mongol army was decimated by a furious common stand. Ultimately, even the Ming Dynasty would bend to the united resistance of the people of Vietnam.

Later, after the Europeans, the Portuguese, the Dutch, the English, and the French all fought over commerce until the French prevailed, Ho Chi Minh and his Viet Minh Party and storm troopers would tear Vietnam apart in one week. The Indochina War was underway and Koan's father would endure a destruction more terrible than World War II. Over ten years, before the Vietnamese would repulse the French. Koan was three years old.

In the Geneva Accord, the country was divided at the seventeenth parallel and the ink barely dry before Ho Chi Minh announced in 1954 that all the people and soldiers of the north and south must unite. Thus was Koan's future sealed, as had been the future of all his ancestors as far back as there were records or memory to call upon. He was not alone, he would not fail, he was patient, they had time, it had always been so, it would always be so. After all, General Giap himself had said, "Every minute, hundreds of thousands of people die all over the world. The life or death of thousands of human beings, even if they are compatriots, represents really very little." Koan would do his part, as his ancestors had also done their part.

25

I T WAS NOW OVER A WEEK SINCE THE disaster of the vertical assault on fire-support base Erskine. Boston could smell them. He finished a breakfast of ham and eggs from a B-1 unit. The sudden appearance of the sun was a shock. If it remained clear, the order would come down to cross the Dakrong. He saw Jake making his way along the lines as he always did just after dawn and beckoned to him, indicating he wanted to talk. As Jake approached, Boston, unable to wait, said, "Sir, they are here. I don't know where but the little fuckers are here."

Jake had learned to respect Boston's sixth sense. That's what he called it, anyway. He wasn't sure whether Boston could really smell them or not, but Boston always said he could. Anyway, he was seldom wrong. Sure, he thought, I can smell them too if they are in large numbers, the fishy smell that comes from their sweat and excrement. And Jake was just as sure they could smell the Americans because of the difference in the food they ate. He decided it wasn't an advantage for them to be able to smell us anyway because they always seemed to know exactly where we were and where we were going. Boston was now kneeling over his water-filled helmet, cleaning his mess kit and finishing a semishave. His light-blond whiskers couldn't be seen much anyway; they were very fine and grew only in patches on his young face.

Jake, still looking at him, asked, "Are you sure, Boston?"

"Lieutenant, trust me, I just know they are here."

"Okay, I'll mention it to Clahan. I'm going up to see him now anyway, and he may want to say something upstairs." Jake turned, leaving Boston to clean up his mess, and continued on up the hill.

Jim Clahan was in a jerry-rigged hootch, which was occupied by three company commanders. It was located at the center of the hill just north of the ammo dump. Jake walked up to the hootch and stuck his head in and upon seeing Clahan asked, "You gotta minute, Skipper?"

"Sure, Jake. Incidentally, while you're here, the battalion wants to take Pringale out of the bush and send him back to the world. Apparently they had already notified his parents that he bought the farm and now they're afraid he will do it for real. Anyway, there's a resupply coming in later today and I want Pringale on it."

"No problem, Jim. Listen, Boston says he smells the gooners. He knows they are here somewhere."

Clahan, arching his brows, said, "Well, no shit, Jake. Of course they are here. They're all over the fuckin' place."

Jake, wearing something of a smirk, replied, "Oh, come on, you know what I mean. Boston's good; if he says he smells 'em, he does. I think we should at least send a couple of extra perimeter patrols out."

Clahan, now standing, said, "I know Boston is good, Jake. I was here before you, remember. I'll pass the word along, but Boston's sense of smell is not going to impress the battalion Six, in all probability."

Jake, countering, said, "Jim, you can send out as many patrols as you want. Let's send out a couple, not more than two or three hundred meters, just to check it out."

"All right, Jake, let me think about it. The colonel's going to be paying a visit in the next day or two and I want to be sure we are ready for that. By the way, how's Karen and the baby?"

Jake, absolutely taken aback by Clahan's interest, responded, "Just great. I really miss her. I can't imagine how it would be to hold Harmony." Jake, a little flustered now, just shook his head and said, "To tell you the truth, I try not to think about it much; just when I get the letters. I think if I thought about it too much it might screw up my effectiveness, if you know what I mean."

Clahan, looking down at his feet and seeming to ponder Jake's remarks, said, "Yeah, Jake, I know what you mean. You want to get home eventually, so you sacrifice the short term for the long term."

"Yeah," Jake said, "something like that. Listen, I gotta go. I'll make sure Pringale gets on that bird. Catch you later."

Stepping back into the sunlight, Jake found himself squinting to be able to see. He went back along the south side of his lines to check what he had missed on the way up to see Clahan and was once more struck by the beauty of the country. The temporary sun hung like a bright patch against a steel-gray background. He found Boston, Sugar Bear, Dragin, and Alex Scott shooting the bull.

"Hey, Alex," Jake greeted his friend with a slap on the back. "How's the Preacher doing?"

"Okay, Jake, how about yourself?"

Dragin was sucking on a butt and Jake mooched one off him.

"Alex, I was just up talking to Clahan," Jake said. "Colonel Dagomar is supposed to come in the next day or so. I'm not very excited about that. I don't feel very good about that guy."

"Did he say anything about when we might cross the Dakrong?" Alex queried.

"No, but it's got to be a matter of days, even if the weather doesn't hold. What were you guys grousing about, anyway?" Jake asked.

Dragin answered the question, since it had been directed to no one in particular. "The lieutenant here," said Dragin, flipping his thumb at Alex, "was just asking us what we were going to do when we got back to the world."

"Well, what are you going to do, Dragin?" Jake asked.

"I don't know, actually," Dragin said, "I just want to make it to tomorrow; I don't think about it much beyond that."

"How about you, Sugar Bear?" Jake continued.

Sugar Bear, who was using a stick to pick mud clots out of the soles of his jungle boots, looked up and said, "I haven't thought about it much, either. I've thought some about staying in this green mutherfucker."

Jake, who was still thinking of himself as a gung-ho lifer, was secretly glad to hear that; he hoped Boston was thinking the same way. Dragin rolled his eyes when Sugar Bear made his comment but Jake ignored him. He felt that he loved these guys no matter how they viewed their future. They had shared experiences that nothing would ever match.

Alex was sitting on a couple of empty ammo boxes and listening intently when Jake asked Boston what he thought he might do back in the world. Boston thought for a minute, scratching at the stubble on his chin, and said, "Well, lieutenant, you know my dad has run a grocery store in Newton, Massachusetts, since I was a little kid. I know he'd like me to take it over, but to tell you the truth, I don't know whether I could stand the quiet now. I know all the people in the neighborhood. I've watched my dad get up at o-dark-thirty and go the farmer's market to get vegetables and then come back and stay forever in that little store. Something's happened to me here. I'm different now. I don't think I could ever do what my dad has done. I need excitement; maybe *adventure* is a better word."

Alex, picking up the conversation, said, "That's what we are all searching for, Boston, that sense of adventure. In fact, that's what the hippies, Jane Fonda, student demonstrators back home, and so many of the others who think they have found their cause in the antiwar movement are looking for."

The gathering either stood or sat looking collectively at Alex, not quite sure what he meant.

Sensing the confusion, Alex continued, "Look, how many of you were boy scouts as a kid?"

All but Sugar Bear raised their hands. Dragin said he had been a cub scout and then quit. Then Sugar Bear pointed out that there weren't any boy scouts in the ghetto.

"Well, did you join a gang or a club?" asked Alex.

"Sure," Sugar Bear responded, "all the brothers either belonged to the Skulls or the Night Riders."

"It's the same thing," Alex said, "Baden-Powell understood that when he created the boy scouts; in fact in many ways some people attempt to remain scouts all their lives. They get their highs from wearing juvenile uniforms with mysterious decorations. Some stay locked into one stage of excitement or adventure their entire lives. They never seem to understand that the law of adventure is that the adventure itself must die in order to be born again. In fact, God said it first."

A chorus of "here we go again" emanated almost simultaneously from the listeners.

"No, no," Alex said, "come on, give me a break, you guys. Actually, God did say all of that first in John, chapter 12: 'Except the grain of wheat falling into the ground die, it abides alone; but if it die, it bears much fruit.' The point is, it is in the continual dying of our most exciting adventures that we reach maturity, physically, emotionally, and spiritually. That's how we grow from being less fruitful to more fruitful and from the infantile to the adult. Once again, God said it this way: 'When I was a child, I did childish things and when I grew up, I did grown-up things.' The problem is," Alex went on, "that many people never come to grips with the death of their adventures. They go everywhere in search of some stimulant or purpose that will relight the torch of their passion. I predict that some of these people fifteen and twenty years from now will still be looking back here, longing and yearning for this time, regardless of how it turns out. Remember what we are talking about today. It will be true for the Fondas, the hippies, the Vietnam vet, and the student protestors. Each with different positions, each searching for the same thing. It could be worse for our generation over here because many of us will never be able to find anything again that compares to what we have gone through." Suddenly Alex stopped when Dragin, walking away toward his hootch, muttered, "fuck this shit!"

Sugar Bear and Boston looked at each other, their round eyes betraying confusion. Jake said, "Well, just what are all of us doing here, Alex?"

Without hesitation, the Preacher responded, "seeking change to free ourselves from the fear that our lives are worthless or lack purpose."

"I remember," Jake interjected, "reading about Papillon, a prisoner on Devil's Island, who used to dream night after night the same dream of being tried before a tribunal and being found guilty of living a worthless life."

Dragin, not yet out of earshot, yelled back over his shoulder, "I'll take life, period. Worthless or not, just give me tomorrow!"

"Go smoke another joint," Boston shouted back, eyeing Alex and Jake as he did so.

"Hey, man," Dragin said, wheeling around, "I know what meaning in life is and what purpose is, and as long as I can still get one up I can participate. How about that for meaningful, Preacher?" Dragin glared at Alex. "Do you think about that at all or has God relieved you of that responsibility as well?"

It was hotter. Rivulets of sweat ran down Alex's chest and mingled with the dried dirt that had taken up a position there for several days now. Several more troops had joined Sugar Bear and Boston. The Preacher was now attempting to respond to Dragin's question, and, turning to those left, he said, "Solomon said that all is vanity. We are born, we live, suffer, die, then others come and do the same. They get up, go to work at the same place, doing the same work until they aren't needed anymore and are told they will never be forgotten; but they will be and they know it. They work, sleep, enjoy themselves, eat, make love, and it all starts over gain. Nothing is ever really new and man can't seem to get outside the restraints of his own nature. Dragin is doing the same thing. He is just seeking life, he even said it. That's what all of us are doing, only we are in an environment where we can't ignore death."

"What do you mean by ignore death?" Sugar Bear asked.

Bo Lawler had shuffled up by this time and was listening while he sipped on a warm Carling's Black Label. Alex, noticing him, lifted an eyebrow in recognition and continued.

"Think about it, Bear, we can't ignore death because it is so much a part of us every day. We see it, anticipate it, expect it, and yet, for the most part, even here, feel it will happen to someone else and not us. In the States, on the other hand, people not only feel it will happen to someone else but that it will never happen to them. Here, we know it will happen. That's why Corporal Dragin says, 'just give me tomorrow.' We all feel the same way but we are learning in the middle of this adventure how to face death because we cannot ignore it, just as at some point in everyone's life they will not be able to ignore it. That is why I am always on you guys to accept the Lord. Everybody comes face to face with him someday. You must be prepared for this because it will not only be the single greatest adventure you will ever have but will be the only one that will never die."

"Shit," Bo broke in, "I'm not worried about accepting the Lord, I'm worried about him accepting me. Besides, I really don't fear death or hell," he said sententiously. "I've already been there and so has everyone here."

Alex thought for a moment and then responded softly: "Look, Bo, I'm not really trying to convert anyone. I just want my life to speak for itself. You can't contradict people in respect to religion because you only deter the weak and those who are not yet committed to their own adventures. The real adventurers are defending a doctrine; they are defending their treasure and are nearly immovable until they learn the truth for themselves. Even then, they will cling beyond what is rational to what is now already a lie, as in many cults. This war may already be proving my point. Subjective experience can't be the basis for proof of any position, because the moment someone believes unreservedly, he experiences a further assent that his cause is just. He now has a goal, an answer to life's problems, and life has meaning."

"And the meaning for your life, Preacher?" Jake asked.

"I have told you, Jake, to serve Christ and grow in his likeness."

"But aren't you subject to the same objections and qualifications you just raised about other people?"

"Of course I am," Alex responded. "But as with all adventures, the truth will remain or die and a new adventure will begin. God likes the men and women who can dedicate themselves to an idea they feel is worthy of their devotion. But, remember, what is the source of great joy and triumph can be the source of great pain and tragedy when two immovable objects meet, each with total commitment to their cause. What is happening back home is that the sense of adventure that took us so easily into this war, as it has with every war, is becoming deadened. Our nation is becoming claustrophobic and without the commitment necessary to win. The North Vietnamese are fueled by the adventure brought to them through a thousand years of war. If our only purpose is to survive in the field, as Dragin says, then we have already lost. The amount of power we possess makes no difference. It is the spiritual power that counts. And, yes, man outside of God does possess a spiritual power."

"Oh, come on, Alex," Bo interjected, "we have never lost a war and we will never lose a war."

"That's true, Bo, but up until now, we always possessed the purpose that continued to give life to the adventure of cause. Where is it now? Who are we really trying to convert? How many politicians, clergymen, Americans in general, are committed to this cause? How many of us understand it at all? I don't even think the president understands it."

"How about you, Preacher," Jake broke in, "do you understand it? I asked you before but how about one more time—why are you here?"

Alex stood staring at Jake and then the others clustered around him in various states of repose. He stared into each face, a few looking away from his gaze. Finally, he said, "For you, Jake, and Sugar Bear, and Boston and the others, and for me. It is my adventure, too." And with that, looking like he might be close to tears, Alex got up abruptly and made his way back toward his platoon CP.

At the foot of fire-support base Erskine, Nguyan Koan moved forward three feet, because there really was nothing else for him to consider.

26

L ATER THAT DAY, WHEN THE CHOP-
pers came out of the mist, the early
patch of sun had already disappeared
into the gray. Three CH-46s flew toward Erskine. On board were C-
rations, extra C-4 plastique explosive, ammunition, three twinks, SP
paks for each platoon and Colonel Smith Dagomar. Jake was near the
landing zone as the birds approached. The colonel stalked out of the rear
of the helicopter like MacArthur landing in the Philippines. He wore a
chrome-plated helmet with full bird insignia emblazoned on the front,
while a gaggle of combat photographers fluttered about him snapping
pictures for posterity. The clutter that inhabits every LZ was picked up
and thrown around the area by the rotating blades. Dagomar spied Jake
and called to him, "Lieutenant. Come here a moment. I'd like to chat
with you."

Jake, surprised by the attention, hunched over as he neared the slowing helicopter rotors.

"What's your name, son?" Dagomar questioned.

"Jake Adams, sir."

"Well, lieutenant, how's it going for you out here?"

"Just fine, sir, but we're all concerned about when we will be stepping off across the Dakrong."

The colonel, stopping Jake short, said, "I think we need to be concerned about what we are doing while we are on this hill, don't you, lieutenant?"

Jake, taken aback, paused and then said, "Of course, sir, that's not what I meant at all. I was just . . ."

Interrupting him, the colonel said, "I think the policing of this area is terrible, lieutenant. Who's responsible for that?"

Jake could not believe his ears. What the hell did this guy mean? What did he think we were doing out here; sitting around scratching our balls and playing poker?

He was so astounded, he didn't respond quickly enough and the colonel asked again, "Did you hear me, lieutenant? Who is responsible for the policing of this area?"

"Uhhh, sir, we had a chopper shot down during the insert on this LZ. We are just barely in place and it's standard operational procedure for the troops to toss their used C-rat cans over the wire and down the side of the hill. I mean, what else could we do with them?"

"Don't question the reasoning behind my concern, lieutenant," Dagomar responded. "Where is your company commander?"

Oh, shit, Jake thought, now he's going to lay into Clahan and he doesn't need that either.

"Sir, he's up at the common CP, just above the main ammo dump, near the saddle," Jake said, pointing up the hill.

Dagomar, now pushing, said, "What about your extra utility trousers, lieutenant? I have already noticed a couple of marines walking around here with their asses hanging out. Are you carrying your extra utilities?"

Astonishment on astonishment. Jake had not seen an extra pair of utilities since he had been in Vietnam. In fact, he had worn one pair of trousers until they practically fell off. If a pile of new or clean ones came in, Jake and his men would discard the ones they were wearing, put on the new trousers, and continue to march.

"Sir," Jake said, "we really aren't carrying an extra pair of utilities because each marine is carrying extra C-4 for this operation."

172

The colonel, apparently put off by the response, just looked at him and then turned to depart. Jake stood there wondering at the lack of understanding on the part of this man who had obviously lost touch with the bush and the men in it. Dagomar turned to his aide, making a remark loud enough for Jake to overhear, about the fact that the lieutenant had not saluted him either before or after the conversation. Salute him, Jake thought, what an asshole. You don't salute anybody in the bush unless you wanted to get their head shot off by a sniper. Well, hey, he thought, maybe that's not such a bad idea. If I could be sure they would shoot him instead of me, I might try it. One thing is for sure, this guy fits my initial impression: he's a real dork.

Clahan and the other company commanders soon knew the old man was on board. Since Clahan was the only first lieutenant among the COs, he deferred to the captains. It was one time he was glad to play a supporting role. Dagomar made himself comfortably unwelcome by displaying the same attitude to the group of COs that had endeared him to Jake. It was quickly apparent that his primary reason for making a personal appearance at Erskine was to announce, as he had at Razor and Cunningham, that in two days they would cross the Dakrong. Enough heavy-lift choppers had finally arrived to get all the guns in place, so the artillery was ready. He just wanted to impress upon his company commanders the importance of the operation and the value it would have for the entire cause in the south. And of course it would reflect on him as well, so he wanted it to go well. If the measure was the body count, they would get a body count. He had already forgotten his conversation with Jake, so he didn't ask to speak to Lieutenant Clahan. In fact, he didn't really remember much of anything he had said. It was magnanimous for him to be in the bush anyway with these men, he thought. They should be grateful I am here at all to provide them moral support. He felt good about it, actually, as he doffed his chrome helmet, responding to his aide's warning that the chopper was ready.

Jake was listening to Jerry Dollar talk about what he knew of Smith Dagomar. Jerry was leaning against the side of the artillery CP, watching Dagomar and his aide approach the LZ.

"You know," he said, "Dagomar missed ground combat in Korea by filling in administrative billets and I think he's running scared that he might screw up his career in the bush. It's clear to me that he focuses in on the petty bullshit to avoid the bigger decisions."

Jake saw Jerry scrunch his eyebrows together in a questioning fashion as he looked toward the LZ. Turning his attention as well, he saw Clahan in conversation with the colonel and then they both looked toward Jerry and Jake. That's when it dawned on him.

"Oh, shit," he said to Jerry, "I was supposed to have Pringale down by the LZ to go back on Dagomar's chopper." With that he scrambled over to Pringale's hootch and gathered him up with remarkable speed, pushing him toward the landing zone. As they approached Colonel Dagomar and Lieutenant Clahan, Clahan took over by introducing the colonel to the private and, together with the contingent of newspeople and his aide, the entire entourage embarked on the chopper.

The two lieutenants stood looking up as the helicopter disappeared in the low cloud cover but said nothing. Clahan turned to go back to his hootch but as he did so he flung back at Jake, "You should have had Pringale on the LZ, Jake." He paused, staring back, and then smiled, saying, "but that guy Dagomar is still an asshole."

It was about thirty air miles back to Vandegrift Combat Base and Dagomar wanted to swing over fire-support base Cunningham, so he had the chopper turn northeast. Passing over Cunningham they were parallel to Razor when the radio alerted them that a patrol from Razor was in contact. The crew chief came back and yelled into the colonel's ear what the situation was and asked, since they were so close, if they couldn't try to get the wounded out. Dagomar was perplexed. If he refused, he might be thought a coward. Yet he had an out; he had this kid Pringale with him and he certainly needed to protect the private's life, not to mention his own. Still, he knew that was pretty weak, so he decided to make the extract. The helicopter changed course and Pringale, still carrying his weapon, moved forward to stand beside the machine gunner. The landing zone had been blown in a small clearing they had used to insert into the jungle several days earlier. The circular pattern of descent began into the dark cloud created by the smoke grenades that the ground troops had popped. That's when the rounds began coming up through the deck of the chopper.

174

Heavy fire was being concentrated on the helicopter while, like a shark going in for the kill, it moved in ever-tighter circles, closer and closer to the LZ. The crew chief was directing the fifty-caliber fire to general rather than point targets; the patrol on the ground poured small-arms fire away from the perimeter they defended. PFC Pringale moved to a position to the left of the gun team and was firing over the mounting brackets of the machine gun.

Colonel Dagomar was on his feet, heading toward the cockpit to order the pilot to lift off, because he felt they were in danger of being shot down. The pilot had already decided to touch and go because he knew that mortar rounds would soon be coming in. If the ground troops were out of position, he wasn't going to wait; he did have the old man on board.

The chaos and intensity of the firefight obscured the death of PFC Pringale. One round found its way through the side of the helicopter. It entered the left side of Pringale's forehead and exited just above his right eye. He sat down in the corner, where the divider separated the cockpit from the cabin, and stared vacantly at the crew chief while his life's blood ebbed out of him. This was the obstacle that kept Colonel Dagomar from reaching the cockpit. He stood staring at the body of the young man he had intended to return to the United States and safety.

The rear hatch of the chopper lowered as four marines humping two wounded buddies scrambled aboard. Lift-off occurred without the colonel's order and Colonel Smith Dagomar had seen action. This day would be a favorite topic of conversation for years to come. A Bronze Star with combat V would be his for his heroic effort to extract marines in trouble. The crew would not receive commensurate reward. For most of them it was just another day survived. For PFC Pringale it was not.

Back on Erskine, the scuttlebutt was that the part of the patrol that had not been extracted was found the next morning tied to trees at the base of fire-support base Razor. One round had been fired through the back of each of their heads. That, combined with the news that Pringale had bought the farm, created a pall that intensified the bad feelings created by the first day's insert on Erskine. They had been on that hill only a week and already it seemed like a lifetime. The troops had secretly admired Pringale for escaping. Because of some screw-up in the system, he was going to beat them at their own game, and each marine was a little envious. He hadn't even been wounded seriously and he was going to go home. But he didn't make it and they all died a little bit with him. They wanted to escape; he had helped to make the dream a little more real. As it was, some of the edge on everyone's hope for tomorrow died with him.

PART THREE

NO GREATER
LOVE

The way to love anything is to realize that it might be lost.

G.K. CHESTERTON

He that shuts love out, in turn shall be shut out from love, and on the threshold lie howling in outer darkness.

ALFRED LORD TENNYSON

Pray that your loneliness may spur you into finding something to live for, great enough to die for.

DAG HAMMARSKJÖLD

How can we lose when we are so sincere?

CHARLIE BROWN ("PEANUTS"), 1968

If we had won in Vietnam, what is it that we would have won?

FATHER OF BOY KILLED IN VIETNAM, 1977

27

JAKE FOUND THAT HE LIKED JERRY Dollar; unlike so many artillery officers, he seemed to be sensitive to and understand the needs of the grunt. Jerry was the executive officer of Fox, Second Battalion, Twelfth Marines, the 105 and 155 battery at Erskine. He had distinguished himself on fire-support base McClintok when it had been overrun and had been awarded the Silver Star for his efforts. The scuttlebutt was that he had picked up an M-16 and joined the troops in the trenches, taking over for a fallen platoon commander and holding his section of the lines.

Jerry had shown Jake pictures of his family, especially his new baby boy that he had yet to hold. In just three more months he would rotate out. Jerry had already decided to get out of the crotch, as he called the corps, and go into business for himself. His boss, the battery commander, was Captain Roscoe Smith, a quiet, surly man. Jake had few conversations with him and, in general, just kept his distance. From his hootch, just below the lip of the ridge on the east end, Jake could see the battery command bunker dead center to the saddle that split the hill below the main ammo dump. The CP was at the end of his lines on the south side of the perimeter, so Jake often stopped there to talk with Jerry. Around midnight on February 9, Jake stopped by for a chat. Four hours later, Koan reached out to his bangalore torpedoes and blew the wire.

Jake was near the end of his lines, between his M-60 emplacement and 106 recoilless rifle. The night was totally black and socked in by intermittent rain that kept the troops huddled in their fighting holes beneath ponchos; the water rose up over their ankles. Miserable was the best way to describe it. There were three simultaneous explosions; one at each natural approach to the perimeter. Only two were followed by troop movement, at the north and south side of Erskine. Approximately sixty sappers made the assault. It was accompanied by mortar and rocket-propelled grenades, fired simultaneously with the initial explosions in the wire. An NVA squad remained in the tree line on each side of the fire-support base to lay down suppressing fire as the others attempted to compromise the perimeter by penetrating the lines.

All three strands of triple concertina were breached at the north and south sides of the hill as the first bangalores went off. Not one trip wire or claymore mine was detonated; the NVA had made a perfect approach. Not one listening post was aware of the movement outside their lines until the initial explosions. Mass confusion prevailed. Jake hit the deck and could hear Boston yelling for his squad to fire the final protective line. All over the compound, rounds were being returned as Koan moved forward with six others to enter the wire. RPGs were slamming into the lines and mortars fell like rain inside the perimeter. The rain of fire was designed to get the marines to go to ground, and it was working. Koan knew there was little time before the marines would fire illumination rounds; it was imperative that they get inside the wire first.

Jake was back on his feet making his way to his hootch and the Professor, who had the radio. He moved in a low crouch, amazed at the amount of ammunition being expended. No one knew who or what they were shooting at, but it was certain they were under attack. The first mortars had bracketed the finger inside the perimeter, blowing up one 105 howitzer on initial impact. The deluge of fire, automatic weapons and RPGs, mortars and bangalore torpedoes, along with the chaotic cacophony of sound accompanying them, took its toll. Jim Clahan, along with the other company commanders, hit the deck. One rocket-propelled grenade looped over the lip of the hill and hit near the main ammo dump just outside the command bunker. Confusion kept most of the company commanders away from their radios. Gunny Jacobsen was already on the hook trying to get a sit rep from each platoon commander by the time Clahan had recovered sufficiently to find out where the radio was.

Bo Lawler, along with the Second Platoon facing the north side of the perimeter, had a 106 recoilless rifle take a direct mortar hit. Pieces of shrapnel were whistling through the air, making noises like the Fourth of July. Bo had a hootch cut back in the side of the hill where he and Alex, Jake, Boston, Dragin, and Bowman had been talking just the day before. He came tearing out of the hootch, trying to figure out what the hell was going on. Barber, his radioman, was already at his side yelling that the Gunny was on the hook. As Bo took the receiver, a string of AK-50 rounds began tracing a line down the side of the hootch. Bo went down, but Barber just stood there looking at the rounds as they made a straight line for him. He was snake charmed as he watched the rounds approach and then tear into his body, pinning him against the dirt wall and then continuing on down the hill. He looked vacantly at Bo as he slumped against the hootch, the handset still in his hand, crackling with the voice of the Gunny demanding a response that would never come from Barber.

Alex, tied in on the south side not far from where Jake was walking as the first rounds went off, had established communication with the command post. There was not much to say; no one knew what was really happening. There wasn't time to find out what the situation was at each fighting hole and then relay information to the command post so that it could be evaluated calmly.

The entire jungle lit up; it was as if someone were taking pictures in a dark room. The flashes from high explosives illuminated men moving in jerky, fragmented movements like figures in an old-time movie. There was no chance to get the listening posts back inside the lines. Privates Wolf, Dickenson, Druschel, and Perkins found themselves sitting outside their lines, being fired at from both sides. Wolf and Dickenson were just outside the south side of the hill, and Druschel and Perkins were outside the north side. They went to ground. Each had two claymores trained at the wire and beyond, but blowing them would give away their positions. Druschel could hear movement to their left, where the first explosion had taken place. He was trying to see, but it was nearly impossible with the amount of fire pinning them down.

Koan was peeling back the wire; they had their hole and all six were inside, edging their way up the side of Erskine. The first illumination rounds finally awakened the sky. Light fluttered from the swaying flares, making everything surreal. Boston couldn't tell whether he could see men moving or not. Suppressing fire continued both ways as Druschel, looking up the hill, saw Koan and his team moving upward. Training his M-16 on automatic, he let go a burst as Dickenson got on the hook to tell the lieutenant that the wire had been breached. Almost as soon as the round went off, an RPG slammed into their position; only pieces of them remained, just an arm or a leg or a piece of intestine. The adventure was over for Druschel and Dickenson. Koan continued to move up the hill.

The mortars were coming in increments, every thirty to forty-five seconds, doing what they were designed to do, keeping everyone down in their holes. A call went out for Puff and Spooky, but they were at least half an hour away at Vandegrift. Koan's counterpart on the north side of Erskine had also breached the wire. Perkins and Wolf had blown their claymores and were trying to get inside the perimeter when the final protective line was fired. They were yelling into the company net to let them in as they were now pinned down outside the lines. But there would be no pause in the firing. Nothing was coordinated enough yet to let them in, and the perimeter was already compromised. The entire compound would go to ground. Anyone who moved would be the enemy.

Jake, Bo, and Alex were working their lines. Hawk had moved as rapidly as possible over to Sugar Bear's position which protected the vulnerable east tip of the finger. Outside of Bo's lines, on the south side of Erskine, there were about twenty-five meters of gentle incline before the fighting holes. Koan's counterpart was approaching that area as Koan and his team hit the center of Dragin's squad. A flare popped in the night and Dragin saw them as they moved into the holes. Three chicom grenades exploded and drove him back into his fighting hole. PFC Speights was lifted completely out of his hole and Dragin was hit in the head with a heavy piece of metal that fell out of the sky. Several gooks jumped over his position, not realizing he was even there. Dragin jumped to his feet, blood streaming down his face, and, leveling his M-16, let several bursts go in their direction. Hawk had moved from Sugar Bear's position to Dragin's. One of Bo's squads had also been penetrated. Hawk got Jake on the radio and told him of the compromise and Jake radioed in to Clahan.

Fire-support base Erskine went to ground. Thirteen men had made it inside the perimeter. Each hole had been sealed off. A late-arriving Puff and Spooky lit up the area, firing into selected targets. Boston was free-handing sixty-millimeter mortars into the area just outside the lines. The entire hill was lit up by Spooky with an eerie glow that turned the night pale green. Cordite and smoke and fog played tricks with the illumination. Anything that moved inside the perimeter would be shot. Jake thought he saw movement outside Fox's Second Battalion command bunker, but it was still difficult to see in the flickering light. Turning to the Professor, who was monitoring the net, Jake asked him if he could make anything out.

Koan had jumped up on the overhead of the artillery-battery command bunker; he was wearing a fifteen-pound pack of plastique explosive attached to a detonator he could pull from a rip cord by his right shoulder. Jake saw him as another flare popped just over the bunker and he grabbed the Professor's rifle. He was sighting in on Koan, who had jumped in between Captain Smith and Lieutenant Dollar. They were both aware of what he was about to do. Neither moved; all three were standing in a hypnotic circle. Jake sighted in on Koan's head as the light shifted back and forth, making the target appear to move. As he hesitated in the flickering light and concern for an accurate shot, Koan, acting with the volition that a thousand years of fighting had imbued in him, thought about nothing as he reached for the cord. Captain Roscoe Smith knew his only chance was to reach Koan. Jerry Dollar was thinking of his new son. Both of their screams, Smith's of rage and Dollar's of futility, were cut short as Koan pulled the cord. Jake, in his moment of hesitation, watched as the entire bunker seemed to lift up out of the ground, his own scream of outrage taking up where Smith's and Dollar's left off, all three subsumed in the explosion.

Each platoon was now sealed off in its own perimeter. Clahan was calling on his PRC-25, asking exactly what was going on. Jake told him what he had seen and said he would get back if there was anything else to report. The marines spent the rest of the night sitting in wet muddy holes watching for any movement, firing in fear at shadows that flickered in the light of periodic flares. The entire sapper team that had entered the wire on Bo's side of the perimeter was cut down in the FPL. Puff had arrived, firing thousands of rounds from Gatling guns mounted in the big C-130. Mortars continued to fall outside the lines, but there would be no further penetration.

Satchel charges were being dropped in the ammunition pits. The remaining sappers waited in darkness behind piles of sandbags until the dump blew. It went with incredible force. Four hundred high-explosive 105-millimeter howitzer rounds at one time. Entire undetonated cannisters spiraled through the air, landing with thuds in the moist earth. The secondary explosion lifted a 105 howitzer, all sixty-four hundred pounds of it, and hurled it twenty meters, where it landed on Boston's sixty-millimeter machine gun, killing the two marines manning the position.

The early-morning light was preceded by intermittent flashes from cannisters cooking off and exploding inside Erskine. Pieces of howitzer carriages, bolts, cannisters, debris, and clutter gouged holes in the earth and redefined the contours of Erskine with each explosion. Fire reached the ancillary ammo dump and set off two hundred beehive howitzer rounds; each round contained nine thousand needlelike fléchette missiles that functioned as antipersonnel weapons. The first explosion deepened the hole that made up the saddle of Erskine.

Fléchettes flew through the air by the thousands, ripping into sandbags and men. Confusion was complete. Every 105 and all but one 155 howitzer in the battery had been destroyed. To the NVA it was even better than rounds coming from the big Vietnamese guns inside Laos; it was the marines' own ammunition hitting themselves with perfect accuracy. Koan had done what all his ancestors had done before him; allowed patience and commitment to underscore effort and wear down the intruder.

Sit reps kept the net alive. Real and imaginary probes kept the mortar and machine-gun fire sporadic, and marines sat in pairs, hunkered down against random mortar and RPG rounds and the incessant explosions of rounds cooking off in the smouldering earth. Twelve Vietnamese died in the wire of fire-support base Erskine; twenty-two more were found inside the wire and another seven bodies outside. Nine of the attackers made their way back down Route 9 toward Base Camp 911, as Erskine continued to tear itself apart in the night.

Morning came to Erskine in relative silence, revealing a landscape vastly altered from that of twenty-four hours earlier. At first light, Jake and the Professor crawled out of their fighting holes to greet desolation. Great guns lay scattered randomly inside and outside the lines, instruments of destruction themselves now destroyed. Walking up over the lip of the hill, Jake stared in awed disbelief at the scene below. Smoke rose in ringlets from the top of Erskine. Fox, Second Battalion, Twelfth Marines, was virtually gone. From where Jake stood, he could see the gnarled tops of trees rising up out of the side of the hill. The valley swept off in the distance to embrace the Dakrong. But on the spot where he stood was Armageddon. The one remaining 155 stood with its nose up in the air just above his hootch, its base and huge tires the last thing still in place from the night before. To his left, two struts and half of the wheel carriage were all that remained above the ground of a 105. To his right, two others lay over the side of the hill. One was completely blown apart; the other, its carriage gone and one tire blown away, lay exactly on top of Boston's M-60 machine-gun position. Jake could see the arm and leg of a marine who ended his tour in Vietnam and this world beneath his own artillery piece.

Movement was taking place all along the perimeter. Cordite, burning flesh, and rubber, mingled with the dampness of the jungle, offered a new smell, foreign and mysterious as death. Clahan was on the net wanting a sit rep and an accounting of casualties. Jake, like Bo and the Preacher, responded that they needed time to find out for themselves. Rounds were still cooking off. Pieces of bodies lay at various places, and brothers-in-arms were given the job of taking plastic bags to gather up the pieces and identify, if possible, the remains. It would never be done accurately.

Perkins and Wolf, who had spent their night of terror lying between the enemy and their own lines, took the early light as an augury of life and began their movement back into the perimeter. Without any idea where their radio was or what had happened to it, they simply stood up, waving their weapons to alert the fighting holes of their arrival. Bo stood watching these two marines move back to what had been the second line of double concertina. They would use the same hole blown by the sappers' bangalore torpedoes. The two men passed the bodies of the NVA who had died in the initial firing of the FPL while Koan was attacking on the opposite side. They had to take a good look at the enemy dead. Perkins moved in the direction of one inert body that still wore its skull cap and green shorts. The only missing thing was the gook boots. Bo, watching, yelled when he realized what Perkins was about to do. It was too late.

With Wolf at his heels, he reached down to turn over the body. They were really just kids. No yet used to war, if such a thing were ever possible. They were curious, that was all. Bo could see the result before he heard the explosion. The NVA had booby-trapped the bodies. This one rose up off the ground as a rag doll might be tossed by a child, and then the torso separated from the limbs, taking Perkins and Wolf with it. Doc Pony, who already was faced with too many wounds to treat, ran toward what was left of Perkins. PFC Wolf would live. He was muttering, "We made it the entire night; we made it the entire night. What happened? We made it the entire night." He had found his ticket home, what the troops called a million-dollar wound, the one that took you back to the world.

The medevac and resupply choppers were coming in. Jake had lost six men to various wounds serious enough to take them out. Two others were dead, both from Boston's squad. These numbers were consistent throughout the company, with the total at twenty-three. The battalion, in general, fared better, with Alpha Company taking the brunt of the assault. There was only one officer left in the artillery battery, and one gun. Both materiel and men would be replaced. Jake found Jerry Dollar later that day, face down, a good twenty-five meters from where he last saw him over the shoulder of Koan, who at that moment had been pulling the rip cord. Captain Roscoe Smith would not be found for three days until vultures circling a treetop fifty meters away would give away the location of what was left of Smith to those on the ground.

The assault across the Dakrong would not wait. It was the morning of the eleventh, and on the twelfth, movement toward Base Camp 911 was supposed to commence. It didn't matter much for the First Battalion; every marine on Erskine would be glad to leave that hill. They were convinced it was a jinx. Maybe now they would have a chance to go on the offensive instead of sitting in these damned defensive perimeters.

28

MAJOR GERSON WAS SITTING ALONE AT his desk when the official notice of the death of PFC Jonathon T. Pringale came to him for the second time. He refused to believe it at first, checking the date, thinking it was simply an error in transmission or a duplicate of the first. He called in Staff Sergeant Benson and gave him the correspondence. Benson looked at his boss, his face reflecting first the pain that was in his own heart and then the anger and sense of absolute futility that could be the only natural response to this entire ridiculous affair. The major thought that Shakespeare could not have written better human tragedy. These men, these boys, they were like candles in the wind, alive with light and service and then in the next second snuffed out by a draft from a different direction. What was left was the darkness. In fact, it was becoming more and more the case that no one even wanted to recognize that these young men had ever burned with light at all. Oh, God, he thought, how do I tell his mother?

"Bill, I'm simply not going out there a third time. If those assholes at headquarters Marine Corps want to go back and tell that old woman her son is dead, let them go themselves."

Benson looked at his boss. Both men knew that Gerson would go and that his outburst was one of frustration and personal pain.

And so, for the third time, the green sedan made its way toward the unobtrusive home of Samuel and Myrtle Pringale. For the third time, Mrs. Pringale was there to see them arrive, only this time she was not anticipating the worst. In fact, she was glad to see them, for it was beyond comprehension that they could be bringing bad news a second time. She greeted them with smiles, as once more they made their way up the steps of her little house. But as she looked in the eyes of the major, she knew something was terribly wrong. Dick Gerson knew that this war and all it represented had ended his career. As he looked again into the face of this woman with whom he had shared such pain and joy, and now again incomparable loss, all the reasons he had served his country and the corps were shaken beyond repair.

Mrs. Pringale had somehow gotten smaller as she sat before the two marines. She seemed to withdraw into herself, unable to relate to what was being said to her. They went through the litany of events and tried to make her understand how such a thing could happen, when they could not understand it themselves. It did no good. One more memory was added to the dust of this house. One more statistic was added to the carnage that was Vietnam. One more tentacle of frustration reached into Middle America and multiplied itself over and over and over again. All these two marines could ask themselves as they left this house that smelled of musk and baking bread was, why? And there was no answer.

In the beginning, Lyndon Johnson had said, "In the long view of history, these years are the early summer of America. Our land is young. Our strength is great. Our course is far from run." The true strength of America was running its course with integrity and honor, caught up in a war that had neither. The true strength of America was being dissipated in the killing fields of Vietnam, where these boy-men asked nothing more than for their country to love them as much as they loved it.

In western Quang Tri Province, the rats were as big or bigger than some cats Bo had seen. He hated rats! Some people couldn't stand snakes; others had an aversion to spiders; almost everybody had something that they really found abhorrent, and for Bo it was rats. The First Battalion, Ninth Marine Regiment, had been on this hill for over a week. It was the twelfth of February and each day more empty and partially empty cans of C-rations arched their way over the side of the hill and into the concertina wire. It wasn't long before the rats came. Big rats, brown and menacing. A rat bite was a ticket to the rear and, even in exchange for the painful rabies shots, a trip to the rear, to some guys, was worth the price. Three or four marines had already been medevaced out to meet the needle. At least one was certainly the result of self-inflicted punctures created by a "John Wayne," the name the troops placed on the small aluminum can opener they carried on their dog-tag chain. But what the hell were you supposed to do, thought Bo; if you were wrong and didn't medevac the guy out and he died of rabies, you would really be up shit creek. What Bo couldn't understand was how anyone could actually bait the damn rats, hoping to get bitten. He would rather face Ho Chi Minh personally in Hanoi than face one of those big, brown, aggressive rats.

On the night of the thirteenth of February, one day beyond the ex-pected departure time, Bo woke up about midnight to check his lines. Curled up in the crook of his arm was something big, with eyes that glowed in the dark and stared at him. Bo let out a blood-curling scream that awakened the entire perimeter. The rat managed to scamper up over the top of his head on his way to safer surroundings. No one really ragged him. Others before him had awakened at night screaming and he certainly wasn't going to tell anyone why he screamed. Shit, five months since I've shared a bed with anyone and it had to be a rat. I hope this won't set a precedent, he thought.

Each successive day brought greater contact with the enemy. On the twelfth, K Company hit a platoon-sized patrol and killed 11 NVA. On the thirteenth, C Company was hit on patrol and killed 28 NVA. On the sixteenth of February, M Company killed 11 NVA on Hill 718, and on the nineteenth of February, Boston and Dragin sat on the side of Erskine and watched the smoke peel off of Co Ka Leuye Mountain as E and G companies killed 45 NVA. Between the tenth and the seventeenth of February, 302 NVA KIAs occurred by body count, one NVA was cap-tured, and 130 North Vietnamese wounded were reported. For the ma-rines there were 61 killed in action and 262 wounded in action during the movement south. Yet the heaviest fighting was still to take place. The greatest loss of life on both sides occurred between the eighteenth and the twenty-second, just as Colonel Dagomar had prophesied.

Dewey Canyon was beginning to take on a magnitude that would separate it from any other operation before it, as the body count mounted. On the eighteenth, the Second Battalion began its attack along the right flank, moving steadily south to Co Ka Leuye. The First Battalion moved in increments off of Erskine, with Alpha Company leading the way on the afternoon of the nineteenth. The regiment was in the attack moving south, with the Second, First, and Third battalions moving in tandem south across the Dakrong toward what would now be known as Base Camp 911. The objective, to control Routes 922 and 548.

The Ninth Marines moved down off of the east end of Erskine along the elongated incline that tapered off the finger and then paralleled the Dakrong down Route 9. The lousy weather was going to continue. The sky was no longer present, nor had it been for days; there seemed to be no end to the fog and mist and the wet that permeated the jungle and enclosed everything in a giant watery web. What was important was that they were leaving Erskine. To every man, the hill had become a place to leave. It inspired a bad feeling, an evil spirit and dread. So it was better to be walking off into the mist and the jungle, deeper into the Ashau Valley, pushing toward Laos, than to stay in this prison of concertina wire and exploding howitzer rounds.

The movement was slow. The incline was steep and muddy; each marine literally had to grab at roots and vines to make his way down the muddy slopes and maintain his balance against his fifty-plus pounds of backpack. And as the men went down, the jungle came up to meet them, the mist coming up to enclose each marine, shutting off his buddy, denying him the comfort of knowing who was in front or behind. Unconsciously, the ranks drew closer together. A great snakelike column of men wound its way off the hilltop, down the side of the finger, and disappeared into the triple-canopy jungle that covered the Dakrong and exhaled earthy smells of moldering leaves and jungle rot.

It was fruitless to attempt to read a map. There was nothing to see, no landmarks or ridge lines. Jake had to walk behind his first fire team with his compass open-faced in his hand in order to know if they were heading in the right direction. Not long after they had reached the bottom of the finger and the terrain began to flatten out, a ninety-degree turn to the left was necessary to stay parallel with the river and move in the general direction of Route 9. Jim Clahan came up on the net and ordered Jake to hold where he was and wait for the rest of the battalion to form up and catch up before moving on. So the lumbering line of troops began to seat itself in whiplash fashion in the mud and wet. They would sit for nearly two hours, waiting for word to go on.

Aching bones and goose-bumped skin greeted the word to continue to march. As happy as marines are to sit down, this was one time when they were happy to get up, just to generate a little warmth. Wet 782 gear and soggy jungle boots slogged in the mud, covering feet that would wrinkle up and contract trench foot if they didn't dry out. The ninety-degree turn to the left, moving the column southeast, was made. The jungle rose up to the left and the Dakrong moved swiftly on the right. As before, Jake moved with his compass open-faced in his palm. They had gone one hundred meters when the claymore went off. A piece of ball bearing took a swatch out of Jake's neck as he went down under a small berm at the left side of the trail. Troops went down like dominoes and then there was silence. Jake lay with his face in the mud, with the bitter warmth of his own blood seeping into the corner of his mouth. Men were groaning; a call for a corpsman went unheeded up ahead. Jake tried to get to his feet and, as he did so, a thirty-caliber machine gun opened up, laying a stream of rounds along the top of the berm. He couldn't move. "Wormand!" he yelled. "Can you hear me?"

"Yes, sir, I can hear you, lieutenant."

"Can you make your way up to me with the radio?"

"I suppose I could, lieutenant, but I don't think I want to try. How about you making your way back to me, sir?"

"Listen, you little shit, don't get funny with me now. I can't move. Every time I move at all, that gooner opens up with the thirty. He can't hit me under the berm, but I can't see him and I can't move. Can you see anything or can you move at all?"

"No, sir, I can't move either."

"Where's Boston? Can you see him or hear anybody behind you?"

"No, sir, I can't see anything."

"Shit," Jake said in exasperation. He raised up just a little bit to see what would happen and the thirty-cal ripped up the top of the berm and snaked its way to the far side of the trail. "How in the hell can they see me when I can't see ten feet?" he wondered out loud.

In the rear of the company column, Jim Clahan was going batshit. Colonel Dagomar wanted to know what was going on, but radio contact had not been made with First Platoon. The entire column was held up; sporadic firing indicated something was going on but no one could see anything and there was no communication. Sergeant Hawkins, moving with his radioman, Sweeney, finally made his way around the bend in the road. He found the Professor lying against the side of the trail, separated from his radio.

"Where's the lieutenant?" Hawk asked.

"About ten meters ahead, I think," replied the Professor, "Laying under that berm on the left. I believe he's been hit, and there are other wounded, but every time somebody tries to move, there's a thirty-cal up the trail that sprays the whole area."

"Lieutenant," Hawkins said, raising his voice, "can you hear me?"

Jake, with his face in the dirt, replied, "Yeah, I can hear you, Hawk. You better get Clahan on the net and tell him what's doing here. A claymore was hand-tripped, I think. I don't know what the casualty situation is; I've been hit in the neck, but I don't think it's bad."

Boston arrived as Hawk was getting the company commander on the PRC-25. When the Professor told him what was going on, he removed his blooper from his shoulder and, squatting, duck-walked around the bend where Jake and the Professor were pinned down.

"What the hell are you doing, Boston?" Hawk said, scrambling to grab his feet.

"I'm going to get the lieutenant out of there," came the terse reply.

Jake, hearing Boston, yelled, "Crap, what the hell are you doing?"

"Hey, lieutenant, where's the frigging gook at . . ." His sentence was cut short as a burst of fire kicked up the top of the berm and then weaved across the trail. Boston without hesitation stood to his feet, ignoring the fire, and let go his first M-79 round. Thooomp, went the blooper, and as quickly as that round went out, a second was pushed into the breech and sent flying into the rain forest as the first exploded in the general direction of the thirty-cal. The machine gun began ripping holes in a whipping pattern back and forth across the overgrown trail. Thooomp, went the third round and Boston stood his ground. Wham, the second M-79–propelled grenade went off directly to the front. Click, a fourth round was breeched as the second and third rounds began taking out five-meter chunks of the jungle. The machine gun was silent.

Alex, at Clahan's orders, attacked through the First Platoon line. To the left of Jake, they found dug into the embankment a small spider trap that had hidden one gook who fired the claymore. Apparently, he had some type of communication with the machine gunner and had been transmitting any movement along the trail. His left arm was badly damaged, having taken some back-shock as the claymore exploded too close. The second NVA–operated gun emplacement was just off the trail, about one hundred meters to the front of where Jake had fallen. As Alex's first squad moved up, they found him dead and hunched over his gun, shrapnel holes in his face, head, and left arm from Boston's blooper. He and the NVA who tripped the claymore had been tied to trees by their own comrades, left to take their toll and die.

The entire battalion was held at bay while this action took place. Colonel Dagomar wanted to move as rapidly as possible as a result of the delay. Still, he gave Clahan orders to hold up while they got someone from G-2 down to take possession of the prisoner. Jake was treated in the field. First Platoon had sustained several casualties, two of which had to be medevaced. The colonel moved C Company up through A company, so that the wounded could be attended to and the battalion movement continued. Doc Pony was dressing Jake's neck wound with a field bandage. "What do you think, Doc?" Jake asked. "It looks like this could be a real shit sandwich, huh?"

"I don't know, lieutenant, but everyone is uneasy. The only saving factor is being able to get off that hill. I think the troops would take almost anything not to stay on Erskine."

"Yeah, I know what you mean. The First Provincial Battalion was moved in to take our place, and they can have it."

"Sir, you're going to have to let me change this every day; I'm afraid of the infection and jungle rot, but other than that, it's not very bad."

"You mean I'm not going to get medevaced, Doc?" Jake asked incredulously. "Why the hell do you think I stood in front of that claymore anyway?"

Pony laughed and said, "Yell for me if you want me to take a look." Jake sat in the trail, looking at the jaunty slant to Pony's campaign hat as he got up to slide through the mud and the weary marines who blocked the path back to this platoon.

Charlie Company had just completed their movement through Alpha.

Two and one-half miles southeast of Erskine, while the Second Battalion was moving on Co Ka Leuye and the Third Battalion was moving toward fire-support base Turnage, the First Battalion sat in with Charlie Company on the point for the night. They sat in line down Route 9, with the individual companies providing their own perimeter security, each tying in with the adjoining company for the entire length of the column. Jake had Bo to his rear and Alex directly ahead of him down the trail. Alex was tied into Third Platoon, Charlie Company.

All three battalions had seen action that day. It was clear that the NVA intended to defend this turf. How much resistance they would put up would be determined in the next two days. Jake was sitting just off the trail with his command group, feeling miserable in the rain and mud. His neck was bothering him. Doc Pony was changing the dressing when Alex came back to see how he was doing. Jake thanked him for coming through and asked Boston to come up. He wanted to write him up for the Bronze Star for the action earlier that day. Jake looked at Alex in the fading light and said quietly, "Alex, I still don't quite understand you. Not that I'm ungrateful or anything, but how do you justify the killing and especially the vengeance with which you attack? I watched you move through us earlier today and you were just as intense as the rest of us; maybe more so. You looked like you would kill every gook in North Vietnam."

Alex, thinking a moment, responded, "In Deuteronomy, chapter 20, verses 13 through 17, God lays out the objective of battle, which is total annihilation. It is kill or be killed. In fact, he says, 'And when the Lord thy God hath delivered it into thine hand, thou shalt smite every male thereof with the edge of the sword . . . thou shalt utterly destroy them . . . as the Lord thy God hath commanded thee.' A lot of people would disagree with me, I know." Alex, pausing, wiped his forehead with the back of his hand and squatted down on the ground next to Jake. "You know, to do what God requires in battle takes courage, battle courage. If you know through doctrine that you are in God's plan and that in war you have a job to do, kill the enemy, that becomes the divine norm and standard. In fact, in Colossians, chapter 3, verse 23, God goes on to say that, 'Whatsoever ye do, do it heartily, as to the Lord, and not unto men.' So, Jake, as a believer, the best testimony is to be the best killer in the outfit, if that's your job. The mothers of America don't like that, but the fact is, if our country is to remain free, it's because their sons became the best killers and killed the enemy as unto the Lord."

"Damn, Alex," Jake remarked, more in wonder, "that's some heavy crap."

"Listen, Jake, there are liberal politicians and there are liberal theologians and they are both deceived by peace propaganda. They are blinded to the consequences of peace at any price. When a country begins to listen to the idealists dreaming of a better world, like ours does today, it's like the blind leading the blind. These people who call themselves doves and peaceniks are actually the greatest weapon the communists have, and the worst element they spew forth is the peace propaganda coming out of the pulpits of America. Every Peacenik in this country is a traitor; that's what it amounts to. He is a weapon in the hands of the enemy. Jane Fonda is merely one example of a misguided person who will one day, in all likelihood, confess she was misguided and did not understand; and, in truth, she doesn't understand. You watch, that will happen, but by then it will be too late. The fact is, the worst traitors we have in this country today are the liberal preachers who are shouting peace, peace, when there is no peace."

It was completely dark now on the evening of the nineteenth of February. Doc Pony had finished repairing Jake's neck and sat down to listen. The Professor, who always had wondered about this huge lieutenant, had also paid close attention to what Alex was saying.

As Alex pushed a clump of fronds aside to get up and go back to his platoon, he said to no one in particular, "If you are a believer in Jesus Christ, you are the only hope for your country. The rest of the world is completely deluded by all forms of socialism and encroaching communism. It's possible the next generation may not even know the meaning of the word freedom."

Jake broke in vehemently, "Crap, Alex, you keep talking like we might lose this war. Have you seen us lose one ground conflict yet over here? Be realistic, if we wanted to, we could nuke the whole damn country. In fact, my solution would be to put all the old people, children, and women on a ship and just flatten the whole damn place." Jake paused for effect and said, "Then we would torpedo the ship."

The Professor and Doc Pony laughed; Alex shook his head in a hang-dog manner.

"Everytime I think I'm making progress with you, the bottom falls out," he said. "What happened to the young man with a passion that I met when I first got over here, Jake?

"He's still inside here, Alex," Jake responded, "and most of all, he's still alive." Jake reflected for a moment about his mother and her faith and the impact that she had had on his life and said, "thank God."

"Jake," Alex said, "you, son, are an ambiguity. This is a spiritual battle. Our leaders and our country have lost their way, we are goalless and passionless. You don't win anything just not quitting; eventually you lose. Remember that, Jake. You talk about losing as if it were an impossibility. I believe our nation is at its eleventh hour and even though the battle is spiritual, it doesn't mean you lay down your arms and look toward heaven with a pious expression. Somehow we've got to wake up our country so that we stop straining at the gnats and swallowing the camels. We need to find our way again."

The Professor looked up at Alex and said, "Lieutenant, sometimes you make a lot of sense. I don't understand it all, but I know it's important for me to feel that there is something meaningful to what we are doing here. I don't want to die either, nobody does, but some of us have a lot more will. I want that to mean something."

"Tom," Alex said, "it does count. A Christian is the salt of the earth and the preservation of his country. That's why I have been trying to say the first solution is the personal salvation of the people."

An awkward silence fell over them and everyone knew the conversation was at an end. Alex continued his journey back to his platoon. Doc went back to his position with Hawk and the Professor, contemplating the words of this big lieutenant, and felt something stir inside him. Jake knew that much of what Alex said was true. He still didn't know where he fit in, that was all. He was still on the search, in the middle of the journey. He did know this, however; Alex was the one guy who seemed to know what he was talking about and even believed it. No one else did. Jake respected that. Not even the president or his advisors, not the colonel or anybody. It wasn't very comforting. Apparently everybody was going to have to work all this out for themselves. Who the hell was leading anyway? Jake thought of processional caterpillars that often get in a circle following each other's scent, and go round and round until they die, without being able to break the circle. I don't want to be one of those, he thought. Besides, I'm beginning to dislike the smell I'm following.

29

ONLY THE FAINTEST SHADE OF DARK gray displacing utter blackness betrayed the coming of morning. The dense fog persisted and the wet mist found its way into every crevice and pore of a man's body. Under Colonel Dagomar's orders, Charlie Company moved forward and up the forward slope of the hill. About four miles southeast of Erskine the attack was rejoined. As they approached the crest of the hill at coordinates 1515H, First Platoon, Charlie Company, hit the front walls of four enemy bunkers. To the rear and down the slope about five hundred meters, Alpha listened to the contact. Crew-served weapons, RPGs, chicoms, and AK-47s could be heard rattling down the valley. Charlie pushed forward, calling down napalm within fifty meters of their own lines. The adrenaline rush of anticipation was coursing through the blood of every marine listening to the battle. Clahan got Alex on the hook and told him to get ready to attack through Charlie Company when the word came down. Jake and the other platoon commanders were monitoring the communication.

Captain "Black Jack" Johnson of Charlie Company was reporting on his frequency to Dagomar that what they faced was an NVA artillery position. They had yet to neutralize the bunkers, but they could see the big tube of a 122-millimeter, the biggest gun in the Vietnamese arsenal, protruding over the edge of the hill. The word came for Alex to move forward. The battle had been a desperate one. The weather made it difficult to do much with the air support, and contact was intense. The NVA did not intend to pull back from this position. Charlie Company pressed on through the bunkers, killing three and wounding seventeen NVA while losing one killed and four wounded. They finally captured the big 122-millimeter gun. Dagomar was elated with the progress. He was already on the radio congratulating Black Jack, even as Alex was attacking through the artillery position at coordinates YD195949, pushing the retreating North Vietnamese deeper down Route 9. Once again, the NVA left snipers tied to trees; they killed one marine and wounded two in Alex's platoon. The rest of the battalion just sat, waited, and listened, anxiously wondering when they would join the battle and who would live and who would die. And they all tried to understand what it was all about. Only Colonel Dagomar seemed to know, for he was very pleased at the progress.

On the other hand, old pros like Gunny Jacobsen and, in many ways, Hawk and, even in his inexperience, Jake, who was developing the sixth sense, wondered what the hell they were walking into. Why were the gooks defending this ground? What were they going to find down along the Laotian border?

The rest of the day was spent mopping up and counting the stores and supplies captured. The Gunny became increasingly worried. Even the Kit Carson scouts were nervous. You can chew over the purpose for all this as often as you want, Bo thought to himself, but you still have to make it to tomorrow.

Dagomar was overjoyed! In two hours of intense fighting, seventy-one NVA had been killed. A 122-millimeter howitzer had been captured. The marine losses were five killed and twenty-four wounded in both Charlie Company and in Alex's platoon. "Great stuff, great stuff," Dagomar kept saying to no one. He congratulated himself that the stigma of not being a fighting marine was over. He had vindicated his past.

Once again they sat in the same position they had overrun. Everyone knew that tomorrow inevitably meant more contact.

Once more the pitch black turned to gray. The column that was the First Battalion, Ninth Marines, shook off the water and moved in the misty shroud south and east of the Dakrong River toward Tam Boi Mountain. From the tenth to the seventeenth of February, 1969, 302 NVA had been killed, 1 captured, and 130 wounded in action. Of the Marines, 61 had been killed and 262 wounded in action, as the movement south toward Base Camp 911 continued. On the twenty-first, while Charlie Company was capturing the North Vietnamese gun emplacement, H Company had moved about two thousand meters west into Laos to protect the battalion flank and had ambushed a North Vietnamese truck convoy.

At 0930 hours on the morning of the twenty-second of February, B Company uncovered a large enemy supply cache and seven hastily evacuated bunkers at coordinates 197053. B Company stayed behind to inventory the supplies while Alpha, Charlie, and Delta companies continued to advance toward the battalion objective in grid square 1903. They had about two grids to move through, of extremely elevated terrain in rapidly deteriorating weather. Jake's neck had become infected, as Doc Pony feared. The wound or the bandages were never dry, no matter how often the Doc changed them. The advance was painfully slow. Alpha and Charlie were moving on parallel ridge lines and Delta was following in trace. Bo's platoon took the point for Alpha Company. As the morning wore on, visibility was better. In many ways, the humidity in the middle of the fog and mist and triple canopy was far worse than the heat. They slogged on through the mud and jungle. Bo, like Jake, walked behind his first squad. At approximately 1100 hours, at coordinates 202053, Bo walked into an L-shaped ambush set out by a squad-sized unit. He took one KIA and one WIA while killing seven of the enemy. As the NVA retreated, once again they left a sniper tied to a tree to die.

In rotation, Alpha Company moved through Bo's platoon and Bravo Company. Alex fell in behind Jake and Bo followed in trace. After nearly two hours on the move, they were struggling up a large incline toward a ridge perpendicular to their line of movement. It was about 1300 hours; Boston had been on the point for the last hour and a half. Jake stopped just short of the last rise before going on to the military crest, or forward slope of the hill. He moved Dragin and his squad up

203

to the front. Boston was bringing up the platoon rear and Sugar Bear had the middle. Hawk didn't like the look or feel of the ridge. It straddled the Laotion border and was invisible in the fog; its presence could be felt. The Professor grabbed Jake's arm and told him that Clahan was on the line. Jake took the receiver, "Six, this is Alpha Actual, over."

"Actual, this is Six," Clahan replied. "What's the hold-up? Let's move up the ridge. It straddles the battalion objective and the Battalion Six wants to move."

"Roger that, Six. We would like to probe a bit. It doesn't look too good from here. Give me about thirty minutes to check it out."

"That's a negatory, Actual. You get on line and move."

"Uh, I roger you, Six, out." Jake gave the handset back to the Professor and turned to Hawk, thinking about the Battalion Six; he muttered, "That guy is still an asshole." Hawk responded with a nod of his head and looked at Jake, his face a mask of dull fatigue and indifference. Jake continued on, "Listen, Alex will be coming up on the starboard side. I want Boston and Sugar Bear side by side with Dragin following in trace. There just can't be any advantage of surprise, even with this lousy weather hiding them and us. The real question is, just how big a unit are we walking into?" Jake stopped, lowering his head in thought for several moments. He looked up with a frown of concern, shrugging his pack into a more bearable position, and then turned his head to the Professor and said very quietly, "Professor, tell Clahan that we're on the move."

30

I T WAS NOT COLD FOR A FEBRUARY day in the middle of Indiana. The cemetery was brand new, the thin grass barely covering the frost-hardened earth. Only a handful of burials had taken place. Jonathon T. Pringale was returning to the soil he had loved and tilled. A tent was erected over the grave site at the top of a little knoll which was roughly at the center of the cemetery. Most of the friends of the Pringales had come to the funeral. Besides, the incredible set of circumstances had made the occasion a media event. The procession to the graveyard was a long one. The press had offered the usual, "can you believe this" sensational story of the double death of PFC Pringale, and they were out in force. The sun was bright; big cottony clouds stretched out to the horizon. Six chairs sat just under the lip of the tent facing the casket. The Marine Corps Inspector and Instructor team, which handled the military aspects of the burial, were there in their dress blues to present the flag which draped the casket to the Pringales. Major Gerson and Staff Sergeant Benson were attending at the request of Mrs. Pringale.

It truly was a beautiful day. There was just a little bite in the wind, enough to remind a mourner of football games, cheerleaders, and a little whiskey in with the hot coffee that sloshed around the inside of your Thermos. Mr. Pringale sat next to his wife; their daughter was on his left; his brother and Mrs. Pringale's sister filled the other chairs. One chair remained empty. It seemed to be a sardonic reminder that PFC Pringale could have been an invisible presence at his own funeral. Was it really him in the casket? Mr. Pringale was morose but not violent, as Myrtle half expected him to be. He simply said nothing: He went about preparing for the funeral, insisting only that Major Gerson attend, much to Myrtle's surprise.

The bugler played taps, the notes carried away by the wind, haunting and then lost over the countryside. The morose melody brought different degrees of pain to the souls of those who heard it. The eulogies had been said at the funeral home. Johnny's high-school coach spoke haltingly about this fine young man and his commitment to God and country. One of his teachers remembered his academic excellence and said that it was a cause of great sorrow when a life full of promise was cut short in such a brutal way. But no one spoke of the purpose of the war, of serving one's country. The time for such language apparently had past. At the grave-side, the preacher committed the body to its creator. As the flag was being folded, Mr. Pringale produced his old service revolver from under his heavy wool suit coat and pointed it at Major Gerson. No one really noticed what he was doing until his arm was fully extended. Mrs. Pringale saw him first and screamed a shout of defiance rather than fear: "No! Sam, no! You can't do this, it was not his fault, it's not anyone's fault. Oh, God, Sam, let it be and let Johnny rest."

The cameras were rolling for the six o'clock news. Women were screaming and men looked on in disbelief, some shouting warnings. The preacher was still holding the Bible open over the casket of Jonathon T. Pringale as the father attempted to make his contribution to the insanity that had killed his son. With one round he could make fifty-seven years of negative thinking and commentary come true. He could justify every single hour of nay-saying he had confessed before his wife for the length of their married life. He could prove himself a prophet. Major Gerson stood alone as people around him scattered in terror when it became apparent he was the object of Mr. Pringale's attention.

206

"You bastards send these young men out to die for a cause you know nothing about. Day in and day out they pay the ultimate price, while the goddamn politicians and the military take the lives of kids whose only sin was being young enough to get drafted or too young to know better. They get killed and then people like you give us meaningless words of sacrifice that, damn it, can never make up for what we've lost."

Dick Gerson stood looking at the father of the latest dead marine in a long line of those he had put in the ground. He really didn't care what Mr. Pringale did. He was finished anyway. He was sick of it all. But, like Staff Sergeant Benson, his only remaining supporter, still at his side, he watched the shaking hand holding the revolver. He watched it as it turned and then he lunged forward, realizing what this old man was intent on doing. The round took away the left side of the head of Jonathon T. Pringale's father, spattering blood and gore across the six seats in the front row. Vietnam, in its own way, had taken the life of father and son. Or the politicians had taken them, or the communists, or the circumstances, or something. But they were dead and the cameras were rolling and the press was getting it all down for posterity and people were screaming and the six o'clock news was going to be a hit. And all across America, families' lives were being altered, never to be the same again. In Indianapolis, Indiana, Myrtle Pringale sat holding the blood-spattered flag that had covered her son's casket as she bore witness to her husband's death.

31

I T HAD BEEN VERY DIFFICULT TO GET the dead and wounded out. In the three days since they had left Erskine, they had used explosives to blast four landing zones out of the jungle and prayed that a chopper could make it down in the bad weather. The first casualties had to be walked back to Erskine at the end of the first day. The weather just would not break. Between the ground cover and the fog, there seemed to be no way of making regular sorties.

Jake was pondering that part of the problem as he made his way forward, trudging behind Dragin's squad. Roots from the banyan trees wound up and out of the ground and looped along the earth. Marines slipped and swore in the mud. Everything was wet and the extra movement didn't help them feel any less exposed and vulnerable. The jungle was alive with rain and wet and falling leaves as the marines moved like ants up the side of the ridge. The contour of the terrain was funneling the movement of the companies up the hill. Jake expressed his concern to Clahan; he felt they were moving toward a natural position of defense where they were bound to encounter a hot reception. Clahan told him to press on.

Suddenly a whirlwind of small-arms rounds coincided with RPGs and eighty-one-millimeter mortars, scything away at and denuding the jungle. The earth shuddered all around Jake. Cries for corpsman had risen above the noise and penetrated the fog. Jake, Alex, and Bo pressed their platoons forward. Dragin had gone to ground and two AK-50 machine guns were doing their best to keep him there. The entire rim of the ridge had erupted and it was difficult to see where the fire was coming from. All three platoons were laying down a base of fire while trying to move fire teams and squads up the side of the ridge as quickly as possible. Clahan had moved up behind Bo's platoon; he was frantically attempting to call in artillery from Erskine and Cunningham.

Dragin could see a small mud trail directly in front of him; it wound its way up a little draw to the top of the ridge. Incoming rounds were falling indiscriminately as he jumped his teams forward, moving up the draw. Then the top of the ridge began to erupt from the artillery 105s and 155s. Then Dragin moved.

Jake was trying to let Clahan know his situation and to find out if Alex and Bo were able to keep up. He was kneeling beside the Professor, who was shaking as he usually did when the shit hit the fan. Hawk was trying to keep Boston and Sugar Bear on line behind Dragin. But no one had actually seen one single gook. The incline was fairly steep but rutted into a corduroylike surface that made it easier to go up the hill. A small hook in the trail led to the top of the ridge. There the first team made the turn in a hail of machine-gun, AK-47, and SKS rifle fire. The first two marines came tumbling back down the incline—one straddling a banana tree, wearing a look of surprise on his face; the other nearly taking Dragin's feet out from under him. Both were dead before they hit the trail and lay still.

Jake made his way up to Dragin. "What do you think is up there?" Jake asked. "Hell if I know, lieutenant, but I think the whole goddamned gook army is around that little hook and I can't see a fuckin' thing."

Both Boston and Sugar Bear were pressing now and Jake told Hawk to hold them up. On his left, Alex run into pretty much the same thing. His was a straight assault, but again the lip in the crest of the hill was eclipsed in the fog and mist, making it all but impossible to see the enemy.

His entire platoon was bogged down under the enemy's suppressing fire and mortar rounds. Bo was in a similar situation, although he might be able to get around the end of the ridge and come up on the main finger, if he could just move another one hundred to two hundred meters. Jake started to move back down the hill after telling Dragin to give it one more try.

As it was, the entire company was bogged down in the mud, fog, and enemy fire. There had already been eight casualties, and they were in danger of expending more ammunition than they wanted without making the top of the ridge. Charlie and Delta companies were about one click back, waiting on parallel ridge lines. At this point, Colonel Dagomar gave orders to back down the ridge about one hundred meters and try to get the dead and wounded out. Then, he reckoned, they could make another run at it the next morning. As that decision was being made, Dragin had penetrated deeper into the enemy's position than the rest of the platoon. With poor visibility and the chaos resulting from the firefight, he hadn't noticed the separation, and Jake and Boston were unable to keep up. Dragin had actually breached the first line of defense, a complex of three bunkers that gave way under the pressure. Pushing forward, the momentum carried them a good thirty meters out, so Dragin just pushed on to the crest of the ridge.

A lull in the firing made Dragin aware for the first time what had happened, but by that time it was already too late; the hole in the NVA lines was sealing over. Dragin, Bohanin, Johnson, and Sealy found themselves inside the NVA perimeter. The second line of bunkers was directly in front of them, about twenty meters up a gentle incline. There were gooks everywhere they looked. Both Johnson and Sealy went down with the first bursts of fire. Dragin started to head back down the hill but then realized they were cut off and that the first squad wasn't behind him.

The first thing that came to his mind was that he could be fucking his eyeballs out in Olongopo City. Then a squad-sized detachment appeared out of nowhere. Dragin looked over at Bohanin, who was already on his knees, having dropped his weapon. Dragin, looking around at the NVA, dropped his M-16 on the ground and shouted, "A live dog is better than a dead lion," and then he flipped them the bird.

Screams bounced off the ridge line during the night. It was difficult to tell if it was Dragin or any of the rest, but the effect was the same. About 0300 hours, rounds were fired, two or three seconds apart. Then more yelling and screaming, and then silence. The NVA had shot holes in their hands and strung barbed concertina wire through the holes using the excess to tie them back to back. Thus, any movement, however slight, caused extreme pain in the partner. The Vietnamese had spaced the shootings out through the night for maximum impact on the listeners. All three marines but Dragin lost consciousness as the barbed wire was pulled through their hands.

At 2200 hours, Bo was carrying a casualty back down the hill, a young marine who had taken shrapnel from a Chinese communist grenade in both legs. His wounds were superficial but he had broken his left leg when he fell. Bo laid him down in a bamboo thatch at the base of a banana tree.

"How you feeling, Santos?" Bo asked, as the corpsman worked over his legs.

"Okay, sir, I guess this would be a ticket home in most cases, huh?"

Bo looked down at this young man, wondering what he meant.

"I mean if we could just get a chopper in, I could get out, but we haven't been able to get that done for days and now we are really in the crap, sir. Do you think we will ever get out of here, lieutenant?"

Bo, squatting down next to Santos, said, "You bet we will, and we will get you out of here tomorrow, you just wait and see."

Doc Emery had ripped Santos's utility trousers back to reveal a half-dozen wounds in each leg.

"Nothing here really serious," he said to Bo. "I've dressed both legs, but it would be a good idea if we could get him out of here as soon as possible."

"Yeah," Bo responded, "I know. Listen, Santos, you hang in there, hear; we'll get you out tomorrow."

"Thanks, lieutenant, I appreciate it," Santos responded, without much conviction in his voice.

Doc Emery asked if he could talk to Bo privately, saying, "I gave him some morphine to hold down the pain, lieutenant; but he may wake up feeling it in a few hours."

"Okay, Doc, thanks a lot. How's everybody else?"

"Well, we took three WIAs, but Santos here will be the only medevac if we can get the choppers in."

Alpha sat in on the side of the ridge but didn't expect any movement during the night. Bo worked his way over to Jake to see how things had gone. They traded stats on the dead and wounded.

"I've only got one that is bad enough to medevac," Bo said, referring to Santos, "but I think he's going to give up because he doesn't think we are going to get out of here. He doesn't seem to be hurt that badly."

"They're just kids, Bo. I just can't seem to get it out of my mind. One replaces another, ad infinitum."

"The gooks are like that, not us. It seems like they have an endless supply of bodies and they have been divvying them out for a couple of thousand years."

"Yeah, that's true, but we haven't been doing it for two thousand years."

"In a way we have, Jake. Maybe we haven't been doing it that long, but we've sent our share into combat."

"Alex says that war is divinely inspired. He claims that if our motives are right, we can expect victory, just like Israel in the Old Testament," Jake said, rubbing his eyes from the fatigue he was feeling.

"Don't you think the gooks pray?" Bo asked.

"I don't know," he replied. "If they do, it's to a different god," Jake suggested.

"Well, what about two opposing forces that pray to the same God? What then?" Bo inquired.

Jake thought for a minute and then said, "I guess that's a problem for God. Besides, Bo, you're beginning to sound like Alex. He acts like we could lose this war, and we've never lost any war."

Bo, moving up close to Jake in the dark, tried to see his face, his dark brows nearly touching in concentration. "Listen, Jake, some of us have lost a war. We understand what total defeat really means. My family and every old Southern family knows in its bones the meaning of defeat. My great grandpappy was totally defeated and then the South suffered under the federal boot for a decade. I know defeat because it was bred into me. There is no lesson like it. In fact, Jake, in the South, military academies and football tradition were spawned out of that defeat. There are lessons that can be learned no other way than by defeat. Maybe God lets us experience defeat in order to learn lessons we couldn't learn in any other way. I know one thing, my grandpappy was sure he was going to win too."

Jake was once again thinking about Jehovah's throat and how many young men had been called home. Perhaps all of these conversations were already dialogues of the dead. "God," he said to Bo, "we are all too young to die. I haven't lived enough yet to die. Many of these kids are dying innocent. Dying with instruments of death in their hands, killing others and yet innocent themselves."

The Professor broke up the conversation to tell Jake that the Skipper was on the hook wanting a sit rep. Bo turned to go and said, "I'll catch you later, Jake. Don't get too deep in all the philosophy, hoss, just keep your eye on the bouncin' ball, you owe it to yourself, hear?"

"Yeah, Bo, I hear you, see you at the top of the hill . . ."

Bo trudged on a couple of steps and then turned once more toward Jake: "Sometimes, Jake, remember, even in losing, you win." And then he disappeared into the night. Jake wondered what he meant by that. The Preacher had said almost the same thing to him back on Hill 418. He really did love these guys, this "family"; he respected their courage and will to live. He had been questioning many of the beliefs by which he conducted his own life. He had been defining himself through his role as an officer, but now the way he perceived it was changing dramatically, and with it his definition of himself had to change. Damn, everything seems to be in limbo, he thought sadly.

As they suspected, the NVA were content to wait until morning to see if the marines had the intention of crossing over into Laos. The NVA knew it was a no-fire zone. Bo woke up with water running off his nose and down his chest. He tried to get the ache out of his joints, but with each night in the bush it had become more and more difficult to do. The LPs had already returned; the men were squatting in the mud, eating biscuits, cheese, and cold C-rats all along the line.

Doc Emery went over to check the wounded and found Santos dead. He told Bo that he thought the kid just gave up. "He just wasn't hurt that badly, lieutenant; like he said to you, he didn't think any of us were going to get out of here and I guess he decided to take his own way out." Emery paused and then looked at Bo: "Do you think he's right, sir?"

"Knock that shit off, Doc. Of course we're gonna get out of here and not only that, we are gonna kick gook ass all the way to Hanoi in the process. Now get your gear together and let's get ready to mount up. I think we are going to have a busy day." As the little corpsman turned to go, Bo stood looking up the hill. What he saw was mist and gray and jungle, and what he felt was doubt.

It was almost dawn on the morning of the twenty-first.

Once more, just as they had been briefed back at Vandegrift, they were on line and would try to make it up the side of the ridge. During the night Delta had moved up behind Alpha; Charlie remained behind on a parallel ridge. Alexander Scott was ready when the word came down. He moved his platoon forward and to the right of the finger to angle up the main approach from the southeast side of the hill. Jake and Bo moved forward. Once more the NVA guns opened up. Mortar tubes popped, signaling the explosions that would once again tear up parts of the jungle and the marines that were in the way. But the 105s and 155s had begun to do their work, and under the cover of howitzers and mortars, Alpha Company moved.

It was a battalion bunker complex. There were one hundred and seven A-frame bunkers that rested in the military crest of the hill. Underneath the ridge a tunnel complex ran two hundred to two hundred and fifty meters. B Company had counted sixty machine guns, fourteen mortars, and one hundred tons of artillery, mortars, and small-arms ammunition, yet it was nothing compared with what would be discovered as the First Battalion, Ninth Marine Regiment, moved toward Laos. The closer they came to the border, the more the enemy resistance stiffened. However, the North Vietnamese were not positioned for in-depth defense. They had the advantage of terrible weather, difficult terrain, entrenched antiaircraft guns, and, since Base Camp 922 abutted Laos, there could be no flanking attacks; but even so they would still employ a hit-and-run offense.

Alpha came on line as well as they could in the triple-canopy jungle. Clahan kept the artillery coming from YD197053 to YD197049. The marines were in tight as they moved forward. From somewhere up the ridge a fifty cal was ripping apart the banana trees; they fell as if cut in two by an invisible scythe. Small-arms rounds from AK-47s and SKSs began by popping randomly, like corn in a skillet, and then picked up in volume, sending down a hail of death to be intercepted by some unlucky marine. The sixty-one and eighty-one mortar tubes thumped from over the ridge, like a bass section counterparted to the higher-pitched smaller rounds, and the symphony of death played on.

As difficult as the terrain was and as miserable as the weather continued to be, somehow platoons managed to move more or less in unison. Although the members of the separate platoons didn't know it, they were all nearly on line at about the hundred-meter mark from the ridge top. Clahan was moving behind Bo's platoon when the end of the third squad made sight contact with the first bunker. Mortars, bloopers, and suppressing M-60 fire did a fair job at keeping the gooks dug in. Neither side had fire superiority. Movement by the marines had largely been in fire-team wedges and squad vees. Now they flanked in a series of rushes, firing and maneuvering as best they could.

Alex suddenly found himself on top of the line of bunkers on his end of the finger, and then he and his men broke over the ridge line before they even realized it. A series of smaller bunkers sat about twenty-five meters farther up the hill behind the line Alex was now facing. The firing was intense; the only possible movement into the complex was alternating short bursts of speed and then falling to the deck, returning as much fire as possible. It was difficult to determine how many casualties the marines were taking. Alex had seen several marines go down in the attack. Cries for corpsman floated over the chaos.

The elephant grass had not been cleared in front of the first few bunkers. Alex, slipping, fell in an open bunker on top of a lone gook who apparently was hoping to escape notice as the marines went by.

They were both surprised and scrambled to get away from each other in the small space. The smaller man, the North Vietnamese, tried to raise his SKS rifle and succeeded only in knocking it against the side of the bunker as Alex, recovering, lunged for him, grasping both man and weapon in one huge bear hug. Face to face with the NVA soldier, Alex inhaled the odor of rice and betel nut. Like a hooked fish, the man thrashed until Alex could feel the steel of the rifle begin to rasp against arm and leg bone. His breath came in a rush as it was squeezed out of his lungs, eyes bulging inches from Alex's face, eyes that recognized impending death. Alex squeezed with his massive arms until he felt bones break and the body quit protesting. Alex let the NVA fall to the bottom of the temporary home he had created for himself days earlier. He stood over his kill, breathing heavily, flushed with the act. Suddenly he felt someone behind him. Wheeling around, he lunged for the figure towering over him and, catching a boot, pulled what turned out be his radioman, Lilly, down on top of him.

"Jesus Christ, lieutenant, don't kill me too. I saw you go down and I thought maybe you were hurt. Shit, let me outta here," he said, scrambling up the mud-slick side of the bunker.

Alex sat down in the bottom of the pit, straddling the dead soldier, staring up at PFC Lilly, apparently unable to speak.

"Lieutenant, lieutenant, are you okay?" Lilly asked, not quite sure what to do.

Alex remained still, sitting on his trophy, harshly breathing in the life-giving air that he had denied his victim.

"Lieutenant Scott, what's the matter with you, sir?" Lilly asked again.

This time Alex looked up and half stumbled as he got his huge frame up, balanced on his feet and heaved himself up over the top of the bunker. "I'm okay, Lilly, I'm okay. Let's keep moving. Where is the rest of the platoon? Have we kept moving? How long have I been down in that hole?" he asked in machine-gun fashion and, without waiting for a reply, turned and began moving up the hill. Lilly followed his lieutenant and kept silent, but he was worried about this big man.

Jake was finding the heaviest fire leveled at his platoon in the middle of the ridge. Bo's men had nearly breached the first level of bunkers and, like Alex's platoon, were engaged in hand-to-hand combat in the fighting holes. As the gooks retreated once again, they tied snipers to trees, leaving them to die. The bloopers were doing their work, lobbing grenades into holes spin armed to explode as they went and blowing men apart on the receiving end. Bo finally broke through the first line of bunkers, only to encounter intense fire from the second line of defense. Here a fifty-cal was sending spurts of steel rain pouring down the hill.

Bo and his first squad killed a number of NVA in their holes. Several mortar rounds traced their way down the slope, the last round hitting within twenty meters of their position. Three marines went down, shrapnel ripping away chunks of bone and flesh. The big fifty-caliber machine gun, sitting about thirty meters ahead, began punching out rounds in the same direction. Bo found himself in a position where he could not go forward or turn back. Sweeney, who was still humping his radio, had been hit and he couldn't get to the handset. His third squad was trying to move up and through but also bogged down just below the first bunker complex. Bo could see little shocks of black hair bobbing up and down directly in front of his lines. He lay still, hoping to avoid drawing any more fire, until he heard Clahan's voice shout out directly behind him and then pitch to a scream as he ran by with what was left of the third squad. He was still screaming as he went by, firing an M-16 as he went. As Bo, transfixed, watched, they traversed the thirty meters to the machine gun, laying a suppressing fire against the chugging fifty-cal. Bo, now on his knees, could see Clahan firing into the machine-gun nest as rounds from the big gun found their mark and lifted him completely off the ground, appearing momentarily to suspend him in midair. Then he dropped to the ground and out of sight. The charge had broken through the suppressing fire and other marines including Bo were now up and over the top, killing the four NVA manning the gun emplacement. The rest of the platoon was now on its feet, running and firing and shouting and moving.

Bo walked over to the lifeless body of Jim Clahan. He had taken eight fifty-caliber rounds up the center of his torso, nearly splitting him in two. He looked down at this black man who had saved his life and possibly the platoon—hell, maybe even the company—by creating the momentum to take the hill. Sitting down on the ground beside him, Bo picked up the body and held it in his arms, pools of blood soaking through his utilities. Red blood, he thought, not white or black, but red blood. He looked at the wide nose spread over Jim Clahan's face and the thick lips, and he held him closer, unable to comprehend his own feelings. No greater love, the Preacher would say. No greater love but that a man give his life...a black man, for me?

32

J AKE COULD SENSE THE FIGHTING
going on farther up the ridge,
beyond the point he had reached. He
knew that Bo and Alex had made better time, but his casualties were
mounting from the mortars and suppressing fire. Every time he tried
fire and movement, he would get beaten back down. He yanked the
handset from the Professor but couldn't reach Clahan. In fact, he
couldn't get anybody up on the company freq. He told Boston and
Sugar Bear to bring up their machine guns for a frontal assault and
put all his blooper men on line. Giving the order, they started up the
hill again, offering as much suppressing fire as possible. Boston was
pumping as many M-79 rounds out as it was humanly possible to do.
Then, with a shout, they moved and felt the line give just a bit; with
a communal roar they reached the top of the ridge in a half-lope
half–run-walk movement.

Doc Pony was doing his best to attend to the wounded. There were
already seven casualties in First Platoon alone. He was putting a battle
dressing and a tourniquet on a young marine who had his arm taken off

at the elbow by a section of the base plate from an 81 mortar, when a stray round shattered one of the protective plates in his flak jacket and knocked him unconscious.

"Doc, Doc," his patient cried, "you can't get hurt, Doc, you have to take care of me." But the Doc could not hear him.

Jake was still pushing his platoon as best he could. Hawk, moving at the rear, kept pushing and cajoling and urging in order to maintain the momentum. Chaos was, is, and always will be the only word to describe a firefight. Instinct and training make survival and order only faint possibilities. Sugar Bear had his squad moving and firing. Boston, just in front of Jake, was nearly incoherent as he got caught up in pumping out blooper rounds and urging his squad on. He barely noticed the round that glanced off his helmet, but he did notice the one that ran up his left arm from the forearm to the elbow and exited just below his biceps. Jake saw him go down, but they were cresting the hill and the forward movement had a life of its own. Carried to the top by the momentum of the assault, Jake yelled out for the Professor to get a corpsman up for Boston. Sugar Bear was dropping grenades like calling cards into each bunker they passed. It was difficult to determine how many NVA were being killed in the holes, but there were many.

The 814th NVA regiment was pulling back from the first line of defense. As before, they would hit aggressively and retreat, leaving snipers tied to trees to wreak havoc and die. Alex had flanked the ridge by coming up the east end of the finger and was now tying in with elements of Jake's platoon. Bo's platoon had already met with the left side of Jake's; hasty perimeters were being established and body counts being done. Boston made it to the top of the hill and was refusing to be medevaced, even if they could get a chopper in.

Jake, still at the center of the attack line, saw Dragin and Bohanin first. Johnson and Sealy were farther to the left and also dead. Shot through the head, apparently as the NVA were preparing to leave the hill. Dragin, who had somehow been either forgotten or missed in the confusion, was still alive. His pockmarked face bore the same vacant stare that Jake had seen on him when he was smoking dope. Since

Doc Pony couldn't be found, Doc Emery was waiting to treat Dragin's wounds once they cut the barbed wire from his hands. The wire barbs had ripped horizontal tears above the gunshot wounds. Dragin was in the merciful clutch of shock.

"Lieutenant," the doc said, "he's not going to make it if we don't get him out. I've given him plenty of morphine for the pain but he needs plasma and we are running short of everything. There are at least a dozen others that we need to get out as well, not to mention the KIAs."

"What's the count, Doc?"

"Well," Emery responded, "we've got four dead and twenty-two wounded; not all need to be medevaced. I don't know what the hell we're going to do if we don't get a break in the weather. Besides, every time we get even a small break, by the time we blow the LZ the gooners bracket it with mortars and then the sky guys don't want to try to come in; or as soon as the first round hits the deck, they split."

"I know, Doc, we've tried seven times already and I suspect we will give it another try; if not today, in the morning." The Professor interrupted Jake to tell him the colonel was on the line. Jake took the handset, wondering once again where Clahan was.

"Six, this is Alpha One Actual, over."

"One Actual, this is Six. What the hell is happening out there and where is Alpha Actual?"

"Wait one, Six." Jake turned to the Professor and asked if he had heard from Clahan. "Sir, I think that the Skipper was moving behind Lieutenant Lawler's platoon and I haven't seen either of them."

Jake, returning to Dagomar, said, "Six, we have breached the objective and are pursuing the little people with fire. I will get back in about one-five minutes for a better readout, four."

"Ten four, Actual, that's fifteen, out."

Jake walked behind Boston, who was messing with the tight wrap on his arm. They went back over the lip of the ridge and down to where Bo had last been seen. They traveled about ten meters when Jake turned to Boston and told him to gather up a fire team from

221

Third Platoon for security. When they were joined by the other marines, they started back down to the first bunker line. About halfway down sat Bo, still holding the remains of Jim Clahan. Jake, bending over the two, grabbed Bo by the shoulder: "Bo, what's happening, man?"

Bo looked up, still cradling Clahan, and responded, "Hey, Jake, I'm sorry, man. I didn't mean to bail out on you. I was just sitting here with my man Clahan. He went and did a pretty damn stupid thing, you know."

"No, Bo, I'm not sure what you mean," Jake replied. "What did he do?"

"Well, he saved my white ass from dying on this fucking mud hill and, in the process, got himself split open like a watermelon, can you believe it? A nigger saving my ass. I was just sitting here thinking about it. Now why do you suppose he went and did something like that?" Bo questioned indifferently, all the while trying to knock some of the dirt and gore off Clahan's body.

Jake looked at Boston, who was standing next to another black marine. All four were staring at Bo, who still held the remains of the company commander.

"Listen, Bo, let's talk about this later. We need to get Jim's body up the hill and get set in. Hell, I don't know what kind of tunnel complexes are in this hill and they might turn around and hit us here. Let me take . . ."

Bo said firmly, "I'll carry him. He was a good son of a bitch. I'll carry him. I owe him and I can't repay him and I swore that I would never owe a black man nothin' and now I do and I can't do nothing about it."

Bo picked Clahan up in one graceful motion and began the mournful walk up the ridge. Jake was thinking about the first time he had seen Jim Clahan back in Quang Tri and remembered how he had expressed the desire to go home and get out of the corps. He was thinking about the fact that he had only about fifty days left in-country. "No greater love," he heard Bo say.

Gunny Jacobsen met them at the top of the hill. He couldn't stop talking about Lieutenant Clahan's assault on the fifty-caliber emplacement.

"Damn, lieutenant," he said, "I've never seen anything like it. He literally broke through by himself and then carried the movement up the ridge. I don't know how many gooks were up there, but there are over one hundred bunkers stretching the ridge line in layers, and I know for sure there were more of those little bastards than us."

"Gunny," Jake interrupted, "where were you when Clahan bought it? I thought you were moving with him."

"No," the Gunny responded, "he told me to move back with the radio and run what he called a communication center until we took the ridge. I mean, what the hell is a communication center in the middle of all this shit? Then he said he wanted to move forward with Lieutenant Lawler's platoon."

"Why do you think he wanted to do that, Sam?" Jake queried. "And why would he want to, for all practical purposes, give up his strategic command when his company was moving to contact?"

"I don't know, lieutenant; he's been acting kind of funny since we left Erskine. He kept talking a lot about having forty-five days and a wake-up and wouldn't it be ironical to buy the farm now. Either way, I'm going to write him up for the Medal of Honor. I don't know whether he will get it or not, but he deserves it. If we had been turned back a second time, I know the casualties would have been much higher. Either way, it doesn't really make much difference, I guess."

Bo, having laid Clahan in line by the other dead, said, "You bet your ass it meant something. It meant something to me and I'm going to make sure people know about it."

"Lieutenant," the Gunny interrupted, "I don't think anybody back in the world wants to know what is going on over here unless it fits into their preconceived position. It doesn't make any difference to them whether we are cowards or heroes. I've watched this damn war get crazier and crazier through three tours and I'll tell you this, we are being chalked up along with the whole war as worthless and undesirable. It all boils down to doing what we do for each other. You have got to have a really special reason to do what Lieutenant Clahan did." He blinked and swallowed hard, fighting to keep his composure. "I know, for the first time, I'm looking forward to retirement. I've earned it and I'm ready, like a lot of the other old-timers." Gunny Jacobsen absently scratched at his three-day-old stubble and said, "I wish Captain Wolf were here; I sure could use some of his whiskey." Jake, with a contemplative look on his face, said, "Well, my friends, that I may be able to do something about."

33

ALEX, BO, JAKE, HAWK, AND THE Gunny were sitting in the middle of the perimeter formed by Alpha and Delta companies. The Professor was monitoring the net. It was night, the twenty-first of February.

"It doesn't look too hot, does it," Hawk said more than asked.

"Did you ever stop to think, Hawk, that back in the States people are gorging themselves at McDonald's and Hardee's right now?" Jake asked.

Hawk looked up and said, "No, not lately, lieutenant."

"Well, I was just thinking how great it would be to eat a huge salad, Hawk."

Bo cut in, "Frankly, lieutenant, I'd like to eat some pussy, but I don't think either one of us is going to have our wish come true unless we get out of this fuckin' place."

"Let's look at what we've got," Jake said.

"Colonel Dagomar says we've hit a battalion-sized unit. Our Third Battalion has made fire-support base Turnage. The Second Battalion, Ninth Marine Regiment, is at Co Ka Leuye, just above their objective on the border. We've made our objective but, like the dog chasing the car, now that we've got it, what the hell are we going to do with it?"

Firing erupted off in the direction of Delta's lines. The Professor, listening intently into the handset, reported that Delta had movement in the lines.

"There are holes all over this hill," the Gunny said. "No telling how many gooks are underneath us."

Jake took a drag off of a cigarette he and Bo were sharing, cupping the butt so the burning ash couldn't attract attention.

"Here it is," he said, "about three days southeast is a mountain named Tam Boi at grid 2404 on your map. If we can get a resupply and a medevac, we will step off in the morning. If not, we will leave the dead and wounded with Delta. Charlie Company will be joining them here along with Bravo. We'll move to Tam Boi to be there on the twenty-fourth, and we can hope the rest of the battalion will join us later. The real advantage of air support has been lost to the weather and the number of antiaircraft guns that the gooners have up here. Once we are all on Tam Boi, we will extract from there." Jake paused, trying to see each man in the darkness or at least sense some kind of reaction.

Everybody was filthy, with their utilities in different stages of destruction. The wetness had not even allowed the jungle rot to dry into hard scabs; instead the sores, caused by cuts usually made by the sharp edges of elephant grass, stayed open and raw. Jake picked at his own sores, including the one on his neck, while Bo, open-shirted, his dark chest hair matted and rising up to meet his unshaven face at the neck, was busy scraping mud from the toe of one jungle boot, using the heel of the other as a wedge. The Preacher, attentive as usual, was sitting on a poncho liner munching four or five C-rat crackers at one time. The Gunny and Hawk were kneeling over their map, using a small map light to search out the elevation lines. Flak jackets, some reclining, other standing at attention, cluttered the area. An M-16 lay across the Professor's lap. He sat Indian-fashion to the side of the other five. Every face, could they have been seen clearly, betrayed the strain of all that had taken place since they had landed on fire-support base Erskine. Dark eyes, mouths drawn down into nearly permanent grimaces, helmets adorned with bottles of insect repellent or partially empty cigarette packs. Hand grenades, hooked here and there, the jewelry of the combat soldier. They were grunts, field marines. Kin to every soldier who ever sat in the open and wondered about tomorrow. Jake, looking behind their faces, was thinking about a story he had read somewhere. It was about some reporter during the Korean War asking a marine in the Chosin Reservoir, if he could have anything in the world he wanted, what would he choose? The reporter was sure it would be his girl or a big juicy steak or something like that; but instead, peering from behind his scraggly, ice-covered beard, he just looked at the woman reporter and said: "Just give me tomorrow."

Gunny Jacobsen broke Jake's reverie. "What's it gonna be, sir?"

Jake, jolted back to reality, scratched at his neck absently and then jumped at the pain that resulted. He continued to think for a moment and then said, "Well, unless any of you have any better ideas, and if we can get a break in the weather, we'll try to blow an LZ at first light and get the KIAs and WIAs out of here. Then we'll move along this finger down into the valley and make our way toward Tam Boi. I'd like to get there by the twenty-fourth. That's when Dagomar wants us there and that's when we will get there."

Captain Ferring from Delta Company moved into the circle in time to hear Jake say that they would leave the casualties with Delta if the medevac didn't work.

"By the way, Gunny, what does the Doc say about Dragin, Doc Pony, and Boston?"

"Pony is going to be okay; he was just knocked unconscious. He's gonna have a hell of a bruise on his chest, but he's okay. Dragin is still out. He moves from consciousness to unconsciousness. The Doc's got him doped up; I think he's pretty worried about him. Boston needs to get out of the bush, but that's moot if the medevacs don't get in, and besides he doesn't want to go anyway."

Captain Ferring more or less reiterated what Jake had already said as a result of his talks with Colonel Dagomar, and the war council was over.

"Let's tighten up the fighting holes and stand two awake and two asleep per fire team all night. If the troops have any heavies left, try to get them to eat, but eat them cold; no heat tabs."

Jake told the Professor to get Dagomar on the hook. Both the recovered materiel and the casualty report were impressive. Alpha had suffered 13 wounded and 5 dead on the ridge assault. They had killed 27 gooks in their fighting holes and routed at least a battalion-sized unit. Since the beginning of Dewey Canyon, the battalion had incurred 61 dead and 262 wounded. They had captured one M-16, 2 French Mausers, 724 SKS rifles, 84 AK-47 bayonets, 187,260 7.62 rounds of ammunition, 300 sets of cleaning gear, and one 122-millimeter artillery howitzer.

34

THERE WOULD BE NO MORNING MEDE-vac. It rained throughout the night. Sporadic firing kept the lines alert, and either real or imaginary movement urged marines not to hunker down as much as they would have liked. Fighting holes filled with water. The rats had left during the night; now it was time for the marines.

Morning brought only faint light. The night, not wanting to give up its claim, overwhelmed the sun with more fog and mist and rain. At least it would be just as difficult for the gooks, Jake thought. They could not be any happier than us, right now.

The men and materiel for war were gathered along a ridge line in western Quang Tri Province. Bo and the Third Platoon would lead them out. Alex would follow, and Jake, with First Platoon, and the Gunny would bring up the rear. Once more, Alpha would slog through the mud, hampered by weather and terrain, moving toward someone else's idea of a goal. Command set the goal because they felt they had to, because a long time ago someone else had started all of this; the problem was, no one else could remember either the political or the military reason. At least no one seemed to be able to articulate those reasons. The war was like a committee that had long since outlived its reason for being and now existed only to perpetuate itself. But the purpose no longer mattered to Jerry Motley or Bohanin or Sealy or Johnson or Jerry Dollar. Their purpose, which was to survive, was no more.

For the better part of the month the men of Alpha had fought the terrain and the enemy. Enormous amounts of supplies and materiel were being captured. The body count was high on both sides; everyone was aware that this operation was something out of the ordinary. If the weather had been clear, Alpha Company could have seen Tam Boi rising up out of the jungle to the southeast, a foliage-encrusted pyramid, the exit door from the Ashau Valley, marked "use in case of emergency."

So they moved down the valley, playing a macabre game of tag with enemy snipers and hit-and-run NVA aggressors. There were always some shackled to trees to provide the ultimate cover for the withdrawing enemy. Like lethal gnats, they pestered and provoked and picked away at the men and morale. Two more days and nights of sleeplessness and exhausting effort, pushing forward with little or no food, gathering water from the rain and condensation in upturned poncho liners, savoring cigarettes or chocolate bars like a reward offered to an obedient dog. Now it was as if they were being pulled by the magnet, Tam Boi. Moving mechanically, in near silence, they concentrated simply on getting there. No one could see beyond Tam Boi; it had become an end in itself.

Militarily, Dewey Canyon was already a success. Route 922 and its arterial flow of men and materiel had been disrupted. The build-up by the NVA in western Quang Tri Province had been halted by the Ninth Marine Regiment. The enemy losses were enormous and all three objectives had been achieved. Colonel Dagomar was euphoric; he couldn't lose now. He had kept his frustrations to himself. There was no real victory; not in the larger sense. There were simply no absolutes—except life and death. How do you measure success anyway? Even for me, Dagomar thought, it is survival; getting through this tour without committing some unpardonable obscenity among the lesser obscenities that were committed every day. Where was the glory? he pondered. It was very difficult to be sure that what he was doing fit into a larger picture when he didn't know what the larger picture was. Maybe he really didn't want to know.

Alex also found it difficult to see how what they were doing was going to fit into a larger picture. He told Betsy in a letter he wrote the night after the assault on the ridge that his commitment had to be spiritual, for that was the only understandable purpose. He went on to say that he was overwhelmed with the guts and determination of his brother marines. As his sausagelike fingers pushed the black, government-issue ballpoint across the soiled Third Marine Division stationery, he found momentary peace thinking of Betsy, and for a few moments he escaped from Vietnam.

Even as Alex was thinking of her, on the other side of the world Betsy was preparing for bed. In just two weeks she would be flying to Honolulu to meet him. She had decided that he had made the right decision even with this separation. His letter had been so full of love for her that she thought she might explode with the ache of missing him. He had written of the men and sometimes described his attempts at sharing the Lord with them. His efforts, he said, seemed so futile. He wished there were something more he could do to demonstrate God's love. It was still difficult to understand the change in this man she had married.

Since she had received advance notice of the trip to the islands, she had been preparing her wardrobe and trying to decide what she would take. Her parents had lent her the money for the trip and everything was set. She thought she would leave early and visit her aunt and uncle in San Francisco on the way. Just a couple of weeks away and once more I will feel those strong arms around me, she thought. She felt herself blushing with pleasure at the thought of the reunion. Her parents had taken her to pick out travel brochures and plan the trip and the places they might go. She thought about how near to those beautiful islands was this terrible war with its carnage.

Betsy looked at herself in the mirror, brushing her long golden hair, and then opened her robe, placing her hand on her breast and allowing it to drop down across her navel and rest on the slight bulge above her pubic hair. The announcement of the trip to Honolulu had come in conjunction with the confirmation of her pregnancy. She wanted to tell him face to face. Oh, he will be so happy, she thought; it will give him another reason to come home. That would be the only thing that could make me any happier; to have him home for good.

She pulled back the covers on the same bed she had slept in through high school. I don't think I'll be able to sleep for the next two weeks, she thought. We never really took a honeymoon and this will be just perfect. Betsy's mother stuck her head through the door to say good night. "You look like the cat that just caught the mouse," her mother said, smiling.

"Oh, I was just thinking about Alex, Mom, and Honolulu and how great it will be to be with him again. I truly love him."

"I know you do, honey; he is a fine young man and we are all proud of him. God has blessed us all. Now, you get some rest or . . ."

"Okay, Mom," said Betsy, interrupting her, "but it's just like Christmas used to be. Remember how I couldn't sleep nearly the whole week before Christmas and dad would tease me about Santa not coming if I wasn't good? I just want it to be Christmas morning again, that's all."

"I know dear," her mother said, "I love you, good night."

"Good night, Mom, I love you, too." As Betsy drifted into sleep she dreamed of Alex and Christmas mornings when she learned that she had been good and that dreams do come true.

At first light a collective sigh was felt all along the line that was Alpha. Once more, the weary, stretching aching bodies signaled a reluctant return to life for all of them. Their feet planted in the mud of Vietnam and their souls rooted in the heart of home. The indiscriminate bullet or piece of shrapnel unable to discern the difference.

Sometimes you just know things. And Jake knew as this new dawn broke that this was going to be bad. While Erskine had developed a bad reputation as a jinx, Tam Boi was grimly forbidding, yet it beckoned to them. A way out with a price to pay to the gatekeeper. Just who was the keeper of this gate? he wondered.

It took most of the day to reach the top of Tam Boi. The jungle opened up, displaying gnarled trees, some defoliated. Banana trees, many ruined and standing desolate in a place that had once been lush and beautiful, bore witness to the devastation and despair that prevailed.

Maybe I was wrong, thought Jake. No movement, no contact, no snipers, no nothing. Like Alex, he wondered if maybe the NVA had decided not to defend this mountain. Alpha sat in. Three platoons with interlocking fields of fire and final protective lines. M-60s, M-72 LAAWs, 106s, and marines looking back down into the jungle and the Ashau Valley from where they had come. Again they waited in mud and rain and humidity. Waited for word of an extraction or a resupply or for Charlie to do something. Listening posts were assigned and the defensive posture was taken, not a comfortable position for marines, yet one that they were required to take many times in this war.

The Professor had Colonel Dagomar on the radio, and Jake was listening to the success of Charlie and Bravo and Delta companies. All three objectives were secured now that Alpha was in place. Alpha was to hold its position for the time being until the decision was made to make separate extractions for the other companies or until they joined Alpha on Tam Boi.

The word flew through the company; for the first time in weeks they could feel the lift. Vandegrift Combat Base might not be the world, but it sure as hell wasn't the Ashau Valley. They all wanted to get a break from the constant strain; just some hot food, a shower, a book, or a chance to think about home. Squad-sized reconnaissance was the daily activity around Tam Boi. Then came the monotony of the wait from the twenty-fourth to the twenty-fifth, and then came the twenty-sixth and still no definite word.

They knew the gooks were there. At night they often heard the ghostly sputtering of the mortar tubes in the distance. The First Battalion, Ninth Marines, had uncovered the largest supply caches in the war during this operation. It had taken Charlie Company nearly two days to inventory all the materiel. The last forty-eight hours had seen another 122-millimeter artillery piece captured and the casualty toll was mounting up on both sides.

If they were not on patrol they were talking, usually in small groups, rapping about the guys who had not made it this far. No one had been in this much contact over this long a period before. Sugar Bear had been closed-mouthed and pensive ever since Lieutenant Clahan had been killed. The Gunny was just plain uncomfortable. He didn't like where they sat and he didn't want to stay there. He kept telling Jake that they needed to get their asses off this fucking mountain.

Late in the afternoon of the twenty-seventh, about the time the first enemy probes began, the word came down that they would be taken out on the twenty-eighth at first light. Boston had refused to be medevaced, even though his arm was infected and of little use. Jake didn't protest too much since he figured that they would be out shortly anyway. Doc Pony, his chest still sore and bruised, just couldn't manage to keep all the minor wounds clean. They had built a tight perimeter, without wire but set in the best positions to defend the roof of the hill. The Gunny was becoming more and more anxious. He told Jake that they needed to be reinforced or gotten out; the gooks had had far too much time to observe and mass if they wanted to. "But there's contact all over the area, Gunny, the other companies have been in it just like us," Jake said. "They wouldn't be massing here. Besides, we have had little or no activity up to now."

"That's what bothers me the most, lieutenant. We kicked their asses on that last ridge and the history of the First Battalion, Ninth Marines, is not good here; they hate us more than anyone else."

Jake tried to convince himself that the Gunny was showing the strain of being a short-timer, but he had to admit that, from the beginning, he had also felt a feeling of dread.

The whoosh of the first 122-millimeter rocket went overhead, sending every marine into the hole. It exploded harmlessly over the lip of the hill on the side of the mountain. The second came and fell short on the other side. Inside each marine, the shock of what being bracketed by rockets or artillery augured, lit the fire of fear. The third round landed near the center of the top and then they came in volleys, 107s and 122s, tearing up the top of the mountain and its sides, wreaking havoc and chaos and despair among Alpha, sending more trees and dirt flying before the silence came. Jake looked up to find the Gunny scuttling over to see him. They all expected the attack, but it didn't come.

"Lieutenant," Gunny Jacobsen said, "now they have us pinpointed, you know they are going to hit us."

"Look, Gunny, we are getting out in the morning..."

234

"Yes, sir," the Gunny interrupted, "but we have to make it to tomorrow or there is no tomorrow."

Jake stood there looking at Gunny Jacobsen, not responding immediately, and then said, "Damn it, Gunny, I wouldn't have expected this kind of shit from you. Just get the troops tightened up and let's make it, period, huh?"

Jacobsen looked at Jake, hanging his head a bit, and blushed. "I guess you are right, lieutenant. There isn't anything we can do anyway. We're not going to get any reinforcements in here tonight and we aren't going to get out until the morning. But at least do this," he continued, "call some artillery TOT in, just in case we need it."

"That's a good idea," Jake responded. "Like I said before, you give good advice. Thanks, Gunny."

Jacobsen turned and made his way along the lines, urging his charges to dig in deeper and make sure they were alert; he had a feeling about this night, and it wasn't an encouraging feeling.

35

THERE WERE ELEVEN MAJOR TUNNEL complexes in and around Tam Boi. Just after darkness clamped down on the jungle, from tunnels fifty to one hundred and fifty meters long, the North Vietnamese spewed forth from the earth. They would not make a night assault, but they would move en masse as close as they dared, prepared to move at first light and take the top. They had waited and watched; now they felt the time was right. The mountaintop was bracketed with 122s and 107s and both eighty-one and sixty-one mortars were available for the assault. They would pound the hill and then hit it from all sides. The main thrust would be right at Boston, who sat in the natural approach to the top.

About midnight, the first LP called in possible movement. By one-fifteen, all three LPs in Alpha Company had reported possible movement. Alpha waited. Every man was on the line. Alex and Bo were constantly moving up and down their lines and Jake never stopped wandering from position to position. The Gunny, with the Professor, kept monitoring the net and telling Dagomar what was happening. The lift was still on and would be in the air at first light. "Charlie and Delta were moving to you," he had said, and would lift off at Tam Boi as well. Shit, thought Jacobsen, if there's anything left when they get here.

Alex had stopped Jake as he was checking the platoon positions. "Jake," he said, "they are all over the place. I don't know why they're not hitting us."

"I think you're right," responded Jake, "but all we have to do is make it through to the morning and then get out of here."

"Listen, Jake, I don't want to be melodramatic but . . ."

Oh, no, Jake thought, here we go with another Jerry Motley routine . . .

Alex, continuing, said, "I have a letter here for Betsy and I wonder if you would be sure she gets it if anything happens. I'll probably end up giving it to her in Hawaii next week anyway, but, just in case, would you take care of this for me?"

"You know, Alex, I've always admired your faith. In fact, it has strengthened my own convictions. I've even been reading the Gideon Bible my dad gave me before I left. I wouldn't think of preaching to you; after all, you're the Preacher. But I would like to share what I found just opening up the book back in the valley. Check out Psalm 56 when you get a chance."

Alex, reaching into his pack, said, "Hold on a second, I'll do it now." He retrieved his Bible from his utility pocket; kneeling down in his fighting hole and using his penlight, he read: "Mine enemies would daily swallow me up: for they be many that fight against me. O thou most High. When I cry unto thee, then shall mine enemies turn back: this I know; for God is for me. In God have I put my trust: I will not be afraid what man can do unto me. For thou hast delivered my soul from death: Wilt not thou deliver my feet from falling, that I may walk before God in the light of the living?"

Alex, looking up, said, "I'm glad you are moved to read God's word, Jake. It is all that really matters. When all of this is gone," he said, "it will be all that is left."

Jake, looking down into the darkness at Alex, responded, "I just thought you might find that interesting." He paused, searching for the right words: ". . . uhm, the words were meaningful to me. You know something, Alex," he said, kneeling close to the Preacher, "I don't know why you guys just assume it will be me that will make it through all of this. Why is it you don't think it will be you who ends up telling Karen about me?"

"You'll make it; God has a plan for you, Jake."

Jake was beginning to feel edgy again. "Listen, Alex, I've got to get back and see what's happening," he said. "Give me the letter and I will give it back to you before you leave to meet Betsy in Hawaii." Taking the letter from the outstretched hand of the Preacher, Jake said, "check you later," and his voice trailed off as he walked away.

The night came and went with the first break in the weather in twenty days. It wasn't much and it didn't look like it would last, but by early morning there were actually ribbons of sunlight striping the top of Tam Boi. The choppers could be heard through the cloud cover long before they were actually seen. It may have been the sound of their approach, or the result of a well-coordinated attack, but nothing happened until the first bird hit the landing zone. The chilling sound of mortar tubes echoed across the mountaintop and from ridge line to ridge line as marines dived for their holes. Six rounds slammed into the hill in quick succession. The first three caused the pilot to take to the air seconds after he touched down.

The fourth tore out the side of the helicopter as it began to lift off. Like a wounded bird, it circled first to the left and then to the right, finally plummeting to earth and exploding on impact. Black and gray smoke circled up, blocking out precious sun; the second volley of mortars went aloft. There were 122s and 107 rockets also screaming in the same bracketing pattern that had been established the day before; the marines of Alpha were finding out what suppressive fire was all about.

It was clear that the NVA had taken advantage of the confusion of a lift-off involving many helicopters. It was a lesson the Marine Corps still had to learn, to control the air traffic at regiment level. As if to reinforce the lesson, when the second chopper hit the deck, and while Bo was trying to get his platoon on board in sequence, the shit hit the fan. The first fire team of his third squad approached the CH-46 as additional mortar rounds found the hill. The pilot was nervous. As the second round hit the deck, the pilot had had enough and took off nose-first, dropping the last two marines out the back end of the chopper from about twenty-five meters up. They hit the ground, in a flurry of arms and legs; one was knocked unconscious, the other snapped his leg just below the kneecap. Bo was screaming at the chopper, yelling, "you ball-less, motherfucking Yankee bastards." The third bird was making its way to the ground. The random destruction of the mortars was compounded by the hair-raising screams of the rockets as they made their way into Tam Boi.

The mortar tubes began popping less frequently when the North Vietnamese finally moved on Alpha. Bursting out of the jungle on every side, they moved under the cover of their own mortar fire. Six M-60 machine guns opened up in unison, with a sustained rate of fire of one hundred rounds a minute, each one traveling twenty-eight hundred feet a second. Marines were free-handing sixty-millimeter mortars, dropping them within range of their own lines. Boston was pumping out blooper rounds as fast as he could reload the breach of his M-79. The assault was ferocious, the overwhelming numbers unexpected. The NVA had simply waited in their tunnels until the time was right. Later, in the command chronology, it would be deemed imprudent to sit in one location for more than forty-eight hours.

Dagomar had decided to stop the lift when the first copter got shot down. He reckoned that they could wait until the rest of the battalion tied in with Alpha. But that was before the enemy ground troops hit the mountain. The heli-flight had already turned back toward Vandegrift when they were ordered to return to Tam Boi. None of the pilots wanted to go in, but they came back, their courage an answer to Bo's curses.

It would be only a matter of time before Tam Boi would fall under the pressure of the sheer number of NVA troops. The marines had to get to the choppers as quickly as possible. Jake was requesting fixed wing if he could get it. The battle was joined; if Alpha continued to use ammunition at the present rate, they were going to run out. Jake made that clear to the colonel. Dagomar was thinking how he could explain why an entire company had been wiped out, or, worse yet, captured. That's when he turned the helicopter flight back toward Tam Boi.

The barrels of the M-60s were beginning to turn red. Boston was running out of rounds, and he suspected that everyone else was too. Sugar Bear yelled: "I can see the sons of bitches; and they're coming in."

Jake couldn't figure out how to break the perimeter to get the men on the birds that were on their way back. He could barely be heard on the radio for the firing, and had told Dagomar, who wanted to know how long he could hold out, to get the helicopters in there or he wouldn't have anybody to talk to who didn't speak Vietnamese. He finally broke off by saying, "Six, I can't talk. Just get 'em in here." He gave the handset back to the Professor, who took it with a shaking hand and said, "Lieutenant, I'm scared shitless."

Jake, still finding room for laughter, said, "It's okay, Professor, so am I. Now let's get done what we can get done."

Jake grabbed a loose M-16 and ran in a crouch over to the Gunny, who was trying to figure out where the heaviest fire was coming from. The air was filled with the crack of AK-47 and AK-50 rounds. Bo called in that his lines were weakening; Alex reported the same. The intensity of the fire was awesome; mortar rounds and occasional rockets continued to slam into the perimeter, almost paralyzing the marines. Then, abruptly, inexplicably, it stopped. Maybe they wanted to test the initial response or to see how the first assault would be handled, or maybe they felt they could suck in some more helicopters, but for whatever reason it stopped. Mortars popped occasionally, but the NVA had simply broken contact.

The helicopters came in waves, landing three at a time. Jake decided to pull the perimeter in by tightening the circle and keeping the gun teams on line so that the heaviest fire possible would be concentrated along the final protective line. Chaos is difficult to describe because in any description there is some order, but there was neither order nor sanity on Tam Boi. All three LPs had been brought into the perimeter when the first mortars began to fall. They filled in the gap left by the marines from Bo's platoon. Jake took advantage of the lull to improvise a contingency plan.

In a final brief meeting, Jake passed the word that at his command, Alex and his men would drop back twenty-five meters from their fighting holes and take cover behind a natural berm in the mountaintop after the first wave of helicopters lifted off. They would hold from that position until the second wave of choppers set in and, if need be, then tighten the perimeter again. If they needed a third extraction, they would simply repeat the process until everyone was out. All weapons would be on automatic. The M-60s would stay until the end and be left behind, if that was necessary to get the men out.

"Conserve your blooper rounds and grenades for a final stand," he said. "Go ahead and use your mortars if you have any left. Well, that's it. Let's wait for the sky guys and get the hell out of Dodge. Incidentally," he said, "we will lift out one squad from each platoon in each wave. That way, we keep the perimeter integrity and no one platoon has to pay the total price of being last. Order of movement will be First, Second, and Third platoons, then Weapons. All right, I guess that's it. " Jake, pausing only a moment, looked at each platoon commander and then stopping with Alex said, "Preacher, now is the time for a savior. May God bless us all."

The sky was filled with helicopters coming in at different altitudes and from every direction to Tam Boi. The Huey-gunship escorts were moving in, at Jake's direction, to take lateral courses to the hilltop and keep the gooners' heads down. Three more rockets whooshed overhead, a prelude to a volley of mortars. Once more the battle heated up; small-arms fire rose to a crescendo. The first wave of three helicopters hit the deck amidst exploding mortars. At least one squad made it to each chopper, carrying their dead and wounded. The Hueys were coming in low, firing rockets and miniguns. Then the helicopters were up and away.

Jake gave a sigh of relief and popped a red-smoke grenade as a signal to bring the perimeter in tighter. Bo, Alex, and Hawk moved the men back in precise, orderly fashion. The Gunny set up in the center of the new perimeter with the Professor and the other platoon radiomen. The circle of marines was now no more than seventy-five meters around. Jake was grateful the lines were holding and that no one had panicked and run to a chopper to which he wasn't assigned. He knew that they all wanted out; hell, he wanted to grab a copter skid and fly out himself.

Moving back had cost them the high ground. There were about twenty-five meters of open ground covered with elephant grass that the gooks would have to get through to get to them. Everything came down to time, numbers, and heli-lifts. They would make it or they would not. If the gooners were lucky with the rockets or mortars, it wouldn't make much difference. He ordered each platoon to retain two claymores until the last moment. He felt that they might be needed to keep an all-out assault back and that minutes or seconds might make the difference between life and death.

The second wave of helicopters came in, and three more choppers landed almost simultaneously. This time the mortars were on target. One bird took a direct hit, lifting off the ground in a great shrug with gasoline, hydraulics, and sparks exploding in a giant fireball that caused the other choppers to lift off. Once more, the 814th Sapper Regiment pressed the attack. Two 46s were down on what was a small landing zone to begin with. One was outside the perimeter and one was inside. The heat from the burning chopper was unbearable at the rear of the perimeter; the NVA were pressing from the front. Three more helicopters sat in on what available space there was and marines were running through the center of the perimeter, scrambling into the back end of their respective aircraft. No one gave thought to the courage and valor displayed by the men on the ground and in the air. They were simply doing their job. Here were the small unnoticed acts of selflessness and commitment that lifted soldiers above the squalor of war. This was the memorial!

Bo had lifted out along with the last squad from his platoon. As his chopper pulled away, he watched as two waves of fixed wing dropped daisy chains all along the lip of Tam Boi and Huey gunships kept their miniguns busy just outside the tree lines. He could see the North Vietnamese massing, apparently intending to overrun the mountaintop before the next wave of helicopters could get in. That was the last thing he saw as the helicopter he was riding in turned and headed back for Vandegrift.

The machine guns on the south side ran out of ammunition. Jake could see Sugar Bear and Boston; he wondered why Boston wasn't out yet. A surge on the south side was about to break the new perimeter. One more chopper sat down in the only available place. The pilot wanted to get everyone out, and it was clear that this time he had no intention of coming back.

The gooks were so close that they were throwing chicom grenades at the helicopters. Boston grabbed an ammo box and was running at full tilt toward the gun emplacements when a mortar landed just behind him. Jake and Alex watched him go airborne, one leg severed at the knee. He landed, seemingly trying to rise and run on his stump for two or three paces. The box of M-60 ammo broke apart and spilled its contents in the dirt. Boston picked up his shattered leg, pushed the stump into the dirt, and started firing the machine gun. His left arm, already damaged, hung at his side and he was howling in rage and pain above the chatter of the gun.

Gunny Jacobsen, observing Boston, moved quickly to the other gun position; he held the line while the remaining troops moved to the choppers. Now everyone, including Jake, was on their feet in the assault position, firing as they backed up to the birds and boarded. One chopper lifted off, a second went, rounds were slamming into the deck, snapping through the air, peppering the helicopters. Mortars fell and the earth trembled and shook. Jake went back to one knee, firing into the elephant grass where black shocks of hair and pith helmets separated the waving grass. Then Alex and Jake set off the remaining claymores, blowing swathes of death back across the front of the remaining approach to the helicopter. Jake saw Sugar Bear jump onto the helicopter. Gunny Jacobsen started to get up from his gun emplacement when Jake saw him go down. Jake ran toward him.

In the midst of the confusion Doc Pony was trailing at a low crouch with the Professor. All that remained in the small perimeter were the Doc and the Professor, Jake, the Gunny, Boston, Alex, and one helicopter. Alex was coordinating suppressing fire from in front of the helicopter; time was running out. Gunny Jacobsen had crawled back to his M-60 and was busy fitting some of the stray belts from Boston's ammo box into the breach. Jake, firing while hunkered down, belly-flopped between them. The Gunny had been gut shot. Boston was clearly in shock and living on some incredible reserve of energy and will. The perimeter was collapsing.

"C'mon, Gunny, let's get the hell out of here." "Boston," he yelled, trying to be heard over the cacophony of both machine guns, "let me try to help you back."

Boston stared into the elephant grass and kept firing.

"Get out, lieutenant," the Gunny yelled, grimacing in pain. "Shit, I didn't really want to retire anyway."

Doc Pony was at his side now. Only the two M-60s and the 50s from the helicopter were keeping the gooks out. The Professor was yelling at Jake, "Lieutenant, Lieutenant Scott says it's now or never. We've got to go."

"Oh, shit," Jake said to himself. "Damn it, Gunny, come on. You can make it and I can help Boston." Tears of frustration and anger were coursing their way through the mud on his face. "You crazy son of a bitch. Come on, let me help you get out while there is still a chance."

Doc Pony could see pieces of intestine pushing their way out through the fingers the Gunny had pressed against his own abdomen. Boston slumped over his gun, finally succumbing to the loss of blood and shock. Jake unholstered his .45 and gave it to the Gunny. "This is for you and Boston if you need it." He stood there holding his weapon out toward this man who he realized had meant so much to him. As the Gunny grasped the .45, Jake reached out and touched the back of Boston's head. Without looking at Jacobson, he said, "I love you, you know, you stupid bastard." As he said those words an AK-57 round split two plates in his flak jacket, driving into his shoulder blade. The pain, like a hot flash, took the air from his lungs. He could hear the Gunny's machine gun begin to chatter again somewhere over his shoulder.

The Doc was halfway to the remaining bird. Alex was pouring rounds to the three opposite sides of their position along with several other marines and Sugar Bear. Jake pushed himself to his feet as rounds were coming in to the chopper and from the chopper back toward the perimeter. A second round smashed into his left thigh; exiting just above the kneecap along the inseam. He went down again. Everything had gone into slow motion; the noise of the battle seemed like a distant echo. Jake, looking up from the ground, could see Alex looking at him and beckoning him to come.

Mortars were falling again. They couldn't hold off the gooks any longer. Jake knew he had to make this last forty meters. It seemed like such a long way. Why did Alex seem to be moving so slow? Bam, Bam, he heard two .45 caps busting behind him. Jake thought, the Gunny has cheated those little bastards one last time. He was trying once again to get to his knees but his damn leg wouldn't work right. The chicom seemed to echo when it thudded into the dirt to his right. The ensuing concussion lifted him off the earth, and all he could think about was how his finger went numb when he had held a cherry bomb too long as a kid. This is the same thing, he thought, only my whole body feels like that finger. As he rolled over, Jake once more caught a glimpse of Alex, who seemed to be closer. But the sound of war was gone; in its place a voice, calling his name from somewhere in the distance, reverberated in his head. Was it Alex, he wondered, or was it Jehovah's throat?

Sugar Bear and Alex hefted Jake between them. There was simply no time. All the remaining marines were on the chopper and the pilot was watching the last three move toward his plane. His crew chief was working overtime on the fifty-cal; he knew he had to get out. The North Vietnamese were everywhere. Sugar Bear had reached the back of the apron on the 46 first and was pulling Jake inside. Alex turned and sprayed the pursuing NVA with his M-16. He could see them coming; they were in the open area. He wanted to buy just a few more seconds, just a few more seconds and everyone would be safe. The helicopter blades were pounding furiously; above the din he could hear Sugar Bear yelling at him. Alexander Scott, the big man they called the Preacher, emptied his last magazine and turned to mount the helicopter, only it wasn't there. About twenty meters up, he could see Jake's boots still sticking out the rear. Sugar Bear was looking at him with an incredulous expression on his face.

"Oh, no," Sugar Bear said out loud. "This is not right. This is not the way this is supposed to happen. Oh, God surely. . ."

Alex, catching a motion to his left, turned to see the NVA sweeping over what had been the gun positions for the Gunny and Boston.

So he stood there, this big man, praying, as the soldiers of the 814th and the 813th North Vietnamese Regiments swarmed over the mountaintop of Tam Boi. They took one prisoner alive, a big muscular marine who was on his knees by the time they reached him. They mistook his position for one of surrender and weakness when, in truth, it was one of victory and faith.

36

ETSY LEFT THREE DAYS EARLY TO stay in San Francisco with her aunt and uncle before meeting Alex in Honolulu. On the fourth day, they took her to the airport where she boarded a United Airlines flight for the big island. She had been uneasy for the last two days. Nothing she could put her finger on; just uneasy. She boarded the plane and the feeling persisted. It frightened her that at a time when she should feel so happy about seeing Alex again, she would have this concern. Then it hit her. She was feeling exactly as she had on Christmas Eve when she was a little girl. She was afraid that Santa might not come. She had done something wrong, as her father used to tease her, something that would take away her surprise. It helped her to think about that and she tried to relax for the long trip, but the anxiety persisted as the huge airplane roared toward Hawaii. It persisted as she stepped out into the jetway. It persisted as the first strains of the island songs reached her ears and the Hawaiian girls began to place leis around the necks of some of the passengers. She searched the waiting crowd frantically, looking for Alex, until she heard the public-address system asking her to report to the United Airlines desk. Well, she thought, Alex has been delayed. That must be it. Two marines in dress blues were waiting at the desk as she approached. Greeting her politely, and without hesitation, they told her that they had some unfortunate news.

She stood looking at them. They represented everything that Alex had wanted and everything she had agreed to commit to support. Her mind was racing through her time with Alex that led her to this moment, until one of the marines interrupted her. "Ma'am," he said, "are you all right?"

"Yes," she said, "I know. I've done something terrible this year and Santa won't be coming."

The two marines looked at each other, the tall one saying, with a questioning look, "Ma'am, I'm not sure I understand."

"It's okay," Betsy replied. "It's Alex, isn't it?"

"Yes, ma'am. Lieutenant Scott is listed as missing in action. It is believed that he has been taken prisoner. I'm truly sorry, ma'am. We tried to reach you at your aunt's but we just missed you."

Betsy looked around the terminal and at these two marines. "I wonder," she said, "if you could take me to my hotel. I think I would like to rest and maybe speak with you tomorrow."

"Certainly," he replied, secretly glad that he would not have to stay near this sorrow much longer. He took her arm and escorted her to the waiting staff car.

The sun was already setting on the Hawaiian Islands as the green car made its way along Oahu Boulevard. The two posterboard marines sat at attention in the front seat as the young woman riding in the back looked out at the sunset over the ocean, silent tears ruining her makeup. Betsy Scott was about to begin to test the faith she and her husband shared; it would subject her and others like her to years of uncertainty as America tried to resolve the dilemma of prisoners of war and those still listed as missing in action.

"Oh, Alex," she whispered, "where are you? God, I thought that I would know if he were alive or dead." She thought back to the conversation she had with Alex when she persuaded him to seek his ministry in the military. "Oh, my God," Betsy Scott said out loud, "what have I done?"

37

JAKE WAS MEDEVACED TO CHARLIE Two in Quang Tri, the same hospital where he had seen Captain Romero lying on the landing zone just five short months ago. It was there that he had seen so many men being medevaced in and out. It was there that he had wondered whether or not he would make it. But he would make it. He would spend two months in the hospital in Okinawa, where alcohol-soaked bandages would be stuffed into his shrapnel wounds, causing pain he would never be able to forget.

His last memory of the battle was the Preacher beckoning to him from the rear of the helicopter. Jake was aware that his parents and Karen had been notified about his being wounded in action, and the letters were coming in, full of concern and love, as he lay in his bed. He was grateful to be out of hell; and he missed being with his men, his brothers, in the bush. Some irrational feeling of personal guilt made Jake ashamed that he wasn't carrying his load. In one letter, Bo wrote to Jake that he had been written up for the Navy Cross.

Sugar Bear was the only other person who wrote to Jake. He couldn't believe that Alex had not made it out. The war had taught him how to numb his feelings, but he mourned Boston and Gunny Jacobsen and so many of the others who, like candles that flickered in the wind, were extinguished by a hurricane of political and military confusion. It was in this period of pain, confusion, and guilt that Jake began the selective suppression of memories.

Alpha First Battalion, Ninth Marines, went back to Vandegrift Combat Base to heal its wounds and wait until its sister companies had been pulled out of the Ashau Valley. The entire regiment was extracted by the eighteenth of March. Bo was the only officer left in Alpha when the last chopper touched down at Vandegrift.

The repercussions of this operation were felt all through the Third Marine Division. Representatives of the Marine Corps Historical Archives were waiting to interview participants while events were still fresh in their minds. Dragin would live. He would serve out the rest of his enlistment in Japan. Jake would soon be on his way to Okinawa. Alex would eventually be listed as a prisoner of war.

The survivors walked up from the landing zone at Vandegrift in ragged groups. Hawk and Bo, Sugar Bear and the Professor, his radio dragging at his side—the scarecrows of war. They were filthy, bedraggled, exhausted; barely human yet magnificent in the tattered rags of endurance and survival, having accomplished what every soldier who ever fought had accomplished—facing the enemy and themselves successfully. They would never be the same again.

Like grains of sand tumbling back into footprints on a beach, the gaps and holes of Alpha and all of the Ninth Marines would be filled with replacements. Bo became acting company commander until replacements could be brought in. Then, it was learned, the Ninth Marines would be pulled out of Vietnam as part of the first withdrawal of troops by President Nixon. The Ninth Marines had been the first in, so they would be the first out. Initially everyone laughed in disbelief, but the rumors persisted. Less than two months later, Alpha would be standing on the dock at Da Nang, the first element of the American troop withdrawal from Vietnam. The politicians and the generals called it "Vietnamization."

38

BO STOOD AT ATTENTION IN FRONT OF Alpha Company on the hot, black-topped field for two hours that Monday, listening to the praise of South Vietnamese officials and then from Lieutenant General Nickerson, who said, "The freedom we together have been fighting for we can continue to win . . . we will win. We are proud to have been engaged with you in this effort of free men to remain free. This withdrawal is the turning point, when victories on the battlefield and progress in the pacification struggle permit the government of South Vietnam to say to their American friends, "We can do more, we ask you to do less."

Bo and Sugar Bear and Hawk and the rest of the First Battalion squinted and sweated, clad in their jungle utilities and helmets, stealing glances at the USS *Paul Revere* that would take them to Okinawa. Navy frogmen swam around the *Revere* on guard against enemy underwater saboteurs. The chairman of the Da Nang Citizens Council got up to speak, listing the distinguished guests and then reviewing the history of Vietnam from French domination, to the Geneva Accord in 1954, which separated the country, to the present struggle against the invasion of the communists. He thanked the Allied nations for sending troops and materiel and declared it an outstanding and praiseworthy deed. Then he went on to say, "Now then, President Nixon decided the time was favorable for the pullout of a number of United States troops from Vietnam. This serves as an example for the North Vietnamese communists at the Paris conference table. In fact, it is a very remarkable and helpful decision aimed at termination of the strenuous war in Vietnam at the earliest possible day, and the return of peace to our motherland. My dear United States officers, NCOs, and enlisted men, before you leave Da Nang, speaking for the Da Nang Citizens Council, I want to thank you for your incomparable consecration to liberty and justice. We are greatly impressed, for you left your family behind to assist this remote country of ours to fight this costly war. Never shall we forget your favors rendered to us. May God bless you, and please extend our most sincere regards to your families."

It was over! They were moving in long files up the gangplank; at the top, officers shook their hands and sailors saluted, and everyone sweated in the tremendous heat. The marines of Alpha, First Battalion, Ninth Marine Regiment, stood around looking at each other, unable to completely comprehend what was happening. Clean sheets, a bed, chocolate milk, and salads. The journey from the Ashau Valley back to the world had been a long one.

Jake, prone in his hospital bed, opened his eyes and thought he was still dreaming. Dreaming of Karen and Harmony and then Ashau, the valley of death. His blurry eyes seemed to be seeing the forms of the Professor and Bo and Hawk and Sugar Bear. But that wasn't unusual, for he had dreamed of them often in his weeks in the hospital.

"Lieutenant," Sugar Bear said, "how you doing, sir?"

"You compromising piece of shit," Bo interjected, "you couldn't even hail from a state that could make a decision of which side to be on; you're just damn lucky those weren't Southern gooks, your ass would really have been had."

That's when Jake knew they were really there. He struggled to sit up, with the pain still shooting through his arm and leg. He looked at this group of men he had come to regard as his family, trying to focus in on each face. "I heard you guys were coming back," he said, "but I wasn't sure when." He wanted to make some joke about why they were pulled out first but he just couldn't do it. It was so overwhelming seeing them. "My God," he finally heard himself saying, "it's good to see you. You might not believe it, but I would rather be in the bush than in this stinking place. This is the pits. I'm going to go dinky dau if I have to stay here much longer."

There was a moment of awkward silence and then Hawk said, "Lieutenant, we, uh, brought something to celebrate the reunion." As he said those words, he took a bottle of Wayco Wolf's famous Jack Daniels black label out of a small valise he was carrying.

"Wow," said Jake, "let's do it."

He grabbed some paper cups on his bed stand. The Professor stood at the end of the bed, finally saying hello after remaining silent the entire time. They all looked so different here; it was as if they had been other people from some other dimension where all the rules were different. He wondered if they would be able to adjust to what was supposed to be normal.

The Professor, who looked small and so terribly young to Jake, seemed to be struggling to say something. He finally blurted out, "Uh, we, uh just wanted you to know, lieutenant, how glad we all are that you made it out okay, uh, and . . . for everything you did back there."

Jake was embarrassed and quickly interrupted him, "Hey, Professor, knock that shit off. We all did what we had to do." Then slowly, looking at each of them, he asked quietly, "any word on the Preacher?"

"Nothing more," said Sugar Bear, "but I'll tell you this, if there is anyone that can make it out, he can. He's one tough son of a bitch."

Then came an awkward silence; Hawk used the opportunity to fill the paper cups with whiskey, as Sugar Bear said firmly, "He saved us out there, you know. He kept the gooners down just long enough to get that last bird out. It was the Preacher that helped me carry you out, sir. You know, he lived what he preached. He really did care. I believe that. I've never known anybody quite like him."

Jake was thinking about the many conversations he had had with Alex and how in the end he had lived the truth in which he believed. He was remembering his promise to go see Betsy if something happened. He had never even had the opportunity to read the letter Alex had written to Betsy. And when the doctors had cut the clothes off him to treat his wounds it was apparently discarded. But he knew what he would say to Betsy, for he knew the heart of Alex Scott.

"Lieutenant, lieutenant, are you okay?" asked Sugar Bear. Jake looked up, raising his paper cup to cover the lump in his throat. "To the Preacher," he said.

"To the Preacher," they said in unison, cups lifted in tribute to Alexander Scott.

At that moment the door opened and a fifth visitor walked in. The others turned to stare at him. He stood for a moment, his bushy eyebrows raised in mirth, the corners of his mouth cracked with the beginnings of a smile.

"Holy shit," said Wilbur Akins, sporting his National Defense ribbon. "I told you not to go over there and get your ass shot off, Jake. As special services officer, I just thought I'd drop in and see if you were well enough to get your prod pounded yet."

Everyone was laughing much too hard and Hawk poured a drink for Wilbur. Jake shook his head, trying not to laugh because of the pain it caused him. Some things just never change, he thought, and yet everything has changed.

"To the corps," shouted Wilbur, lifting his paper-cupful of whiskey, "To the corps."

"To the corps," the chorus rang out.

EPILOGUE
WASHINGTON, D.C.

IT WAS SNOWING HARDER NOW. JAKE suddenly realized he was looking for his own name on the black granite and he was amazed that it was not there. Why had he not died with the rest of them? Why did he make it back and not them? There were still no hard answers but, as Alex had so often said, maybe the answer was bigger than all of them. Had he not given his life to prove it? Isn't that after all what the Gunny, Boston, Jim Clahan, Jerry Dollar, and so many others had done? What was certain was that this war had become a common denominator for everyone in his generation. Ill-conceived, ill-advised, ill-planned, it was a tragedy of such magnitude that it could not be covered up. It had turned aimless teenagers into heroes, who found courage they never knew they had. It turned normal college kids into draft dodgers. It crippled some who went, and gave others a direction in life. It took some young men of promise to their deaths. And it brought most home to no welcome, almost as if they had never left. This generation holds beliefs set by this war, beliefs full of doubts and ambiguities that Vietnam left behind. So Jake was standing at the Memorial, finally facing these questions and thoughts that had haunted him for so many years. He was hoping to find peace. If not the answers, at least peace.

He had one more thing to do. Reaching into his pocket, he pulled out another slip of paper, peeling it from its sticky backing. He searched the granite wall until he found Alex Scott, designated MIA. Jake placed the slip of paper bearing one name just above that of Alex. He knew it wouldn't stay in the cold and wind, and even if it did, the park maintenance crew would scrape it off. But it belonged there, for, just as the other names on the walls represented men and women who paid the ultimate price in Vietnam, so did this name of a man who died before the age of thirty-eight of liver and lung cancer. His first child had been born with birth defects, a sure victim of the chemical war in Vietnam. Lieutenant Bo Lawler.

He could feel the cold now. Caressing the names of his fallen brothers, he sighed, tears freezing to his face in the agony of recollection. And then it was over. Taking a deep breath, he turned to walk away, his icy breath preceding him with each step.

Two men in jungle fatigues stood in his path. In their mid-thirties, sporting full beards, they stood arm in arm looking at the wall. Jake kept his head lowered to avoid eye contact and muttered "excuse me," as he tried to pass. They both looked up, and the heavier of the two said, "Were you there, man?"

"Yes," Jake said, already emotionally exhausted and not wanting to get into a conversation.

"Who were you with?" the big man persisted.

"Ninth Marines," Jake said and tried to go by them.

"Hey, wait a minute," the smaller of the two shouted adamantly, as Jake continued on.

He stopped, turning his back to the icy wind, and stood looking at these two living legacies of his own generation. Refugees from a time that would never be duplicated again.

"Hey, man," they said in unison, each sticking out their hand, "Welcome home!"

GLOSSARY

Actual: the unit commander

A.O.: area of operation

ARVN, or RVN: army of the Republic of South Vietnam

AWOL: away without leave

Azimuth: a line from point to point shot with a compass

B-1 Unit: light meals

B-2 Unit: heavy meals

Bald eagle: a company-sized reaction force unit

Berm: small rise in the earth

Brown bar: second lieutenant

C-4: plastique explosive

Claymore mines: antipersonnel mines

Click: one thousand meters

CP: command post

C-rat, or C-ration: field rations

Crew served: refers to weapon requiring more than one man to operate

Crumps: sound of mortar rounds hitting the earth

Daisy chains: clusters of small high-intensity explosives, delivered from aircrafts, that explode with a chainlike effect as they hit the ground

DMZ: demilitarized zone, separating North and South Vietnam

Doggie regiment: army regiment

Finger: ridge line narrowing off into a low area

Fixed Wing: jet

Flechette: small needlelike missile or bomblet fired out of a Howitzer round

FMF: Fleet Marine Force

FNG: fucking new guy

FPF, or FPL: final protective line of fire

Frag: to wound or kill someone using a grenade

FSB: fire support base

G-2: Intelligence unit

Hachimaki: the yellow bandana worn by the Japanese kamikaze as he dived to his death in World War II

H and I: harassment and interdiction

H.E.: high explosive, usually referring to artillery or mortar rounds

Hootch: a hole dug in by ground troops used as a living hole and/or a fighting space

ICTZ: I Corps tactical zone

In trace: one behind the other

KIA: killed in action

Kit Carson scout: repatriated enemy soldier

K-rats: quick-dried field rations

LAAW: shoulder-fired sixty-six-millimeter rocket, made of fiberglass and disposable after one shot

LP: listening post

LZ: landing zone

MAF: Marine Air Force

MOS: military occupational specialty

Net: radio frequency

NVA: North Vietnamese soldier

0302: the military designation for an infantry officer

Passing the dap: a form of handshake used by blacks in Vietnam

PRC-25: radio

Puff: aircraft-mounted Gatling gun

Rear pogue: marine assigned to rear duties

Request mast, or Requestment: to ask for permission to see the commanding officer

RPG: rocket-propelled grenade

Saddle: depression between two hills

Scuttlebutt: rumors

782 gear: a marine's field gear, webbed belts, and so forth

Short-timer stick: a cane with notches depicting the days left before leaving Vietnam

Sit rep: situation report given by radio

Six-by: truck

Skirmishers: squad attack formation

Sky Guys: pilots

Sling arms: holding rifle by having the sling looped over one's shoulder

SOP: standard operating procedure

Sparrow hawk: a platoon-sized force waiting to fly in and help a unit in trouble

Spooky: reference to both an aircraft that drops high-power illumination flares, and to the flares themselves

SP pak, or SPs: cartons of candy and cigarettes sent to the bush marines

Squid: Navy personnel

Tax collectors: Viet Cong who coerced the South Vietnamese villagers to "contribute" to the war effort with money and sexual favors

T.O.: table of organization

TOT: "Time on Target," pretimed artillery fire on a target

Twinks: new replacements

WIA: wounded in action

ACKNOWLEDGMENTS

Every character herein, although fictional, has a model in the factual past; every occurrence its roots in reality. There was an Alpha Company, First Battalion, Ninth Marine Regiment operating in Northern I Corps, South Vietnam in 1968–1969. There did occur an operation named Dewey Canyon, taking place largely as depicted. I have, however, taken liberties with certain time sequences: As an example, in the book Dewey Canyon takes place after Operations Apache Snow and Cameron Falls; in fact, the opposite occurred.

I have also included a glossary of terms, not to be deadly dull or enrage you, the reader, as Charles Wallen reminded me might happen, but rather to aid those unfamiliar with the military terms and colloquialisms of the bush, such as *saddle* or *finger*, without damaging the reality of the text.

I am deeply grateful to the United States Marine Corps; and, in particular, to Lieutenant Colonel Terry Murray, without whose help this work would not have been completed; to Major Charles Lowder, whose initial encouragement was so meaningful. My deepest thanks must go to R. Emmett Tyrrell, Jr., for without his assistance and encouragement this book would not have become a reality.